THE
GIRL
MOST
LIKELY
TO

Also by Julie Tieu

The Donut Trap
Circling Back to You
Fancy Meeting You Here

THE GIRL MOST LIKELY TO

A Novel

JULIE TIEU

AVON

An Imprint of HarperCollins*Publishers*

THE GIRL MOST LIKELY TO. Copyright © 2025 by Julie Tieu. All rights reserved. Printed in the United States of America. No part of this book may be used or reproduced in any manner whatsoever without written permission except in the case of brief quotations embodied in critical articles and reviews. For information, address HarperCollins Publishers, 195 Broadway, New York, NY 10007.

HarperCollins books may be purchased for educational, business, or sales promotional use. For information, please email the Special Markets Department at SPsales@harpercollins.com.

Avon, Avon & logo, and Avon Books & logo are registered trademarks of HarperCollins Publishers in the United States of America and other countries.

FIRST EDITION

Interior text design by Diahann Sturge-Campbell

Instant messaging illustration © Bold Yellow/thenounproject.com

Library of Congress Cataloging-in-Publication Data has been applied for.

ISBN 978-0-06-324523-5

24 25 26 27 28 LBC 5 4 3 2 1

This one's for me.

THE
GIRL
MOST
LIKELY
TO

 *Prologue*

February 2003

There should be a how-to guide on meeting your online friend for the first time. Setting a date and time was easy enough. I told him to look out for the girl wearing a red shirt and black glasses. But then, struck with the latent fear that maybe the boy I'd been chatting with for the last four years was a serial killer, I threw out the first public place I could think of that had internet access. If I'd given myself some more time and put more thought into it, I would have suggested the library, not the internet café where most of the boys from Commonwealth High School played Counter-Strike The library would've been free. Free of cost and of boys who wore too much Axe. The offensive smell was making me woozy.

Alternating commands erupted from stations across the room.

"Go, go, go!"
"Take the shot!"

This wasn't my brightest moment. If I was about to meet a serial killer, it wasn't smart to bring him into a first-person shooter LAN party. Even dumber to show up forty-five minutes early. Punctuality was my blessing and my curse.

I found an open station in a dark corner and hid away from the crowd. The last thing I needed was someone from my class seeing me log into AIM. I mistakenly typed "dangracheldang" out of habit and quickly backspaced. That was the screen name I used if I needed to contact my classmates about homework, but that was rare. As far as my peers knew, I rarely logged into the instant messaging platform. I made sure no one was around when I entered my first-ever screen name: "xxaznxbbxgrlxx."

When I came up with it, I was fourteen and clueless about the internet. With no good ideas of my own, I riffed off my older sister's screen name. Angela didn't mind. She was used to me taking things from her, like her jeans or Alanis Morrissette CD. But xxaznxbbxgrlxx took on a life of her own. She wasn't quiet Rachel Dang, straight-A machine, always afraid of saying the wrong thing. xxaznxbbxgrlxx could be anyone she wanted to be. She could have an interesting life and friends, free from the grind that came with being at the top of her class.

Things changed when I was scoping out a 626 AOL chat room one night. Angela had left for college and I didn't have anyone to talk to. Ma went to sleep early because she had to open her hair salon the next day, while Ba went to his print shop to catch up on film he hadn't processed yet. When I entered the chat, people had moved past divulging their age/sex/location and were throwing out questions typed in alternating capital and lowercase letters. It felt like a bunch of people shouting at the same time.

"AnYoNe fRoM MpK"

"wat is westco?"

"Click here for the new Kai single!"

"lollicup or tapioca express???"

markdog69 left the room

Reading the messages hurt my eyes. I was about to give up when a new chat window popped on my screen.

SuperxSaiyan85: hi

Who was this random guy?

                                                        xxaznxbbxgrlxx: a/s/l

SuperxSaiyan85: 14/m/westco. west covina, in case you didn't know.

SuperxSaiyan85: u?

I wasn't sure why, but it felt safe to reply. We were the same age, and he lived far enough away from Alhambra. There was no way we knew each other.

                              xxaznxbbxgrlxx: 14/f/Alhambra. That's Alhambra, in case you didn't know.

SuperxSaiyan85: ha-ha. Name?

My fingers flew and hit enter.

> **xxaznxbbxgrlxx:** Call me bb

I wasn't trying to be mysterious. Stranger danger kicked in, and I gave him the first name I could think of.

> **SuperxSaiyan85:** Call me Goku

That was how we met. We never learned each other's real names, but I did know this.

He was Chinese American like me, except his family came from Vietnam while mine came from Cambodia. He moved around a lot, mostly in California except for a brief stint in Texas. He was a *Dragon Ball Z* fanatic (obviously), and he liked to browse through chat rooms while he downloaded music from Napster. The guy was looking for a way to pass time while I blabbed on and on about how much I missed my sister, how I was afraid I would never see her again even though she was only an hour away. Goku mentioned an older brother who taught him how to skateboard, his preferred pastime when he was bored, unlike me. I didn't have time to be bored when I had so much homework to do, but if I ever had free time, I channel-surfed like any normal person.

It didn't sound like much, but we fell into a routine, logging into AIM almost every night around nine. At first, it was because my mom wouldn't let me use the dial-up during the day, when she was receiving calls from her friends. But Goku and I kept our schedule after my parents finally upgraded to DSL two years later because by then Goku started a new job, which later turned into two. There were breaks here and there, coinciding with the times he had to move. If we didn't talk for a while, it was usually because of that. When it was time to create a screen name that was less embarrassing to share, I couldn't let go of "bb." I didn't want to lose what I had with Goku, a stranger who, in some ways, knew the most honest version of myself because I never censored myself when I was with him.

So when he told me he had finally saved up enough money for a car and asked if I wanted to meet, I said yes and picked this forsaken internet café.

I slipped on the headphones as my Buddy List loaded. Goku hadn't signed in, of course. There were still forty minutes to go. I debated if I should kill some time by copying my notes for *The Canterbury Tales* or coming up with new ideas for this year's prom theme. Senior year showed no signs of slowing down, not when there was still so much at stake. Some of my friends stopped volunteering or showing up to clubs after we got our college applications in, but not me. There were still school awards and scholarships to be won, and it wasn't the time to start slacking off.

Forget about valedictorian. Commonwealth allowed for multiple recipients, so there were twelve other students in line to receive the distinction. It diluted the prestige, if you asked me. That's why my eyes were set on winning Student of the Year. The highest honor bestowed upon a graduating Commonwealth student, it was given to the most well-rounded student with the high academic achievement. Despite my rigorous courses, I stacked my schedule with as many activities I could fit into a day. I even volunteered to tutor Danny Phan—the new spiky-haired kid rumored to be the principal's nephew. I thought it would win me some points with the administrators on the selection committee, but Danny slept through our tutoring sessions, if he bothered to show up at all. He had practically jumped for joy when I canceled today's meeting. Apparently, becoming the Student of the Year required the patience of a saint.

At this point, my best shot at any unique accolades was Most Likely to Succeed, which was nothing but a popularity contest since it was voted on by the senior class. It was probably going to go to Mariana Sanchez, a varsity water polo player who, like Freddie Prinze Jr.'s character in *She's All That*, was both ridiculously smart and well liked among the student body. I had to remind myself that there was no point competing against someone like her, though such a thought had never stopped me before. I always wanted more than I could have.

I had complained to Goku that I wished I could enjoy my last year of high school when he suggested meeting up. It would be fun, he promised. I liked the sound of it, so long as he wasn't a middle-aged creeper pretending to be a teenager.

I had to stop watching *Law & Order: SVU*.

There wasn't anything to worry about. Our relationship wasn't like that. It had always been platonic. He'd tell me about crushes he had, but confess that he was too nervous to ask anyone out. I'd wished we were friends in real life because it was hard to imagine a boy who wasn't a horny dork like the guys I knew.

An AIM notification of a door creaking open sent my heart racing. SuperxSaiyan85 was online.

Was he here early too? I smoothed down my hair, even though he couldn't see me through the monitor.

But as soon as his screen name appeared, it disappeared. Then, to toy with my emotions further, a message popped up.

SuperxSaiyan85: Had to go invisible or else my friends would IM me.

SuperxSaiyan85: you're here...?

Four years in the making and my first instinct was to duck. This was a bad idea.

SuperxSaiyan85: Are you having second thoughts?

More like twenty thoughts racing simultaneously.

Honestly, I wasn't scared that this guy would turn out to be a fugitive from *America's Most Wanted*. I was scared that I idealized him. Online, he was helpful and funny and nice. That somehow translated into a mental sketch of a cute boy. I had built this guy up in my mind, and what if whatever we had on-screen couldn't stand up to reality? And what if he did the same to me? I didn't think I was ugly or anything, but what if he saw me and I wasn't what he expected either? I started to feel self-conscious about things I never worried about before, like my deep voice, or my jackhammer laugh, as my friend Nat lovingly yet annoyingly dubbed it.

I threw all my stuff into my backpack and shot to my feet,

which I shouldn't have done if I was trying to be discreet. Standing up pulled the cord to my headphones taut, whipping them off my head. They landed on the keyboard with a loud crunch. Maybe it was loud only to me, because nobody glanced up from their screens. They were too busy playing games.

I kept my head down, trying to hide my face with my hair as I walked toward the exit. There was still a chance I could make it out of here. Later I could pretend I was at home and say my internet glitched.

"Watch out!" someone shouted from a distance before the warning was swallowed by the sound of muffled explosions and *pew pew pew*, what had to be part of a team raid. The warning might as well have been for me, though, because out of nowhere some guy wheeled back and flew out of his seat, sideswiping me and making me drop my books and my Sanrio pencil bag.

"Look where you're going." I knelt down and gathered my things.

The perpetrator stopped and helped me up. "Sor— Rachel?"

Danny? Of all people.

"You should be sorry. I wasted an hour waiting for you yesterday. Is this what you've been doing instead of showing up for tutoring?"

I immediately felt guilty about scolding him. I sounded like my mom, a thought that made me shudder. It wasn't his fault he knocked me down while I was emotionally imploding.

"I'm sorry," I rushed to say. I could tell my outburst shocked Danny. Rachel Dang, teacher's pet, never yelled at anyone.

"I'm sorry," I said again. I tried to readjust the straps of my backpack, but Danny was still holding on to my arm.

What was his deal? His face was frozen, eyes wide like when our physics teacher threw chalk at him when he dozed off in class. Danny finally let go of my arm, leaving goose bumps where his hand had been. With the shock of falling wearing off, I was feeling out of sorts.

Still stopping me from leaving again, he said, too soft to be an accusation, "You." The word sounded like...recognition. His eyes lingered on my glasses. Self-conscious, I pushed them up my face. Then his gaze dropped to my favorite red shirt.

No. It was impossible.

I shuffled back, leaving room for the unspoken questions I had. From far away, Danny looked like the same guy who wore a gray hoodie and baggy jeans every day, who walked with a slight hunch like his backpack weighed him down, but he wasn't the same person anymore. Not to me. Not when I knew too much.

"Let's get out of here." Danny lifted his backpack off the floor and moved toward the exit. Because I didn't have any better ideas, I followed him outside. In the daylight, the shadows on his face were more prominent, like the ones under his eyes. It made sense now why he fell asleep all the time and why he left so fast after our tutoring sessions.

Goku had two jobs, which meant Danny shouldn't be here right now.

"How are you here right now?" I asked. Did he get the day off?

"I'm surprised to see you too," Danny said, misinterpreting my question. I nodded anyway because my mind hadn't fully wrapped around the idea that I'd been chatting with Danny this whole time. If I hadn't volunteered to help Danny catch up with his classes, I don't think he would've ever spoken to me. Despite sharing some of the same classes, our social circles didn't mix. If we were online, xxaznxbbxgrlxx wouldn't have any problem jumping into a conversation with SuperxSaiyan85. But now, standing in front of each other, the silence was painful.

This was worse than the time I misspoke at my fifth-grade play and said Chinese New Year was celebrated all over the world except China. "Let's forget about—"

"Do you still want to—" Danny said at the same time. He ducked his head to try to meet my downcast eyes. "Is that what you want?"

It was finally sinking in that Danny knew everything about me too. How much I hated being treated like a run-of-the-mill nerdy Asian girl when my dreams were bigger than high school. But the only way to break out of this town was to work my ass off, thus perpetuating the stereotype. He knew how I wished I could be a risk-taker and stand out in some way. So his question wasn't looking for confirmation. It was egging me on to take a step outside of my comfort zone. It stirred something inside me.

"Where are we going?"

A smile crept over Danny's face. His face was rarely off his desk, so I never noticed how much his face brightened with that small curve of his lips. "Wherever your heart desires."

I snorted. It sounded like some corny thing SuperxSaiyan85 would say. It really was him.

Danny tried not to laugh at me, but he failed. "Are we actually laughing out loud right now?"

It was awkward, talking in person, yet it felt familiar and comfortable and strange all at the same time. Like rewatching your favorite movie and seeing a detail you missed before. Any misgivings I had before melted away. SuperxSaiyan85 was my best friend online. Who's to say Danny Phan couldn't be my best friend for real?

Chapter One

Present Day

THERE WAS NO SUCH THING AS KEEPING A SECRET IN LA. I WASN'T even referring to the paparazzi, who had no moral objections to sharing unsavory photos of anyone giving off the slightest whiff of fame. I was talking about everyone in my favorite coffee shop, located three blocks away from the FreeStream studio. In the first five minutes of waiting in line, I overheard the writers in front of me talk about the sitcom pilot they were working on. The woman behind me was giving someone a play-by-play of a juicy hookup with an A-list celebrity's personal trainer.

"Rolf is massive," the woman gushed.

"*Everywhere?*" Her companion was asking the right questions.

"Ev-er-y-where. It almost didn't go in." The woman sighed like she was still drunk on this man's dick and proceeded to go on and on and on about his stamina. At this point, it was sounding less like TMI and more like a romance novel. Surely this type of man existed only in fiction.

I continued eavesdropping because whether Rolf was real or not, hearing about him was more entertaining than my life. Dating at thirty-eight was a chore. Half of the time I matched with some guy named Seth who worked in the industry, and once he found out I worked at FreeStream he'd switch from courtship to networking in zero seconds. It wasn't like I had much to report on the work front either. FreeStream was running on a lean staff after the last round of layoffs, so my days were long. I'd come home only to hop back on my laptop to prepare for the next day.

The woman was still going on about her sexy escapades when it was my turn to order. I was going to miss the ending of her story, but if the trainer was as famous as she claimed, there was a chance I could catch a summary on DeuxMoi. I stepped up to the counter. "I'll have a regular matcha latte and"—browsing the display of pastries, I pointed at the croissant as big as my face—"I'll take one of those." The coffee shop didn't have the best croissants in town, but I'd needed more carbs to get through the workday lately.

Lively chatter lowered into feverish whispers when I walked to the other end of the counter to pick up my drink. The shop was frequented by FreeStream employees, and I wouldn't have blamed them if they were talking shit about me while I stood there.

It had been three days since *Variety* reported the sale of FreeStream to the media giant America's Broadcasting Network. From the public's perspective, it didn't make sense for any company to want the little unknown streamer that played old B-list movies. ABN had its own streaming services for its extensive catalog. But insiders knew that ABN wanted to reboot a cult classic action franchise about a renegade with a talking motorcycle that FreeStream owned the rights to. Rather than dealing with the process of securing the rights for one series, ABN bought FreeStream outright in case it wanted to stomp on any more of my favorite childhood shows.

In the press release, ABN assured viewers that there would be no interruption to their FreeStream experience and that it would continue to provide quality entertainment. But I knew better. I'd been at FreeStream since its inception eleven years ago. I considered myself an industry veteran, and I'd seen that every time a merger happened, restructuring was inevitable.

Since I was part of the team that worked on the deal, I was a target for everyone's hate. I wanted to shout at them that I'd come into this business because I loved TV and film, but once you're labeled a heartless traitor, no one believes anything you say. So I waited for my drink in silence.

"That's not what I heard."

I immediately recognized the voice of Tara Klein, the executive assistant to FreeStream's CEO, Martin Carr. I peered over my shoulder and located the back of Tara's brunette head. She seemed to be talking to herself until I spotted her white earbuds. She was at the drink station, swirling her beverage with a wooden stirrer. "The announcement's going out today, and you know who's going to deal with Marty's angry emails? Me."

I turned my head, pointing my ear toward Tara like a satellite. Whatever she was about to say, I wanted it to transmit nice and clear. I was morbidly curious about how they were going to "streamline" the workflow when our company was already short-staffed. Our primary audience was older than the coveted eighteen-to-thirty-four advertising demographic, so we weren't rolling in cash like the power players in the streaming space.

"It's going to be bad," Tara said as she snapped the lid back on her drink. "I heard Marty say half."

The barista had to wave me down. I didn't hear him call my name for my drink. The word "half" overtook my brain. "Half" could refer to anything. Half of our budget? Half of the staff? Neither was good. Both would have devastating impacts. By the time

I recovered, Tara had walked out of the coffee shop before I could hear the rest of her conversation.

I grabbed my drink and hurried to my car, which, of all days, I'd parked two blocks away on a narrow neighborhood street. While I'd lived in LA for over a decade, I was never brave enough to parallel park on Sunset Boulevard. Not that the neighborhood street was much better. When both sides of the curb were lined with cars, there was room only for one car to go through in either direction. Driving in LA was like a game of luck. One day you could find street parking with time still left on the meter. Another day you were sitting in bumper-to-bumper traffic on a five-lane freeway, reliving every mistake you ever made in your life.

Today I was going to need all the luck I could get.

I REFRESHED MY email. Five seconds later, I refreshed it again.

"I wouldn't be worried if I were you." Zoe, my assistant, plopped onto the small sofa in the corner of my office. "You know how it is. It's always the assistants and entry-level folks on the chopping block."

I didn't argue with her in case I got to keep my job. It'd be insensitive of me when she was right. Her job was more at risk than mine. I'd put in the time to oversee FreeStream's global business development. I was proud to have climbed up the ranks in my department. I worked hard for it because I was under the impression it would give me a seat at the table to take our fledgling channel to broader audiences. Now that FreeStream was folded into ABN, with its wide audience reach, there was no longer a need for me. I'd become another redundant cog in the big entertainment machine.

How did this happen? I used to be such a go-getter, but somewhere along the line I'd become complacent. I still liked bringing old TV shows and movies into FreeStream and giving them new life with a new audience. But as the years ticked by, the job was less about the movies and more about needing to keep a roof over my head amid skyrocketing rent. But who was I to complain when people came from all over the world to break into this cutthroat business? I was lucky to have gotten my foot in the door and to have a job that gave me a steady paycheck.

A notification chimed on my desktop. It was a mass email from Martin Carr, thanking me (and a slew of other employees) for my service, which was unfortunately no longer needed. As such, I was to vacate the building within the hour.

I shut my eyes and rested my forehead on my desk one last fucking time. I gave this place eleven prime years of my life only for it to end with a generic email. I'd received more personal emails from scammers trying to phish my password. Martin could've stepped up and shown his face over Zoom while he upended the future of hundreds of people. This fake apologetic email was a disgrace.

It was so hard to contain the overwhelming mix of disappointment and worry as I felt Zoe's sympathetic eyes on me. She had access to my inbox. She knew.

"Sorry, Rach." Zoe handed me a box of tissues, but I refused it. I wasn't going to give FreeStream my tears.

"What about you?" I asked.

"I got the email too," Zoe said with a shrug. She was handling the news much better than me.

"I'm sorry, Zoe. If you ever need a recommendation—"

"I'm fine," she said, dumping a ream of paper and a tape dispenser into a filing box. "I was going to call out next week for auditions anyway. This saved me the trouble."

I sat up and kept a straight face. Zoe was twenty-four. She had a bright future ahead of her. I didn't want to infect her with my jaded outlook. I pulled every drawer in my desk open, searching for my badge and key ring. Most of the facilities at FreeStream required key-card access, but not the golf cart.

"Do you want me to get you a box?" Zoe was too good to me. She had no obligation to me anymore, but here she was, helping me off this sinking ship.

"No thanks," I replied. I double-clicked the company shared drive to check for any loose ends to tie up. Sure enough, I was denied access. Damn, that was fast. To think that I once thought of FreeStream as my second home. How foolish of me. If FreeStream was kicking me out, then they didn't deserve any more of my labor. But I still had time before I had to leave the premises, so I was going to make the most of it. That included one last, fuck-you joyride.

I fired up the golf cart and zipped through the parking lot, yelling out my frustration. I must've been delirious, because a part of me felt relief, even though my professional life had effectively combusted. And yet there was something about the wind in my hair and the warm sun on my skin that made me feel invincible.

I pulled up to the soundstage with a screech. They weren't filming, so I let myself in. Nat was in her chair—the one with her name on it—reviewing lines. As the star of *Beyond the Dark*, FreeStream's only scripted show, Nat played Commander Justina Tan, the tough-talking leader on an intergalactic mission with a team of international scientists in search of other life-forms. It read like a *Star Trek* rip-off, but it was a workplace comedy.

I made a pit stop at craft services and swiped a drink.

"I have your green juice, Miss Natalie Huang," I said, twisting off the cap before I presented it to her.

"You haven't lost your touch from your PA days," Nat teased as she happily accepted the bottle and took a sip. "What brings you on set? Are you on your afternoon walk?"

Nat laid on her dramatic actress voice, which she had even back when she was a budding starlet in our high school's production of *A Streetcar Named Desire*. It was funnier hearing it now while Nat sported a serious ponytail and skintight space suit.

"No. I came to tell you that I was laid off."

"Shut up." Nat put her script to the side as she stood and gave me a hug. "Those assholes."

"I should've seen it coming." The writing was on the wall, but surviving previous rounds of layoffs had made me arrogant. "I should've looked for another job months ago."

"Are you going to be okay?" Nat let me go as she asked that loaded question.

I didn't have a good answer. Emotionally, I was a wreck. Financially, I was going to be okay. The severance package along with my savings should keep me afloat for the next few months while I figured things out. All I could do was shrug. "I think so."

"So, what are you going to do now that you have time on your hands?"

"I don't know. Whatever I want." It came out sounding like a question. Nothing in my life, not even the words coming out of my mouth, was certain.

"Like what?" Nat asked.

How would I know? I was laid off only a few minutes ago. Her guess was as good as mine.

"Maybe I can pick up a hobby." I didn't have a routine to follow or a boss to answer to anymore. I was up for trying something new. I ran through a list of things I'd been meaning to do but never had time for. "At the café, I saw a flyer for a beach boot camp class in Santa Monica. Or I could finally clean out my closet and update my wardrobe. I hear Y2K fashion is back in style."

Nat sipped her juice with a sour face, possibly because the juice contained a whole head of kale. "No offense, but what the hell are you talking about? The only cardio I've seen you do was chase after that extra because you thought he was Daniel Henney, and sorry, but you can't pull off Y2K fashion. You didn't pull it off when it was trendy the first time around, and you're not ironic enough to get away with it now."

Ouch. "Remind me why you're my best friend again."

"Because I always tell you the truth and I pay for half of our rent." Right. There was that. I was thirty-eight and still had a roommate who was spot-on about my lack of fashion sense. Hollywood glamour never rubbed off on me.

"You know, I just lost my job. You should be comforting me." Nat gave me a single conciliatory squeeze on the shoulder. "That's it?"

"I don't see you bawling your eyes out, so yeah. That's all you get." I didn't push Nat for more sympathy. People used to say I was determined, but I didn't hold a candle to Nat. She used to go on audition after audition, getting rejected left and right. I didn't know how she withstood the relentless punishment, but she wouldn't be here as the lead of her own show if she hadn't picked herself up and tried time and time again. "Does this mean you're free?"

"Well, since you shot down my ideas, my schedule is wide open. Why?"

"I have some long shoots coming up, and I can't keep up with my email." Nat motioned for me to come closer and lowered her voice. "Remember that indie I shot two years ago? The heist movie where I played a pickpocket with a heart of gold?"

"How could I forget? I couldn't find my wallet or phone when you were rehearsing."

"Well, it's going to premiere at South by Southwest!" Nat threw her hands up and shrieked as loud as a mouse.

I screamed for real, which drew dirty looks from the crew. "I can't believe you didn't tell me."

Nat lowered her hands, motioning me to quiet down. "I don't know exactly when it'll be announced, but I think it'll be soon. My team has been sending me emails left and right about arrangements and stylists, and I don't have time to deal with it. I could really use a personal assistant for the next month or so. I'd pay, of course."

Well, what do you know? I guess I did have a job lined up after all.

Nat made this sound like a temporary, mutually beneficial arrangement, but if we were being honest, Nat wasn't the most organized person in the world. I've had to remind her to pay her bills, and I regularly cleaned expired food out of the fridge. I was already like her personal assistant, only this job would make it more official.

"I hope it wasn't weird to ask," Nat said when I didn't reply right away. "I don't have the time to vet an assistant, and it's nothing you haven't handled before." Nat held up her juice to make her point. "You already know my drink order."

"It's true." If there was anything I felt confident about, it was Nat's inexplicable love of kale. Everything else in my life was up in the air.

Getting laid off was a hard pill to swallow. In my eleven years at FreeStream, I was a manager for only one. I had finally gotten into the groove of my role when the merger threw a wrench into my foreseeable future. But if life was going to deal me this shitty hand, then what the hell. Maybe it was about time I figured out who I was without a job dictating my calendar.

"You're taking the layoff a little too well," Nat commented as she gave me another once-over. "Is there something you're not telling me? Do you have something in the works?"

"I don't." For once in my life, I didn't have a plan, not even a backup one. I'd never needed one before. "This could be good for me," I said, though I didn't fully believe it myself yet. "I can take it slow before jumping into the next thing."

Nat shot me a skeptical glance as she took a long sip of her drink. "If I didn't know you any better, I'd think that was a cry for help. You're always three steps ahead of other people."

"What? I can't try on something new?" Nat acted like I was going off the grid or getting into crypto. I was only taking some time off. It would do me some good, or so I'd heard. I'd jump back into work when I was refreshed and ready. I could get a massage or whatever it was that people did to get some R&R these days.

"If this is your way of saying you want to become an actress—"

I rolled my eyes at Nat's suggestion. I'd dipped my toe in acting when I was an extra, but it wasn't for me. On camera, I was stiff as a board, and I didn't have the stomach to withstand the comments about my appearance. When it came to rejection and unsolicited feedback, I had to give Nat credit. She was tough as nails.

"Excuse me, Natalie." Marcus Gray, the young Black actor who played genius astrophysicist Dr. Caleb Rhodes, threw a thumb over his shoulder. "We're being called to set. Sorry . . . ," he said to me as he walked away, stretching the word because he didn't remember my name. That was fine. We'd only met once or twice before. I didn't care. I was busy eating up his British accent.

"How come you're never that starstruck with me?" Nat asked.

"I don't get starstruck," I said evenly. Not unless it was Keanu Reeves or Michelle Yeoh, who once made eye contact with me at a Women in Hollywood gala and my knees turned to jelly. I took that as a sign from the universe that I was supposed to kneel before my queen. "I was looking the normal amount."

As normal as it can be when you're surrounded by an insanely attractive cast.

"There's nothing wrong with looking," Nat agreed. "If you're feeling shy, I can ask Marcus if he's willing to take a selfie with you."

Shy, my ass. Nat was saying that to get on my nerves. I'd learned quickly that I had to put myself out there to get ahead in my career. When it came to dating, though, I couldn't argue. I hadn't cracked the code to that part of my life, so I had to admit I'd been reserved.

Nat left to take her mark. The director made a last call to quiet the set. I scurried out of the studio before I was locked in. I still had a desk to clean out before I started the new phase in my life: funemployment.

February 2003

xxaznxbbxgrlxx: did you like the movie? I thought it was cute.

SuperxSaiyan85: we should've watched Cradle 2 The Grave.

> **xxaznxbbxgrlxx:** i checked moviefone. The showtimes were way too late.

> **xxaznxbbxgrlxx:** I love Jet Li but you can tell that movie had no plot.

> **SuperxSaiyan85:** oh was that why we watched a romcom? For the plot? It should've been called how to lose a guy in 1 day.

> **SuperxSaiyan85:** I'm picking the next movie.

Whenever that would be. There were only three more months before our AP tests.

> **xxaznxbbxgrlxx:** hey. Are you going to show up to tutoring tomorrow?

> **SuperxSaiyan85:** i can't. My manager scheduled me every day this week.

I don't know why I expected Danny to answer differently. Knowing the face behind the screen name didn't change his situation.

> **xxaznxbbxgrlxx:** the job at the mall?

Nat heard from a friend in Drama Club that they saw Danny at one of those kiosks in the middle of the walkway that sold keychains and accessories.

SuperxSaiyan85: yeah

xxaznxbbxgrlxx: does your manager let you study when it's slow?

SuperxSaiyan85: my manager wouldn't know. I'm usually there by myself.

Even better. What was stopping him from maximizing his downtime?

xxaznxbbxgrlxx: I can drop off my notes after I study or you can call me if you have questions

SuperxSaiyan85: you don't have to.

I wasn't sure why he was refusing my help. He'd complained to me once about how his transcripts were from a hodgepodge mix of schools, how he performed better at some schools than others so his grades came out average. I remembered the day he told me because I connected to that feeling of being so much more than what a piece of paper said about me.

xxaznxbbxgrlxx: It's my job to tutor you. You need to get a good grade so I can look good.

SuperxSaiyan85: you look good anyway

As soon as I finished reading that message, Danny sent more in quick succession.

SuperxSaiyan85: you're going to be a valedictorian

SuperxSaiyan85: you're probably going to get into all the UCs you applied to

SuperxSaiyan85: and all the backup schools

SuperxSaiyan85: and if you get the Merit Scholarship, you'll end up at Berkeley

xxaznxbbxgrlxx: when

SuperxSaiyan85: when? This fall?

xxaznxbbxgrlxx: you mean *when* I win the Merit Scholarship

SuperxSaiyan85: lol you're so cocky Rachel

 *Chapter Two*

I woke up at seven thirty to get a head start on my new-found free life. I made my own avocado toast for breakfast and jotted down a small to-do list in my planner. While I was getting my day started, Nat meditated in our living room before heading out to the studio.

"You're up way too early for someone who doesn't have anywhere to go," Nat commented with her eyes closed. I envied her mental gymnastics, going from sitting still in silence to pretending she was discovering alien life-forms with a ragtag team of scientists.

"That's not true. I have an itinerary for the whole weekend." I read from my planner. "My goal for today is to 'relax at the spa. Deadline: 3 p.m.'"

Nat stretched her arms as she slowly came back to the present. "You gave yourself a deadline?"

"What's wrong with that? It gives me a clear sense of whether or not my goal was completed. Besides," I said, flipping my planner around so Nat could see it, "there's a dedicated column for deadlines and it has these cute little checkboxes."

Checking off those boxes made me feel as good as any drug.

"Planning your free time feels a little . . ." Nat struggled to find the right word.

"Ironic?" I suggested. "See? I do have some irony in me."

"I was going to say counterintuitive." Nat approached the counter to take a closer look at my list, which included balancing my checkbook and scrubbing our bathroom. Limescale was no joke. "This doesn't sound like taking a break. Resting means you should, you know, *rest*. Do less." Nat said this as soft as a lullaby, like she was getting me to lay down the edge in my voice.

"Point taken," I said, trying my best not to sound defensive. Although it was my time to spend, not hers. "Are you firing me, then? Maybe I shouldn't work. I should commit a hundred percent of my time to doing nothing."

"And you say I'm the dramatic one," Nat deadpanned. "I'm not asking you to be on call. What I need is to regain control of my inbox." She pointed at her laptop, which was charging on the coffee table. "You should be able to get into everything. All the passwords are saved."

I settled on the couch and opened Nat's laptop to confirm I had access before she left for the day. "Nat. Quick question. How do you have so many unread emails?" Six hundred thirty-eight, to be exact.

She shrugged. "If it's not important, I ignore it."

My skin crawled. How did she live like this? "It might be faster to set your inbox on fire."

"Ha-ha," Nat said. "Some stuff is important, but not urgent."

"How am I supposed to know that?"

We worked out a system of prioritizing messages she needed to respond to and sending her periodic reminders throughout the day, updating her calendar accordingly. Everything else in her inbox I was free to delete. I couldn't wait to get her inbox down to zero.

"You're going to leave me drunk with power," I said, already unsubscribing her from store promo emails.

"Don't sound too excited now."

"Hey." I stopped Nat before she walked out the door. There were some FreeStream emails, sending reassurances to everyone outside of the corporate office. If I were her, I thought, I wouldn't take FreeStream's word for anything. "You don't think FreeStream would cancel—"

Nat tutted over my voice and covered her ears. "Nuh-uh. We don't say the c-word around here."

Nat was terribly superstitious about anything that could bring bad juju, so I rephrased. "Any word on a season three for *Beyond the Dark*?"

"No," she said with a weary sigh, "but the writers are optimistic. They have Commander Tan and Dr. Rhodes stranded on a desert planet in the season finale."

"Hey! Spoiler much?" As payback, I trashed the next one hundred unopened spam emails.

Nat swatted my hands away from the keyboard. "I didn't mean for you to start now. Go get pampered first."

That was fine by me. I could check something off my list. "Whatever you say, boss."

I SCORED A last-minute reservation for a "rejuvenation package" at a day spa near my apartment in Silver Lake. It included a massage, a facial, and an exfoliation session that promised to leave me restored and renewed.

"It makes me sound like an antique," I joked with Cheryl, my masseuse. She was an older woman with sandy-blond hair tied up in a bun. She smiled kindly as she placed warm rolled towels under my knees.

"Let me know if you want me to make any adjustments," she said in a buttery voice that melted right in with the soothing New Age music playing in the background. "Your comfort is my top priority." Cheryl proceeded to work out every knot in my body with her superhuman hands. "Try to relax," she cooed.

I would have if she hadn't been yanking my arms back, steering my upper body like a bicycle. Her strong grip put my body on alert, like it was under attack. By the time she was done with me, I felt like a blob of kneaded dough. I managed to put on my robe and lumbered to my facial appointment.

My aesthetician, Nancy, began with a quick assessment. Shining a bright light on my face, she asked, "Is this your first time?"

"It is," I admitted.

Nancy squinted as she scanned my face, as though she was counting every single pore.

"You should drink more water," she said finally.

I tried not to laugh. That I did know.

Nancy rubbed two fingers gently on both of my temples, applying the perfect amount of pressure. She moved on to smooth strokes on my cheeks, erasing every thought in my brain. I miraculously forgot about my aching body that had been pulled like taffy. This was the calming experience I signed up for.

"Okay," Nancy said, stopping way too soon. I opened my eyes to see her face, now wearing glasses (safety goggles, more like), and sharp tools where relaxing fingers had been.

"What are— Ow!"

"I'm cleaning your pores," she explained as she continued to prick and press my face with her stainless-steel instruments. "Let me know if it hurts."

She couldn't tell from the way I flinched every time she prodded my face? I was reevaluating everything I ever heard about facials. But I stayed quiet and trusted the process. If this was supposed to help me have the same glass skin as Nancy, then so be it. Beauty required a little pain.

By the end of this self-imposed torture, I contemplated forgoing my last appointment. The receptionist reassured me that the exfoliation session would be gentle and I would come out refreshed from the cascades of water that would wash away my dead skin. I should've walked out the door when I saw my masseuse pull on rubber gloves and boots. The room looked like a laboratory, with a table in the center and showerheads instead of lasers pointing at it. The scraping and scrubbing I expected. But then I was buffed with a moppy sponge that reminded me of the drive-through car wash. For the grand finale, I was doused with water coming from every direction. I returned home drenched, physically and spiritually.

"It couldn't have been that bad," Nat said after I recounted my epic journey at the spa. She'd washed up after coming back on set, but there was still a stubborn smudge of waterproof eyeliner on her eyelids. "You're glowing."

"It's because they scrubbed me raw and then lathered me up in moisturizing serum." I fired up Nat's laptop. "How do people do this regularly?" I found more comfort in scrubbing our bathroom than secluding myself in dimly lit rooms with the constant sound of running water. Oh no, I realized. What if spas ruined the sound of water for me?

"Well, you survived," Nat said, indulging me in my first-world pity party. "I'm sorry the spa didn't work out, but you didn't have to jump right back into work."

"I don't mind. I feel better when I have something to do. Otherwise, I'll do something drastic like get a pixie cut."

"Need I remind you that you *Felicity*-chopped your hair during your Lilith Fair phase? Sarah McLachlan called. She wants you to save your hair and those poor rescue dogs."

"It wasn't that bad," I said, as I trashed an entire page of unopened emails. It was quite cathartic. Not to mention, it was fun to browse through Nat's inbox. There were cool emails in there, like a rom-com script her agent forwarded to her. Nat was finally seen as a leading lady because of the will-they-won't-they storyline between Commander Tan and Dr. Rhodes on *Beyond the Dark*. I blocked out time for her to run lines with me. "By the way, I put the fitting with your stylist on your calendar."

"Thanks."

Nat's calendar was horrifically blank. How did she keep track of where she was supposed to be on any given day? I'd never seen her carry around a planner either. "Are you scheduled to arrive in Austin a few days before South by Southwest or are you jumping into press?"

Nat held up her hands in the perpendicular "T" formation. "Hold on. Time out."

I looked up from Nat's laptop. "What?"

"You don't need to give me one hundred and ten percent, Rach. I'm not going to fire you."

I couldn't be too sure these days. What was the harm in nailing down some details?

"You have a month before the premiere. If we don't book your flight now, you're going to get stuck with an aisle seat by the bathroom, and you don't want that because that's how Keanu Reeves was discovered by a fan. Do you really want to take awkward self-ies with someone holding their pee?"

Nat rolled her eyes. "Are you done?" I nodded. "I'm not that famous," she said, annoyed that she had to say that out loud. "I don't have anything to worry about. And Keanu? How do you even know that?"

"You can find anything on the internet if you try hard enough," I said, which was true in general but not in this case. The mystical algorithm did its thing, and an update popped up on my Instagram. "I'm going to block out your calendar for the whole week just to be . . ." My finger hovered over the touchpad. In Nat's mostly vacant calendar there was one lone event scheduled the weekend before South by Southwest. If I hadn't seen it with my own eyes, I wouldn't have believed it.

The label read: "CHS Class of 2003 20th Reunion."

How did I not know my high school was having a twentieth reunion? Deep down inside me was a pissed teenager wondering why I wasn't asked to help plan the damn thing. But that pettiness was soon overtaken by a heavy feeling in the pit of my stomach. Senior year had been one of the worst periods of my life.

"There's a reunion?" I heard myself say as I toggled out of Nat's calendar and into her inbox. I had to find more information.

"Oh, I forgot about that," Nat said. Clearly, since she didn't even tell me about it. "I RSVP'd, but I'll probably get there late. I have to be on set that day."

I made a note to get Nat's filming schedule. "How come you didn't tell me? A heads-up would've been nice."

Nat crossed her arms, making me wonder if I should be talking to my new boss so casually. It was hard not to when we'd known each other for over twenty years and we were currently sitting next to each other in our pajamas. "I distinctly recall someone telling me they never wanted to relive high school ever again."

Damn, I *was* dramatic. I did say that, but it pertained to one specific person who crushed my heart. "That was a long time ago."

Nat eyed me. "It's not too late to RSVP if you want to go. The invite is somewhere in my email."

"I should look it up anyway," I said as I typed "reunion" in the inbox's search bar. "You know, to enter the details in your calendar."

"Suuure." Nat didn't believe me for one second, but she left me to it. "I'm going to bed. I have an early call time tomorrow."

I waited until Nat disappeared into her room before I opened the invitation.

Dear Miss Natalie Huang,

The Commonwealth High School Class of 2003 invites you back to campus to celebrate its 20th Reunion on Saturday, March 4th at 6 p.m. We would like to honor you and induct you into the CHS Alumni Hall of Fame for your contributions in acting.

While we take a stroll down memory lane, there will be an auction benefiting Commonwealth High School with smart-room upgrades. Please bring your wallet and generosity. To donate prizes, please reply and direct the message to our reunion chair, Mariana Sanchez.

We hope you can join us for an evening of making new memories with old friends. RSVP by February 17th. If you can't attend, reconnect with the Class of 2003 on our Facebook page! Go Eagles!

The CHS Reunion Committee
Mariana Sanchez
Belinda Kang
Winston Lin
Danny Phan
Vivienne Tam-Blake

Danny Phan. After all this time, my chest still tightened at the sight of his name. I had to shove the confusing, contradictory feelings back into the vault of my memory until I knew what to do with them.

I reviewed the names of those on the planning committee again. Who put this team of people together? Seriously, no one thought to ask me?

I swallowed down my jealousy. It was silly. Until recently, I didn't have the time to plan the reunion anyway. I shouldn't be getting upset over having one less thing to do. Still, this list of names confused me. Mariana was our student body president, so her involvement was a given. Belinda Kang was one of the valedictorians with me. She was a college professor now. The last time I saw her was at her wedding to her high school sweetheart, Oscar Castillo. I mean Dr. Oscar Castillo, family physician.

But Winston Lin? He was our class clown. The only thing I could rely on Winston to do was moon the entire school, which he had done on multiple occasions. That boy was weirdly proud of his pasty ass. As for Vivienne Tam, I'd only known the It Girl of our school to attend parties, not plan them.

Then there was Danny. The only thing he was good at was breaking my heart. Then again, I was pretty sure I broke his.

I set aside Nat's laptop and traded it for my phone to search my own email. I tried a few different keyword searches, but I couldn't come up with an invitation. I checked Nat's email again. Her invite was sent to the same email she'd had since high school, which forwarded to her current email address. If my invitation was sent to my high school email address, there was no hope of retrieving it. I couldn't remember my password, and I was fairly confident that the email provider didn't exist anymore.

I checked my Facebook account. I hadn't used it in a while, but I never got around to deleting it. The idea of erasing a bunch of memories and connections with a few clicks scared me. I had to reset my password, but after I logged in, I found the reunion page. There were photos uploaded from names that looked somewhat familiar. I scrolled through images of cliques and varsity teams. It was strange. I used to think high school was so hard, but now, looking at these young faces again, so full of life, I wondered if we had gone to the same school.

In some ways, high school hadn't been that bad. It was the last place where I felt truly accomplished, where there was a direct correlation between my hard work and my achievements. It set me up to handle everything that came after, like my grueling schedule in college while balancing my part-time job and my coveted internship with legendary producer Gloria Miller. That woman opened my eyes to the behind-the-scenes of filmmaking. It took only one phone call from Gloria to get any production assistant gig I wanted. Work had come relatively easily until recently. But when it came to life—the stuff that I was supposed to do outside of work—that I hadn't figured out yet.

I checked my notifications before logging out. I skimmed past old birthday wishes until I found the message I'd been looking for.

My invitation to the reunion was sent by none other than Danny.

It had been waiting for me in my Facebook messages for over a month. The message was a copy-paste replica of the one in Nat's inbox, down to the induction to the CHS Alumni Hall of Fame, except mine was for my contributions to the entertainment industry.

If only they knew I was painfully unemployed. Even if I'd still been working at FreeStream, I hadn't done anything deserving of this kind of recognition. My career met its demise because I played a small part in reinvigorating an old franchise that would eventually get a horrible remake. I didn't push any boundaries or create new art like I imagined I would when I started in this business.

I wanted to delete the invitation until I saw the message below it.

Danny: hope you can make it

Reading those five words sucked the air out of my lungs. The last time Danny and I spoke, I was so angry and I said things I didn't mean. If I'd known they would dissolve our friendship, I wouldn't have said them. Danny was more sensitive than he let on.

I reread his message. He wouldn't have sent me a personalized invitation if it wasn't an olive branch. Or maybe he didn't care anymore. It had been twenty years. The past was well behind us. Judging by his profile picture, time had treated him well. His former hedgehog hair was now longer, swooping the edges of his smiling face. He had more wrinkles around his eyes than before, but he looked like the same Danny I knew.

Damn. I hadn't thought about him in a long time, and here I was, staring at his picture, wondering what he had been up to since he moved away after graduation. The last thing I heard about him was at Belinda's wedding about ten years ago. Someone mentioned that Danny was seeing someone, and I stopped looking him up. Curiously, there wasn't a relationship status on his Facebook page.

I stopped snooping around. I had no right. I had kept my promise and never spoke to him again. But there were times like these when I'd feel low and the nights were quiet, making way for regrets to come roaring back, Danny being one of them. I cringed at how I used to wait by my computer to chat with him, especially after we met in real life. But for that brief period in my life, he was my person. I could tell him just about anything.

Then things imploded because my emotions were volatile and confusing. But Danny wasn't totally innocent either in our friendship's demise. Friends didn't usually kiss friends in a way that altered their brain chemistry. If he wanted to see me again, he better be ready to tell me his part of the story. If he could do that, maybe there was a chance we could be friends again. That sounded kind of nice.

I RSVP'd for the reunion. It was a week away, so I had some time to think about how I could spin the fact that my subscription to *The Hollywood Reporter* was my only contribution to entertainment these days.

I opened my planner and jotted down my new goals.

Date: March 4
Time: 6 p.m.
Goals:
1. Renew friendship with Danny Phan
2. See old friends
3. Relive high school for one more night
Deadline: March 5

February 2003

Things were back to normal when we returned to school. Danny glided from class to class hoping that none of our teachers would call on him. We made eye contact for a second, but it felt accidental. Danny's face was unreadable before he buried it in his arms for a nap.

Before I found out who he was, it made sense that we didn't hang out at school. I knew my reputation. Smart but uptight. Got things done but didn't let things slide. It never bothered me that there was always a "but" because I knew I had people who understood me.

While my parents didn't always get why I was so busy, they trusted me. "You know what you're doing," they'd say as they unwound after work, before calling relatives in Cambodia. They saw the straight As and figured I was doing something right. My sister, Angela, was the one who really took care of me day to day, filling out all of the important school documents that my parents didn't know how to read and feeding me when my parents worked late. Nat had been a good friend ever since middle school, when we discovered a mutual love of movies. She loved the craft of acting and was a verifiable chameleon. My interest in movies was a result of happenstance, in that my parents worked all the time and left Angela and me with our television babysitter.

And then there was SuperxSaiyan85. I could be okay with Danny holding up the status quo at school as long as our online chats stayed the same.

xxaznxbbxgrlxx: have you ever watched the movie, You've Got Mail?

SuperxSaiyan85: Is that the AOL one? With Tom Hanks?

xxaznxbbxgrlxx: yeah. It reminds me kind of like us, except you're not running me out of business

SuperxSaiyan85: thanks for ruining the ending for me

xxaznxbbxgrlxx: you weren't going to watch it

SuperxSaiyan85: now i'm not

I went for it and asked the question I was too scared to ask the other day.

xxaznxbbxgrlxx: did you know that you'd been chatting with me this whole time?

SuperxSaiyan85: nope

xxaznxbbxgrlxx: why did you chat me with that night? there were other people in the chat room

SuperxSaiyan85: i dunno. i was bored

SuperxSaiyan85: if i knew i was going to listen to a girl cry all night about her sister, i woulda IM'ed someone else =P

xxaznxbbxgrlxx: shut up. I missed my sister. She helped me with everything. I was scared about handling high school without her

SuperxSaiyan85: everything turned out okay, didn't it?

xxaznxbbxgrlxx: I guess so. As long as I bring in the grades, my parents leave me alone

SuperxSaiyan85: my parents leave me alone too but it's because they're too busy working

xxaznxbbxgrlxx: same. they're so lucky we don't get into trouble. can u imagine?

SuperxSaiyan85: i know, right?

Chapter Three

MY PARENTS WERE FLOURISHING IN THEIR RETIREMENT. BA started accordion lessons, which was a tragedy for anyone with their hearing intact. Ma got into sculptural paper crafts, which she learned from a neighbor. It was pretty amazing, albeit a little strange, to see them lounge at home and dabble in creative pursuits after watching them hustle to survive all their lives, through war and then after uprooting their lives to come to the US. When they wanted family time, they lured Angela and me back home on the weekends with food. This week's menu was samlar machu youn.

"Stop, lah," Ma called out from the kitchen while Ba played his rendition of "Que Sera, Sera" in the living room.

"You made me lose my place," Ba complained, pushing the bellows together for a discordant sound.

"I'm going to throw that thing away," Ma muttered to herself. She waited until Ba stowed his accordion in its case before putting in her hearing aids. "Lucas zài nǎlǐ? Tell him to come eat."

"He's coming." Angela set the table as the family gathered around it. "We can't start dinner without your favorite son-in-law."

I elbowed Angela. Why did she tease Ma like that? Ma was going to get started on how Lucas was her only son-in-law.

Ma threw a chilly glance at me but refrained from saying

anything. "He likes this soup and he should eat it while it's hot."

She did love Lucas, whether he was the only son-in-law or not. Her eyes positively sparkled when Lucas finally wandered into the dining room and took his seat between Angela and my niece, Hailey. Ma passed him a bowl of soup, heaped with catfish, and watched eagerly until he took the first slurping spoonful of the sweet-and-sour tamarind broth.

"Mmmm," Lucas said, performing his heart out as the steam from his bowl fogged his glasses and colored his pale face with a dash of pink. Satisfied, Ma went back to scooping bowls for the rest of us. When she was out of earshot, Lucas whispered to Angela, "What soup is this again?"

"Just eat it," Angela replied as she dug into her own bowl. I suspected that she was tired of having to once again explain our culture to Lucas, but more importantly, it made Ma happy to see all of us eating together. It was hard to get everyone's schedule aligned to make this happen more often. Angela still lived in Alhambra, only a couple of miles from my parents. But between busy careers and Hailey's school schedule, they came to family dinners as infrequently as I did.

"Jīn wǎn zài zhèlǐ shuì hanh?" she asked, punctuating the question with a Khmer twang as she passed me my bowl of soup, poured over rice, exactly how I liked it. Ma puckered her lips to point at the overnight bag I left by the couch, in case I didn't understand. My Mandarin was rusty, but it wasn't that bad.

I should've given my mother advance notice about sleeping over, but she was the one who always said I was welcome to stay. "You never have to ask to stay in your own home," she once said.

"Until Sunday." I winced as I bit into a hot chunk of pineapple.

The burst of juice scalded my tongue, but it tasted divine. Nothing could compete with a hot meal on a cold evening. "The high school is having a reunion tomorrow."

"I didn't think you were going," Angela said as she served a bowl to Ba, careful not to spill anything on the 3D durian centerpiece that seemed to have made with a million paper footballs. "I didn't go to mine. Why bother when you can check Facebook?"

"Some of us don't use Facebook all the time," I replied. Hailey nodded in agreement. At sixteen, she knew as well as anyone that Facebook was out of fashion for everyone too young to remember that it used to be called *The* Facebook. "How did you even know about it?" I asked Angela.

"I saw the announcement on the marquee when I picked Hailey up from school."

Upon hearing her name, Hailey chimed in. "You graduated *twenty* years ago, Auntie Rachel?"

There was a silent *Wow, you're old* following her question. If I had said anything like this to my aunts at her age, I would have received a lecture about respecting my elders. But I considered myself a cool aunt and let it go. Hailey had likely heard it from my parents anyway.

"I haven't been to the school since graduation," I said. "It doesn't look like it's changed that much."

"Ugh, it hasn't," Hailey lamented. "They don't let us use the lockers anymore because they won't open."

The school was in greater disrepair than I'd thought.

"Will Josh be there?" Ba asked, reminding me why I didn't tell my parents about the reunion to begin with. After three years, they still couldn't understand why Josh and I called off our short engagement. It never made sense when two decent people couldn't make it work, but that was the case. Much of our two-year relationship had overlapped with our MBA programs. As it turned out, two ambitious, highly independent people in a relationship with each other meant that we only knew how to plop each other into our busy schedules. Josh and I weren't as good at building the foundation needed to upgrade our partnership to a marriage. But in my parents' eyes, Josh was a nice man with a job who was willing to marry me and that should've been sufficient.

"I don't know," I replied. Before my parents asked me to beg Josh to take me back, I added, "If he does, maybe I'll meet his new girlfriend."

My fib pleased no one. Ba sucked something out of his teeth. "Two daughters and I only have one grandchild."

"Ba," Angela interjected, like a referee blowing on her whistle. Lucas and Hailey kept quiet to stay out of the crossfire. "Keep me out of it."

"I'm trying, Ba," I said.

"You're trying?" He scoffed. "Mǔ zhū huì shàng shù."

There wasn't any use arguing with him once he started with idiom, but did he have to use this one? 母猪会上树 was the Mandarin cousin to "when pigs fly," except it had a gendered take that I didn't appreciate. I'd like to see a male pig climb trees.

Ma was more discreet with her feelings. She combed her fingers through her silver bangs, as she tended to do when she was worried. "Josh's mom didn't say anything when we went for our walk last night."

When Josh and I were together, I was thrilled that our moms became friends. I didn't think they'd carry on their friendship, though, after we broke up. Fortunately, my mom had nothing to add when it came to Josh. "How's work?"

Normally, I would've welcomed the subject change, but I wasn't about to go down this rabbit hole. My parents knew nothing about my former job despite the countless times I'd tried to explain it to them. Now neither of them was going to take my very temporary unemployed status very well. Ma and Ba had worked since childhood because work decided whether or not they'd eat that day. I didn't expect much empathy for wanting time off to go find myself.

"It's good," I said. That wasn't exactly a lie. It was very good that I no longer worked for a company that didn't value loyalty. I'd spent the last ten years fighting my way up the ranks, but all it took was one email to cancel everything I'd worked for. Getting laid off hurt, but I knew what I was getting myself into when I chose the entertainment business. It was a fickle industry. One day everyone would decide something was the in thing, and the next day it was out. A part of me had hoped that I was somewhat protected by being on the business side of things, but no. The long hours I sacrificed counted for nothing. I was spat out like the fish bone my dad not so delicately hacked into his hand and then dumped onto the supermarket advertisement that lined the dining table.

"Good," Ma echoed, sounding sad. She didn't say anything else, but she leaned in to run her fingers through my asymmetrical bob. It was like she was projecting her worry onto me, or maybe she hated that one side of my hair was longer than the other. It was likely both. The most important thing was that she didn't ask any further questions, saving me from making up some lie. I couldn't shake off Angela quite as easily, though.

My parents were like the CEOs in the family: they only dealt with high-level topics, like when I was going to get married and have children. Angela was like my immediate supervisor who knew the ins and outs of my day-to-day life. She saw right through my vague answers. After dinner, she followed me into my room and sat at my old computer desk, where my humongous Dell desktop still perched.

"When will Ba get rid of this thing?" Angela ran her hands over the keyboard. "I keep telling them to drop it off at an e-waste event."

"Because they're hoarders." Our parents didn't get rid of anything. My bedroom looked exactly as it did when I was in high school. I'd bet a million dollars that there was still a stack of Delia's catalogs underneath my bed.

"I saw the news," Angela said as I unpacked my clothes. "Were you affected by the layoffs?"

Times like these, I hated that Angela and I looked so much alike. It was like I was looking in the mirror having a conversation with myself, except one of us had a steady graphic design career, a husband napping on the couch, and long hair of equal length.

I hung up the outfits I borrowed from Nat's closet. She always had better taste in clothes than me. Angela correctly interpreted my silence as confirmation. "I won't tell Mom and Dad, but do you have anything lined up?"

"No, but I'm sure something will come up soon," I said, taking a shot at optimism, but it didn't land. Angela forged on with her line of questioning.

"Have you started looking? Doesn't it take awhile to find something?"

"Don't worry. I'll get around to it." I shouldn't have been annoyed with Angela. These were all reasonable questions. She was looking out for me, as usual. Angela always had more applicable advice to give than our parents did, whether it was about writing personal statements or getting birth control. But now that we were older, I wished she'd left some things for me to handle on my own.

"Which outfit do you like better?" I asked, hoping to divert Angela's attention with pretty clothes. I held up a drapey black gown. Nat had worn it once to a premiere, and it landed her on several best-dressed lists.

Angela pointed at the cream pantsuit in my other hand, which Nat had worn to last year's upfronts. "You're going to a reunion in a high school gym. Who are you trying to impress?"

"No one," I said too quickly in my effort to sound casual. Angela's eyebrows shot up close to her hairline, closer than the time she tried Botox.

"Hey." Angela's voice dipped, sounding much softer than usual. "I won't judge if you want to get back with Josh." I couldn't help but laugh at her misdirected sympathy.

"Nuh-uh," I said before Angela could let the idea sink roots into her brain. Did she really think I was hung up on Josh? We'd broken up three years ago. Then again, what was time? Here I was, indecisive about what to wear because of someone I hadn't seen in half a lifetime.

"It's going to be the first time I see my classmates in a long time. They're all doctors and professors now," I said to steer the subject away from my love life. I didn't lie to Angela. There was a part of me that wanted to show my old friends that I was just as successful as them—or at least I was before I got laid off. I wasn't going to show up and let them patronize me with their pity either. I held up the suit against my body. "What do you think? Does this say 'sexy Hollywood executive' to you?"

Angela leaned back in her chair as she evaluated the look. "What do you wear under the blazer?"

"Nat didn't wear anything underneath except double-sided tape," I recalled.

"That's not going to pass the dress code," Angela retorted.

I scoffed. "Tell me they've updated the rules in the last twenty years." It never made sense that I had to wear shorts that fell beneath my fingertips when I held my arms by my side, but boys (at least in 2003) could wear baggy cargo pants that fell off their asses. I sifted through my overnight bag and found a black cropped camisole. "Do you think they'll let me onto school grounds wearing this?"

Angela blew out a low whistle. "Call me if they send you to the principal's office." She called Hailey into the room. "What do you think, Hailey? Can Auntie wear that to school?"

Hailey leaned against the doorway as she assessed the suit. "School administrators would say that's the kind of outfit that would quote-unquote 'distract boys.'"

Perfect.

"Angie!" Ma shouted from the kitchen. "Do you want mango?"

"Oh, I gotta go." Angela jumped out of her seat. "I have to stop Ma before she sends me home with a whole box."

I stopped Hailey before she followed Angela out. "Wait. Can you help me with something?"

"Sure. What is it?"

"Don't tell your mom." This had Hailey intrigued. She closed the door behind her and parked herself on my bed. "Can you help me look someone up on the internet?"

Hailey whipped out her phone from her back pocket. "First name, last name, occupation?"

Wow. She was on it.

"Um, Danny Phan. Occupation unknown."

The lack of information didn't stop Hailey from typing. "Who is this Danny Phan?"

The boy who confused me more than calculus. "Just someone I used to know."

"Why is this a secret, then?"

"It's complicated."

"Ugh, boys," she said. *Ugh, boys* indeed.

Hailey flipped her phone around, showing me her screen. There was an image of a museum curator named Danny Phan from Sacramento wearing a quirky pair of clear glasses. "Is this the guy you're looking for?"

"No." It wasn't my Danny.

Undeterred, Hailey swiped to the next search result. "How about this guy?"

Clearly, she wasn't using a discerning eye. The picture was of some gamer named Danny Phan who looked young enough to be my kid. "I'm looking for someone from my high school."

Hailey scrolled through her phone. "There's a lot of Danny Phans, Auntie. You don't know anything else that could narrow it down?"

I shook my head. That didn't turn out the way I expected. "I thought your generation was supposed to be good at technology."

"We are," Hailey said, tapping her screen at lightning speed. "See? I searched your name and found all kinds of things about you, like how you were one of the folks laid off from FreeStream." She scrolled further. "As reported on *Deadline* and in *Variety* and *The Hollywood Reporter*."

"Okay, that's enough." Damn. The one time I made the trades, it had to be about my layoff. "Don't tell your Popo or Gong Gong."

Hailey kept scrolling until her eyes widened. "You have an IMDb profile? What movie were you in?"

I groaned. Nat had a small part in a low-budget, raunchy teen movie and got me in as an extra. Needless to say, the film hadn't aged well. "You don't need to know."

By the time I said this, Hailey had read my short acting résumé. "You were 'Asian Girl #2' in a movie called *The Summer Before Last*? Did you have any lines?"

Hailey should've been able to infer my answer given that my character had no name.

"No," I replied. Thank god, though. I was a terrible actress. I got roped in only because I happened to be visiting Nat on set that day and they were short on extras. "I had to act like Nat's Asian friend."

Talk about art imitating life.

"It sounds bad," she surmised.

"It was," I confirmed. The movie had gone straight to video. Nat played Asian Girl #1, who was only there to wear a skimpy outfit, but her part had enough lines to get her into SAG. Fortunately, there were better parts for Asian American actors these days. The other day Nat received a script for a buddy comedy set at a haunted mansion. She'd play a veteran detective stuck with a rookie on a case. The premise was campy, but the dialogue kept me laughing. I'd jotted down a few notes and was reminded of my days doing script coverage as a production intern. I hoped Nat didn't mind. She hadn't asked me to read her scripts, but it was a thrill to find a gem.

"Don't waste your time looking for the movie." I shooed Hailey out of my room. I didn't need to know more about my career lows. I wanted to know more about Danny, but I guess I had to get to know him the old-fashioned way.

I ARRIVED AT Commonwealth half an hour early, even though I'd tried hard to busy myself during the day to avoid sitting in the parking lot with nothing better to do. I had looked into booking myself a real vacation, but I couldn't commit to it in case I needed my savings a little longer. Then, for fun, I had read a script that Nat's agent had sent to her. It was a romantic comedy about a woman who discovers she's dead and her former boyfriend is a lying scumbag. In the process of taking her ghostly revenge, she runs into her ex-boyfriend's best friend, leading to an unexpected romance. The script was sharp, and the lead part played to Nat's strengths, but the business side of me knew that it was going to have a hard time getting funding. The current marketplace favored large tentpole movies. I had written notes in case Nat wanted to talk about it. That had only taken me until lunch.

There was so little to do at my parents' house. I didn't talk with them very much because they gardened all morning. I was so desperate to do something that I even washed my car in their driveway. I couldn't wrap my head around it. When I was working, I dreamed about having free time. Now that I had it indefinitely, I felt . . . lost. I'd never experienced this before.

Parked in the school lot, I still clutched the wheel. My pulse was pounding under my skin. Why was it so hard to relax?

A knock on my window pulled me out of my head. I couldn't believe it. Danny was staring down at me, with one hand on the roof of my car, probably wondering why I was strangling my steering wheel. His Facebook picture didn't do him justice. His hair, which used to have spikes sharp enough to impale someone, now swooped like the wind. His once-bare face was defined by his goatee. There were some wrinkles and a hint of dark circles under his eyes, but those had been there as long as I'd known him. He'd put on a little weight, but who hasn't? I wasn't complaining about the way he filled his gray suit. He still reminded me of the cute boy

I wanted to talk to the most, but now with the handsome patina of a grown man.

It was getting hot under my blazer, reminding me that my killer suit was meant for a grand entrance. But no. I'd been relegated to reuniting with my former friend in our high school parking lot underneath the shade of solar panels.

Danny's eyes tracked my face, probably noting how I'd changed. Then his lips parted. Those damn soft lips. I had to stop giving his mouth so much credit. We had kissed so long ago. It was possible that the way it turned my world upside down was a figment of my dramatic hormonal imagination.

"How did I know you'd be the first to arrive?" he said when his eyes landed back on mine. The friendly teasing was surprising, but not unwelcome. If Danny wanted to start this reunion with a clean slate, I was game. My life had already unexpectedly started over.

I rolled down my window. "Do I win a prize?"

"Yeah." His head pointed toward the school. "You get to set up the balloon arch."

My manicure protested. "You didn't hire someone for that?"

"Do you know how much that costs? An arm, a leg, and then some." Danny dipped his head, his nose barely crossing the threshold of my window. He was staring, his gaze heavy, probably withholding questions like *How have you been?* and *What have you been up to?* Yet here I was, wondering if I could get an arm, a leg, and then some. This close, it was hard to deny that he was attractive.

"What were you doing out here anyway?" I asked instead.

Danny tilted his head toward the school. "I had to make sure that gate was open."

Gate?

I looked out the windshield. What do you know? I hadn't no-ticed the gate until Danny mentioned it. It didn't exist when we attended school. It was tall enough to make ditching class im-possible.

Danny tapped the roof of my car. "Come on. I'll walk you in."

First the personal invitation, and now this. Present-day Danny was more mature than I anticipated. I rolled the window up and opened the car door. I made an effort to step out calm and col-lected, like I looked this chic on a daily basis. I watched Danny's face, which I could see clearly since we were standing in between two cars with only a foot between us. I followed where his eyes dipped, first to the small gold pendant on my necklace, then trail-ing down my camisole to my exposed navel and stopping where my hands clutched the handles of my Celine purse.

"You don't wear glasses anymore," he said when his attention returned to my face.

"Lasik," I replied.

"You seem to be doing well." Something shifted in Danny's tone, and I couldn't pinpoint why. His voice lifted, like he was questioning me.

"Uh." I looked down to see what he was seeing, in case I was missing something. "This old thing?" I ran my hand against the smooth leather. "I got it as a gift for myself after my promotion."

"Congrats. Doing what?"

"I'm a manager of global business at FreeStream." I heard the present tense of my statement after I said it. It was force of habit, but any attempt at correcting myself stayed in my throat. Without my former job, what else could I say about myself? I swallowed that sad thought. I had to sound more convincing if I wanted to carry this charade for the rest of the night. "You might have heard of it if you've scrolled down far enough in the app store."

Danny made a somewhat agreeable sound as he turned toward the school. I followed him in, trying to decipher what all of this meant. This secretive side of Danny was all too familiar and ever confusing.

"What about you?" I asked. My heels clacked hard against the concrete as I caught up to him. Commonwealth High School was composed of five interconnected courtyards, like the dots on a die. We crossed campus diagonally, taking the shortest route to the gym. I dodged the old tree in the center quad that dropped spiky brown pods that used to get stuck on my cardigans. "What do you do now?"

"I, uh . . ." Danny shrugged, like it was boring, but then he cleared his throat and stood a little taller. "I'm an executive coach."

"You are?" I fished my phone out of my purse and googled "Danny Phan executive coach."

"Why do you sound so surprised?"

Because I was! Whenever I looked Danny up, I never came across an executive coach. Now that I knew his job, it was tragic how quickly my screen filled up with pages about him. According to his own website, Danny graduated from UC San Diego and had a career as a project manager before becoming an international-ally certified professional coach. Below his bio, there were logos of Fortune 500 companies, representing some of his notable clients. I scrolled down with a mix of awe and wonder. What kind of wisdom did Danny have that he imparted to these higher-ups?

Would he happen to have any advice for a failing former executive experiencing her first layoff?

Danny turned around to find me lagging behind because I was glued to my phone, stalking him in every sense of the word. "Hey, don't do that."

He sounded modest, but his website boasted several deliverables. *"Let me help you become a confident leader. Together, we can overcome the self-doubt that's holding you back and create a path toward your goals."* His glowing client testimonials had me eating my words. One was quoted saying that Danny helped their team unleash their potential, leading to increased sales. Who was this Danny they spoke so highly of?

"I'm sorry," I said. I shouldn't have underestimated him. That was what had gotten me into hot water with Danny in the first place. "This is great. I'm impressed."

"I'm glad you think so," he said in a tone that wasn't glad at all. My compliment didn't help, apparently. I stopped in my tracks.

"Are you mad at me?" *Still?* I wanted to add. I was ready to forget our last fight if he was.

Danny stood a few feet away from the weak navy-and-white balloon arch that hovered over the open gym doors. "How can I be mad at you? We've barely said hello."

"What is it, then?" I asked, copying Danny's stiff stance. Whatever it was, I could handle it. Forget about sweeping things under the rug. Anything was better than this guessing game we were playing. "Did I say something wrong?"

Danny's nose flared, and just when I thought things were going to get heated, he shook his head, admonishing me. "You haven't changed."

March 2003

SuperxSaiyan85: have you seen emotion eric?

xxaznxbbxgrlxx: ??

I clicked on the link Danny sent me and up popped a grainy image of an Asian man looking surprised. I thought this was a prank, but as I clicked around I discovered that the entire point of this website was that this Eric guy posted a new picture of himself with a different facial expression, as requested by his "fans," for lack of a better word.

xxaznxbbxgrlxx: uh is this the kind of thing you're into?

SuperxSaiyan85: you don't think it's funny?

xxaznxbbxgrlxx: I think people on the internet are weird

SuperxSaiyan85: don't judge. aren't we all a little weird?

xxaznxbbxgrlxx: yeah but that's what screen names are for. No one has to know my weirdness except me xxaznxbbxgrlxx: and you

SuperxSaiyan85: you mean you're not an asian baby girl? lol

xxaznxbbxgrlxx: don't laugh. you're not a Super Saiyan. Except for your hair

SuperxSaiyan85: that's why emotion eric is funny. It's refreshingly honest

xxaznxbbxgrlxx: you should send him a request to emote "refreshingly honest"

SuperxSaiyan85: nah I'm waiting for his take on "gassy"

xxaznxbbxgrlxx: you do that

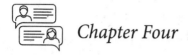

Chapter Four

DANNY'S COMMENT HURT. ACUTE AND SEARING, IT BURNED LIKE he'd put out a cigarette on my heart. Pretending the past didn't exist had been an undeserving wish. It was a stupid one too, because being in our high school gym only propelled me further back in time.

I could see Mariana's touches on the decorations and the whole setup. She went hard-core on the Commonwealth navy-and-silver color scheme for maximum school spirit. In spite of a few upgrades, the gym was the same as I remembered it. The wooden stadium seats were folded against the walls like they'd always been for school dances, preventing introverts like me from staying on the sidelines.

A DJ was setting up on the far end of the basketball court, testing the sound. The first song she played was "Dance with Me" by 112, and suddenly I was transported to junior year—Nat and I bobbing our heads to the song in our matching tennis uniforms during homecoming because our away game ran late and we didn't have time to change. It was odd. I hadn't thought about that day in years, but somehow it felt like it was yesterday.

Was that why Danny was still holding a grudge? Maybe I was stupid, thinking we could ignore how we left things. But I'd changed! Teen Rachel cared so much about beating everyone. I wasn't like that anymore. I didn't give a fuck about any of that anymore. I was too tired to care. If Danny would just talk to me for more than five minutes, he'd see that.

"Why aren't you clapping, sexy lady?" a voice called out. I turned around and found Vivienne clapping, as the song commanded. If it weren't for her playful voice, I wouldn't have recognized her. I was accustomed to seeing her in gym clothes, which was her punishment from the principal whenever she tried to wear rave outfits at school. The Viv standing in front of me was wearing a sky blue, long-sleeved linen dress that looked like something you'd wear if you were about to frolic as though the hills were alive.

"Viv! Oh my god! How are you?"

"Oh, you know," she demurred, leaning in for an air kiss on each cheek like we were European. "Got married. Had a couple kids and started freelancing. Did you know I was a club promoter for a while?" I opened my mouth to say yes, that I kind of remembered hearing that back in college, but Viv kept talking. "Well, after I met my husband, I quit doing that so I could start my own business. You may have seen me on Instagram. I sell high-quality essential oils, and if you're interested, I have samples in my car." My stomach clenched. Strong smells and I didn't mix. "I had to come early to help out, but when you have a second, I can show you what I have. But enough about me. What about you? What are you up to?"

"I—" I was a little dizzy from how quickly Viv recapped her life. My mind was so focused on Danny that I hadn't thought about my life summary. Other than work, I didn't have much to report. I had managed to avoid every major life milestone one was expected to reach by middle age. No house to speak of. No husband. No kids. I was really living the spinster life.

"I work in entertainment." Thank god for Nat. Being her assistant hadn't been titillating, but at least the job allowed me to say something truthful.

"Yes, I see you in Nat's IG sometimes at those red-carpet events." Viv looked over her shoulder. "Where is she?"

That was a good question. "I'm sure she's on her way."

"Well, I can't wait to see her! Who would've thought that someone from Commonwealth would become famous? Oh wait." Viv tapped my hand to stay put. "Mariana put me in charge of check-in." Viv scanned the table until she found my name tag among the many laid out, glancing at it before handing it over. "Love it."

I had to hand it to Mariana. She thought of every little detail. My name tag had a freakishly clear copy of my senior portrait along with my select accomplishments.

RACHEL DANG

2003 Scholar-Athlete (Tennis)

Most Likely to Succeed

Damn. Who knew a two-by-three sticker could be so savage? If anyone made bets that I was going to succeed, they lost their money. I might as well cross off the last line and write "loser" instead. My only consolation was that my portrait looked good.

"Rachel!"

I turned around and found a swarm of old friends, who started taking turns to hug me.

"I don't even remember the last time I saw you," Belinda said. I didn't think it had been that long since I'd seen her, but it must've been because Belinda's natural hair had since turned halfway gray.

"It might've been your wedding to this guy," I said, giving

Oscar a nudge. I spotted the bold "Dr." prefix on his name tag and Belinda's. I wondered if they had matching "Dr." and "Dr." towels in their house, even though they were from different disciplines. Oscar was a doctor who dealt with colds. Belinda dealt with modern art. "Are you still at Cal State LA?"

"No. I'm at UC Irvine now," Belinda replied.

"Tenured," Oscar proudly added.

All I heard was job security. What did that feel like?

Tina Vo greeted me next with a flash of her perfect teeth—a requisite accessory, I imagined, for an orthodontist. "Rachel, you hot bitch."

"Who, me?" I wasn't one to turn down a compliment. I spun around to revel in it while the serotonin boost lasted.

"God, you still look the same," Tina said as she continued holding on to me to examine my face. "Do you use retinol?"

"No."

"Vitamin C?" I shook my head. Tina looked at me like I was a unicorn. "Gua sha?" "Gua sha" sounded like something I should know as an Asian person, but I didn't. Before I could ask her about it, she snapped her fingers. "You don't have kids, do you?"

Tina laughed the question off like she was sure she had discovered my secret, even without confirmation from me. I laughed it off too, to end the conversation, not because I thought it was funny. I knew becoming a parent took a lot out of someone. Angela was exhausted when Hailey was first born. But it wasn't like I was childless for a lack of wanting. My career had never coincided with finding the right person to start a family with. Just wanting to have it all didn't mean I could have it all at the same time.

"Is this your husband?" I blurted out, pointing at the ridiculously good-looking man next to Tina. I was eager to get off the topic of children, but in my haste I must've guessed wrong. Everyone in the group burst into laughter.

"You don't recognize me?" the man asked, even though it was obvious I didn't. He had the chiseled face and shiny, slicked-back hair of a model in a cologne ad.

Model Man laughed, delighted. He finally stretched his lapel over his broad chest and showed me his name tag. "It's me, Bo."

As in Bo Zheng? I almost gagged.

He looked nothing like his senior portrait. Bo had sported a bowl cut all four years of high school and wore the same rotation of Commonwealth shirts and ironed khakis. He was a nerdy nerd, and that was coming from a veritable nerd myself. I stole another glance at his total makeover. It was unreal how tailored clothes and a haircut transformed him into this cdrama-worthy man. "You look . . ."

Great? H-hot? Ew, no. I couldn't even say it in my mind.

". . . different."

Bo flashed a smile that was dripping with swagger. He was loving this. Well, he deserved it. His glow-up was exquisite. "It's great to see you too."

He extended his arms. I didn't have "hugging Bo Zheng" on my bingo card, but here we were. With everyone watching expectantly, I leaned in and got it over with.

"Rachel!" Mariana said, making a beeline toward me from across the gym. At the sound of her voice, my group of friends disbanded.

"We have to get back to setting up. Mariana's got us on a tight schedule," Tina explained in a whisper, not without a quick eye roll behind Mariana's back. Mariana didn't see because she zoomed right into me for a quick hug. "Rachel! Just the person I wanted to see!"

"Here I am!" Unsure what to say next, I took a cursory glance around the gym. There were new banners flanking the upgraded scoreboard. The badminton team had won the state championship from 2017 to 2019 and picked up their streak in 2021 and 2022. "Look at that. Commonwealth was always good at hitting cocks."

Mariana laughed like we were old friends, as she probably thought we were. Mariana never knew she was my rival. I didn't need to look at her name tag to remember her accolades. She was captain of the water polo team and student body president. Twelve of us may have earned the distinction of valedictorian, but the school allowed only one speaker and it was her. I should've known that she'd be a shoo-in for the Student of the Year Award. And her success didn't end there.

Unlike Danny, Mariana was easy to keep up with. She added me on LinkedIn years ago, so I knew she was the CEO of a nonprofit that provided low-income kids in LA with school supplies each year. And when she surpassed ten years of service, she was given one of those pronouncements by the mayor of Los Angeles that looked like a page out of an old storybook. She posted a photo of it with her wife and her child, a toddler at the time. Mariana had everything I ever wanted, then and now.

Old rivalries, even the one-sided ones, never die, apparently.

"How's life?" I said with a big smile, trying to cover the reek of jealousy.

"Oh, you know," Mariana said, flicking her wrist like it was a silly question to ask. "Work. Spending time with family. Same old same old."

"I bet." I didn't know Mariana's same old same old, though. Wasn't that the point of putting together this reunion? "How did you even find the time to organize the reunion?"

Mariana's eyes fluttered as she exhaled a short breath. "Well, last year, I called the school about planning the reunion, and the principal brought up that the school needed some new tech. Naturally, they thought of me to put on a fundraiser."

Mariana was within her rights to brag. She was always good at bringing resources in, whether it was selling boxes and boxes of chocolate bars for new water polo equipment or organizing the school's first food pantry. It made sense that she did this for a living. This was her niche.

"We've got some great prizes. I hope you're ready to spend some cash." Mariana dragged me to the tables set up by the basketball hoop where the donations were displayed. There were a lot of good items up for bid. There was a "Night on the Town" basket with a gift certificate to the local AMC theater and a new brunch spot on Main Street. Someone generously donated a weekend at their rental property somewhere in the woods of Oregon. At the end of the table, a basket donated by the school was filled with Commonwealth swag, including cheerleader pompoms, a CHS hoodie, and a letterman jacket.

"Mmm." I hoped that sounded somewhat agreeable. The school apparel looked cute, but I wouldn't know when I'd wear it.

"Where are they?" Mariana went behind the registration tables and searched the boxes stored underneath.

"What are you looking for?"

"The programs." Mariana huffed as she stood, hands on her hips. "I wanted to show you your profile. We included a picture and bio of all the honorees."

"My bio?" I coughed to recover from my squeaky voice. "Where did you get my bio?"

"I hope you don't mind, but we swiped it from your LinkedIn," Mariana said.

Ah yes. The one social media platform I hadn't updated yet. I should have been grateful that she didn't say my IMDb. Playing "Asian Girl #2" wasn't groundbreaking representation, even for its time.

Our conversation was interrupted when the side door opened. Danny, sans suit jacket, was carrying a stack of chairs over to the registration tables. I couldn't help but notice how his dress shirt was stretched taut against his body. I only managed to look away when Danny caught me staring. Mariana's attention had diverted to the beverages being set up by the buffet tables.

"Is there a bar?" I asked. God, I hoped so. Socializing was hard on a normal day, but today was a whole other ball game.

Mariana made a face that didn't quite qualify as a smile. "I wish. Alcohol is prohibited on campus, but we have some sparkling cider."

Great. Just great. We were being served the choice beverage for kids at holiday parties.

"Makes sense," I said, even though it didn't. No one at this event was remotely underage.

"Where's Nat, by the way?" Mariana asked.

"She's probably on her way." What was everyone's obsession with Nat? No one cared much about her when we were in high school. She was the quirky drama kid people kept at arm's length because she loved breaking out into song.

Mariana frowned. "She told me that she'd donate backstage passes to the *Beyond the Dark* wrap party."

"When did she agree to that?" I couldn't recall anything in Nat's inbox about giving away backstage passes. I would have seen it if the offer had been made within the last three months. "When did you email her about it?" Mariana was taken aback by my sudden questioning, and I realized too late that it was strange of me to ask. Nobody knew I was Nat's assistant. "We still talk a lot," I added, trying to keep my voice nonchalant, "and I would've remembered if she mentioned it."

"Uh-huh." Mariana didn't seem to buy my explanation, but also didn't think too much about it. She tapped on her phone screen. "Do you think she'll reply if I shoot her an email?"

"I don't know. She's probably driving from set," I said. "I could call her if you want."

"Could you? I have so much to do before doors officially open."

"Yeah," I replied. When I didn't immediately take out my phone, Mariana's smile turned extra smiley, implying *Right this second*. I took out my phone and pointed at it to show her I'd step out to get right on it.

I walked out of the gym, far enough away so that no one would hear me. It rang several times before Nat picked up. "Hey, Nat. Are you on your way?"

"Not even close." Nat sounded exhausted. "It took forever to set up the shots, so we're running late today. I don't think I'll make it on time."

Damn. Nat was supposed to be my safety blanket at the reunion in case Viv attacked me with tea tree oil. I shuddered at the thought. "Well, do you remember donating a pair of backstage tickets?"

"Oh shit! I forgot about that. Can't I ship them later?"

"You know Mariana. She wants them here." It made sense. It

was easier to drive up the bids if people could take them home right away. No one wanted to put all their bets on a maybe.

"You know Mariana and I made out once?" Nat said this like she was letting me in on a secret even though she brought this up whenever we reminisced about high school.

"Yeah, yeah, at one of Tao's parties." Tao had a big, boastful personality that veered into obnoxious. People mostly tried to ignore him, impossible as it was, until he started throwing parties as loud as him. Tao graduated from Commonwealth on a high note. "It was the Smirnoff Ice. Everyone was experimenting. She's married now," I said, bursting her bubble.

"I won't let you ruin my memory," Nat said with a huff. "That's the stuff of teen movies. The weird drama kid kissing the most popular girl in school."

"Yeah, yeah." I couldn't let Nat get too far on a tangent or else we'd be talking on the phone forever. It wouldn't be the first time that had happened. "Where are the passes?"

"I think I brought them with me," Nat said, her voice coming in muffled. "Sorry, I'm getting makeup touched up. Let me drop you a pin."

"Wait—"

Nat hung up on me. A few seconds later, a notification appeared on my phone screen. Nat was filming four miles away at the Huntington Library. I wondered which botanical garden a group of fictional space scientists were going to land in. Nat needed to explain that one to me. I checked the time. If I left now, I could get to Nat's trailer and be back before the reunion started.

"You're leaving already?"

My body stilled at the sound of Danny's voice, bracing for an incoming argument. But when I turned around, Danny seemed to not know what to do with his hands. "I— If you're leaving, I want to apologize for earlier. I shouldn't have been— Can we start over?"

Watching him trip over his own words sent my heart tumbling. Danny had no idea how much he'd charmed me with his awkwardness. In a way, it made me feel comfortable with my mediocre social skills, as if two weirdos made a right.

"Yeah. I'd like that." I shook my head when Danny gestured back toward the reunion. "Actually, I have to pick up Nat's auction donation. I should be back soon."

"Oh." He palmed the side of his neck, scratching a spot behind his pink ears. "Do you want me to go with you?"

Yes. The answer appeared in my mind faster than I could blink. "Can Mariana spare you?"

"Everything's done," he said with a sheepish shrug. "Although"— Danny sucked in a breath through a nervous smile—"the last time I got in your car, my life flashed before my eyes."

"Oh. My. God! It only happened that one time!" The excuses were on the tip of my tongue. It was my first time driving on the freeway in the dark. That concrete island near the off-ramp came out of nowhere. No one got hurt. But I refrained from reasoning with him, knowing my words would fall on deaf ears. I'd have to prove to him that I was a far better driver now. "Let's get out of here."

March 2003

Nat begged me to be her date for the Spring Fling.

"I don't have time," I had told her. I'd found old AP test prep books in Angela's bedroom, stuffed in her closet (she was hiding the goods!), and I was going to spend my weekend on practice tests. But I begrudgingly went dress shopping at the Montebello Mall after Nat said my plan was the saddest thing she'd ever heard.

There were so many options, but nothing that fit the occasion. On one end of the spectrum were sundresses that were too casual, and on the opposite end were quinceañera princess ballgowns. I needed something in between. I wasn't sure why I was putting so much thought into my dress when I wasn't planning on dancing. I had nothing against dancing, but I disliked being bad at it. My plan to stay off the dance floor was to serve food, and I didn't need a sparkly dress for that.

I left the dress store, ready to cut my losses with a pretzel, when I was approached by an Asian guy wearing a baggy hoodie and an even baggier pair of cargo pants.

"Miss. You look like you could use some new shades," he said, stepping to the side to reveal a display of sunglasses at his booth. There was nothing unique about any of his merchandise, which included cheap watches and jewelry. They all looked like goods you could get in Chinatown for five dollars if you bargained hard enough.

"No thanks," I tried to say, but the guy was persistent. He pointed at the shelf with necklaces and belly-button rings.

"Perhaps some jewelry for prom?" he asked.

I humored him by picking up a pair of silver earrings that looked cute, but then put them back down. "Next time." I don't know why, but I felt like I needed to give him a reason or else he'd keep trying to sell me something. "I don't have a dress yet, but I'll come back when I do."

"Be sure that you do." The guy clapped his hands, rubbing

them together like they were cold. "My associate can help you too."

I turned around and found Danny, confused by my presence, as he walked up to the booth with a corndog. "Rachel? Uh . . . what's up?"

The mood shifted, and I couldn't figure out why. Danny's posture was rigid, like an action figure without movable joints.

"You know her?" The sales guy's face lit up as he gave me one of those acknowledging nods. "I'm Jimmy."

"Hi." I barely got the word out before Danny shifted to stand squarely between me and the booth.

"Jimmy. I forgot I can't work today. I have to do a project with Rachel. Can I swap shifts with you?" I picked up on the lie and played along.

"Yeah, a project. Got it," Jimmy said as he stole Danny's food and waved us off. "Take my Friday shift."

"Yeah, okay," Danny replied, though it sounded like he would've agreed to anything Jimmy suggested. His hand landed on my back, sending a shock through my body from the sudden contact. He turned me around and nudged me toward the exit. Somehow, my body grew warm, despite the mall's frigid air conditioning.

"Who was that?" I asked as we dodged other shoppers on the way out.

"My brother," Danny said with a bit of reluctance. He shook his head, annoyed. He didn't seem to want to talk about it, so I didn't ask. When we made it to the parking lot, Danny's face was struck with a realization. "Uh, I came with Jimmy. Did you drive here?"

"Yeah."

"Can you take me home?"

"Yeah, okay." Disappointment settled in my stomach. I didn't think Danny would want to do practice tests with me, so I was going to suggest getting some shaved ice or something. Instead, I drove him home.

SuperxSaiyan85: I'm never getting in the car with you again

> **xxaznxbbxgrlxx:** I got scared! That other lane is supposed to yield!

SuperxSaiyan85: we're lucky to be alive

> **xxaznxbbxgrlxx:** it wasn't that bad

I didn't want to spend the rest of the night getting made fun of, so I changed the topic.

> **xxaznxbbxgrlxx:** ask your brother for a ride next time

> **xxaznxbbxgrlxx:** Jimmy seems nice

SuperxSaiyan85: try to avoid him if you see him

> **xxaznxbbxgrlxx:** why?

It took Danny awhile to respond. I thought he had stepped away from his keyboard.

SuperxSaiyan85: he's not the most reliable guy

SuperxSaiyan85: sometimes it feels like I'm the big brother, not him

xxaznxbbxgrlxx: i see

My fingers went still on my keyboard. It didn't feel right to pry. I wished we could've had this conversation in person. I couldn't tell the tone of these instant messages from reading them. I'd offer to meet up, but there was no way my parents would let me out at this hour. I was going to suggest talking over the phone, but it was too late. Then, with the sound of a door slam, Danny had signed out of AIM.

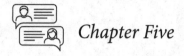 *Chapter Five*

"SEE? WE ARRIVED AND YOU'RE PERFECTLY SAFE. YOU CAN LET go now."

Danny still gripped the handle above the passenger door window like he was riding the subway. It reminded me of how my mom would do the same whenever she sat in the passenger seat, but I didn't think Danny would appreciate the comparison. It didn't reflect well on my driving either.

"I'll let go when we're parked," Danny replied.

The joke was getting stale, but I kept that to myself. I drove past the cartoonishly tall and narrow wrought-iron gates at the Huntington Library's entrance and stopped at the parking booth.

"Sorry, we're closed!" the parking attendant said. "If you drive up, you can make a U-turn and I'll open the gate for you to exit the premises."

That wasn't an option. I couldn't leave here without those passes.

"Oh, I'm with the *Beyond the Dark* crew," I blurted. The attendant eyed me, and it wasn't hard to see why. I was too dressed up to be operating equipment.

"The crew arrived hours ago," the parking attendant said, like she didn't get paid enough to deal with this shit.

"Right," I said. If only I had the FreeStream badge that HR made me surrender when I left my office. I tried to come up with something quick. "Do you have a list? I'm Rachel Dang. I'm a friend of Natalie Huang, lead actress of *Beyond the Dark*. If you call the crew, they can confirm that."

"No, ma'am. I don't have a list." I ignored the way "ma'am" took my ego down a notch. "Unless you can provide proper identification that you're part of the crew, I can't let you in."

I held up a finger to buy some time. I called Nat, but her phone went straight to voicemail. I spied the walkie-talkie strapped to the attendant's waist, but I wasn't sure if anyone would pick up if they were shooting.

"Hold on." I logged into Nat's email on my phone. I'd been avoiding this because she gets so many messages and the notifications would drive me up the wall, but desperate times, desperate measures. I quickly found the email with Nat's call sheet and found the production code, which was usually printed on yellow signs whenever something was filmed on location. "I'm with 'UFO.'"

The code was a little bit on the nose. Productions typically used abstract words to throw people off. I showed the attendant my phone so she could see the call sheet on my screen for more proof.

She stared long and hard at my phone, then emitted a wary sound. Just when I thought she'd send me packing, she lifted the gate and waved me in. I was kind of shocked that it worked.

True to his word, Danny didn't release his grip until we parked. He rolled his eyes at my victorious smile. "Fine. You're a good driver. Are you happy now?"

"Yes." We followed the trail of "UFO" signs inside the garden, past the sparkling reflection pool and down a winding path of desert plants.

"So," Danny said after some companionable silence, "you're like a VIP. A flash of your phone and doors open for you."

Was that his interpretation of the last few minutes? It was hard not to bask in his amazement. "I know how to get around," I hedged.

Danny turned around and began walking backward. "It's not like you to be modest."

"How about humble?" I suggested. I'd been humbled quite a bit as of late.

Danny gave me a questioning look, but there was a teasing glint to it. It didn't last long. "You always liked movies. I'll never forget watching *Better Luck Tomorrow* with you. You couldn't stop talking about it after."

I tugged on Danny's sleeve and dragged him toward the middle of the walkway before he bumped into a spiky aloe plant. "Come on. It was the first movie I'd seen with a cast comprised entirely of Asian Americans in a contemporary setting. The lead was stressing over SATs. That was the relatable teen content I needed."

Danny's eyebrow arched. "What about the crime and murder parts?"

"Okay, that wasn't relatable," I conceded. "But you have to admit, it was a cultural milestone!"

"My point is . . . I can't say I'm surprised." Danny turned back around as the path narrowed, leading us into a different garden with more trees. I couldn't tell what kind of foliage surrounded us now, but I appreciated the shade. "You were the one with a ten-year plan."

I groaned as I dodged a low-hanging branch. In retrospect, the plan was delusional. Graduate college by twenty-two. Get a high-paying job. Find a boyfriend by twenty-five. Date for two years. Be engaged by twenty-seven. Have a baby and a house by twenty-eight. Naive eighteen-year-old me didn't factor in the many, many variables outside of my control. "A flawed plan."

We exchanged wan smiles at the same time. The coincidence of our mirrored faces had a pleasant familiarity, like finding your favorite station after turning the dial on a staticky radio. We had our own frequency that was irreplicable. I'd forgotten how easily Danny could draw me in with something as simple as a glance, and it was still frustrating.

If I had to pinpoint where our relationship went downhill, it was during a murky period when we were spending more time together, supposedly to study. My dad was getting worried about closing his business. Even though he downplayed his concern, I was feeling more pressure to get a Merit Scholarship. It was weeks before we graduated, and days away from our AP tests. I was the one who made Danny cram for our AP English practice essay questions, and I couldn't fault him for actually remembering the things I said.

Of course, it looked suspicious that we both used similar phrasing. When our teacher asked us to stay after school to discuss it, I was so fearful that I was going to get disqualified or that it would go on my permanent record that I didn't hear Danny offer to withdraw his exam. The only thing I seemed to catch was that he received a better grade than me. After that, I don't know what came over me. I was livid. There was no talking sense into me. The things I said were uncalled for.

April 2003

"How could you get a better grade if we basically wrote the same paper?" I folded my essay in half and stuffed it in my backpack.

"Why are you upset?" Danny asked. "What happened to 'I look good when you do good'?"

"I'm just saying, if you want to copy my work, cite me next time."

Danny blinked like he'd taken a blow to the face. "Wow. So that's how it is, huh? You think you're better than me?"

As upset as I was, I knew it sounded bad, which was why I couldn't bring myself to own up to it. "I wanted it more than you."

That, he couldn't refute. So he gave me the silent treatment for a few days before we were back on speaking terms. It wasn't my finest moment.

At the time, my life was about ticking off checkboxes and hoarding as many awards, big or small, as I could. It was laughable how much I blew this test out of proportion—a test that had no real implications for our lives. The problem was that once I set my mind to something I usually achieved it. As a result, the misses were harder to swallow. "How about you? I mean, you're doing well for yourself."

"You could say that," he said as he readjusted his tie, intentionally flashing his expensive watch at me in the process. I'd never seen him with such a smug smile.

I let him gloat. He deserved it. "Okay. I see you."

"What are you talking about?" he asked innocently. Innocent, my foot.

"You're loaded. I get it. You don't need to be so obvious about it," I teased.

"Oh, so I should cancel my helicopter, then?" he joked.

I'd missed this with Danny. Standing close to him, glimpsing the occasional silver strand in his hair, made me ache for the years of friendship we could've had together. "Do you even have space to land a helicopter at your mansion?"

"Actually, I bought a house not too long ago. It didn't come with a helipad."

"Wait. For real?" The real estate market in California was horrific. Buying a house was a feat. "Where?"

"In Alhambra. It was originally going to be for my mom, but she decided to move to Houston to be closer to her family."

"Congrats," I said, belatedly. I wished I sounded more sincere, but I was surprised that he was back in our hometown. "How long have you been back in town?"

"Last year," he answered, but didn't elaborate. Instead, he stopped at a landing before the path turned. "You knew I moved?"

It was a loaded question. Danny watched me carefully, like he wanted to see the words come out of my mouth in case he needed to feed them back to me and make me eat them. "You know people talk. I happened to hear."

There was a bitter tinge to his laugh. "Since when did you talk to people? I thought you didn't want to talk to anyone from high school anymore. Or did that only apply to me?"

Wow. Danny sucker-punched me with that.

A breeze got caught in the corner where we stood underneath an umbrella of trees, rustling the branches. A confetti burst of leaves swirled as the wind carried them away. If only this weak tornado had been strong enough to whisk me away from this conversation. I could acknowledge that I wasn't perfect, but he wasn't totally innocent either. He seemed to have amnesia about all the times he left me hanging, wondering what the hell we were doing. Had he ever stopped to consider his part in how things ended?

I would've accepted any one of several possible answers, like apparently being unable to give me more when he made things complicated by kissing me. Like an explanation for why he didn't show up on Awards Night, which at that point was one of the most important days of my life. What had he expected? I couldn't fix a relationship with someone who wasn't going to put in the same effort as me. I'd reached my limit.

So much for letting the past stay in the past. I hadn't come to the reunion to reignite old grudges. I wanted to show Danny a different version of me than the hotheaded version he last saw, but he was making it so difficult.

I brushed off a leaf that had fallen on my shoulder. "Listen. I don't mean to get off topic. All I meant to say was that I'm happy for you. We're both living our best lives." Well, one of us was. "There's no need to rehash something that happened ages ago."

"Then why does it sound patronizing when you say it?"

It wasn't my intention. The truth was, I was pretending my life was peachy when it wasn't, and I wasn't cut out for acting. Unsure how to salvage the situation, I resumed walking, leading us down a steep concrete path out of the forest. "Let's go find Nat and get out of here."

"Fine. You're the boss."

"What does that even—"

No. I wasn't going to dignify that comment with a response. I hated being the bigger person!

Fortunately, it wasn't long until we found trucks and trailers parked by the set, which ran parallel to an expansive lawn.

"This way," I said to Danny. It helped that Nat's trailer had her name on it. All we had to do was go inside, find the passes, and skedaddle.

We walked around an open truck filled with camera rigs and lights. I nodded a greeting to the crew, channeling top-brass energy as I climbed up the stairs to Nat's trailer. I knocked, but when no one responded, I tried the door. It was unlocked, so in we went.

Nat's trailer wasn't very big, and I'd never seen her carry anything bigger than her gym bag to work. If the passes were here, they wouldn't take long to find. "I'm going to check her purse," I said to Danny, who looked completely lost. "Why don't you check her vanity?"

Danny palmed his cheek, looking befuddled by the bright lights and the makeup lying around. "I don't know, Rach. This feels wrong. I remember Nat being cool, but I don't know her well enough to search her things."

"Fine, I'll handle it. Could you just—" I waved a hand back and forth at his wooden posture. "Could you chill? Take a seat while I look around."

"Nat's going to be okay with that?" Danny asked, skeptical.

"Yeah, we're really close." Like, I've seen Nat scratch her stomach when she yawns first thing in the morning, kind of close. "She won't mind. We're doing *her* a favor," I reminded him.

I opened the closet located at the corner of the trailer and found the tote bag Nat had been using lately. Inside, I didn't see anything out of the ordinary. Phone. Wallet. Keys. Sunglasses. Her favorite lipstick in three shades. No backstage passes, though.

I turned around to search the vanity, in time to see Danny dip a curious finger in the eyeshadow palette and swatch a green color on the back of his hand. "I don't think that's your color."

"I wasn't doing anything." Danny rubbed the evidence off his hand, though a glittery sheen remained.

"Sure," I said, unable to hide my grin. I pulled out the first drawer at the vanity, which held only hairbrushes. Danny moved to get out of the chair, but I tapped his shoulder to stay. "Don't," I said, as I knelt down to search the lower drawers. "I got it."

"I'm not in your way?"

His voice dipped lower, giving me the sense that he wasn't just being courteous to me. I glanced up, to where Danny's gaze held mine in the mirror. I recognized that loaded glance. I'd seen it from a distance, like when I used to pass Danny in the hallways, and I'd seen it up close. That gaze filled my chest so fast it hurt. If one look could unearth feelings I'd buried long ago, I wouldn't be able to keep up with this charade.

Danny looked away first, giving me temporary relief. I thought I was off the hook until I followed the direction of his gaze. He was looking now at his arm, which I'd been holding on to for balance.

"Oh! I'm sorry." The words spilled out of my mouth, but my hands didn't get the memo. I was still touching him. I quickly detached myself. "I didn't mean to do that."

Danny rubbed his arm where my hand had been, like it was a stain. "It's fine."

It didn't sound fine. Nothing was fine.

"I can't find the passes," I finally said, hoping the change in topic could give us some emotional space. "Let's try to find Nat on set."

I opened the door of the trailer and walked right into a burly man. An angry burly man.

"You can't be back here," he said. He was bearded and dressed all in black, like the rest of the crew, except this guy was built like a brick wall.

"I'm a friend of Natalie's," I said.

Beard Man crossed his arms and widened his stance like he was ready to tackle me if necessary. "Yeah, sure you are."

"I can prove it." I pointed toward the set in the distance. "Ask anyone here. I've been to the soundstage plenty of times."

"You and every other *Beyond the Dark* fanatic."

I gasped. I liked *Beyond the Dark*, but I didn't think I passed for a member of the show's small cult following, which was confined to the nerdy eighteen- to thirty-five-year-old male demographic. Sure, my hair was short, but it wasn't that short.

"Excuse me," I said, bringing a pointed finger to Beard Man's face. "I'm not some random fan. I'm a FreeStream employee."

The guy wouldn't budge. "Huh, you sure about that? Didn't they lay everyone off?" My stomach dropped like I'd swallowed an anvil. Danny had been watching our exchange the entire time, but I saw the way his attention seared into me now that I was caught in my lie. Beard Man, oblivious to the tension brewing between Danny and me, wrapped his big hand around my wrist. "Ma'am, I don't know how you got in here, but you need to leave right now."

"Hey, man." Danny intervened and grabbed Beard Man's arm. "Let's not do this."

"Yeah! Let go of me!" I would've complied without force. We were done searching the trailer anyway. I tried to yank my hand free, but the guy was ridiculously strong. He pushed Danny off and removed me from the trailer without much effort.

Beard Man finally let go of me when we made it down the stairs. "Stay here until security escorts you out."

Danny appeared next to me. He lifted my arm, checking it for injury. "Rach. Are you okay?"

I nodded, trying not to make too much of the brief contact. Anything would feel good after getting thrown out.

"That's good," he said, releasing me. "So, is it true? You were laid off?"

I couldn't tell if Danny was confused or surprised. When my mouth couldn't produce a single word, his lips twisted to the side like he was sucking spinach out of his teeth. Danny palmed his forehead as his head tipped back in laughter. "I can't believe this. I knew something was up, but I didn't think you'd lie to me."

"Well, I-I . . ." I stuttered to my defeat. I'd graduated from Berkeley and yet I couldn't come up with a decent excuse. I stretched my eyes to point at the beefy man standing between us and the backstage passes. "Now's not really the right time to discuss this, *Dan*."

Danny's lips pressed into a thin line. He never liked being called Dan, even though he abbreviated my name all the time.

"I don't know what's going on," Beard Man said, interrupting us. "But you need to take that elsewhere." A crackly noise came from the walkie-talkie attached to his hip. He lifted it up to his mouth. "Come again?"

The voice on the other end spoke louder. "Keep it down. Cameras are rolling."

"Sorry, chief," he responded, glaring at Danny and me. "I'm trying to get rid of some trespassers."

"We're not trespassing! We're Natalie's guests!" I shouted. I didn't give a fuck if I cost FreeStream money. What were they going to do? Fire me?

"Is that Rachel? Hi, Rachel!" I stood taller at the sound of Nat's voice projecting from the walkie-talkie.

"See?" I smirked. "I told you." Beard Man was steadfast in his indifference. "Can you let her know we're here for the passes? She'll know what I mean."

It took a few seconds, but Beard Man reluctantly brought the walkie-talkie to his face and asked Nat to confirm that she invited me.

Nat's crackly voice responded. "Tell Rachel that I looked all over my trailer and I couldn't find the passes. They must be at home. Sorry I didn't text," her voice squeaked as she spoke in double-time, "and for making you drive back. I love you, 'k, bye!"

"Well, there you have it." It was Beard Man's turn to be smug, and I couldn't muster the energy to fight it. Not when I had Danny to answer to.

"We'll let ourselves out," I said as I turned back to retrace our steps. Damn. I had to climb uphill in those damn heels. It wasn't worth it when we were leaving empty-handed. Danny gestured to let me go first. He fell into step beside me, and when he didn't say anything right away, I wondered if he'd let my little lie slide. "I can drop you back off at the reunion. I'll go to my house to get the passes."

"I have a question."

My body recoiled in anticipation. I had to tell him the truth. I wasn't fooling anybody. The designer suit I'd borrowed from Nat was now drenched in sweat. I was jobless with no real idea what to do next. I was thirty-eight years old, living in an overpriced apartment with a roommate who, up until recently, had struggled to put up her half of the rent. Our roles had since reversed. Nat was helping me stay afloat by hiring me to keep her life organized and fetching her things. I wasn't sure how I got to this place.

"You and Nat live together?"

"Yeah. For the last seven years." I counted in my head to make sure that number was right. "Same apartment out in Silver Lake. It's near the FreeStream office and close enough for Nat to drive to all her auditions."

Danny glanced at his watch. "I'll come with you."

"You will?"

"It'll take like, what? Twenty minutes to get there and twenty minutes back?" Danny stared ahead as he made another mental calculation. "Mariana planned to kick off the program at six fifteen to give stragglers some time. If we leave now, we'll probably miss the introductions and, at worst, a 50 Cent song or two."

"Are you sure?"

Danny nodded. "That way, you have forty minutes to explain why you've been lying to me this whole time."

"Fuck." My legs wobbled as I tried to climb the cracked, uneven path back to my car. "For what it's worth, I didn't intend to lie to you. I was laid off. It'd be nice if you could spare some sympathy."

"I'm sorry. I really am, but would it kill you to admit that you made a mistake?"

"Yes," I huffed, blowing a tendril of hair away from my face. "I would literally wither away." I sneaked a look at Danny. His mouth was still twisted, but this time he was fighting a smile. It was nice to know that he wasn't impervious to my sarcasm. "I don't know why I lied."

Danny chuckled off his disbelief. "I have a hard time believing that."

"Why? Not everything I do is calculated to the most minute detail. Believe it or not, I've changed!" Danny rolled his eyes. "I have!"

"You need to calm down."

"Don't tell me to calm down!" I hated it when people told me to calm down. All it did was pour gas on the fire. "Maybe you're the person who hasn't changed. You're the one who can't fathom that maybe I'm different. I don't have a five-year plan. I don't even know what I'm doing tomorrow. Unemployment is boring, and if Nat didn't think it was utterly depressing, I'd park my ass on our couch and have myself a *Princess Diaries* marathon. I am, for the first time in my life, completely lost, and I don't know what to do. So forgive me for saving face with my little white lie."

I huffed as I recovered my composure. It wasn't my intention to shout, but my feelings had gotten away from me.

Danny's face softened, little by little, with empathy. He reached for my hand, clutching the side of it like he was holding a stapler. He gave it an encouraging squeeze, and I could hardly believe that the warmth from this odd clutch stole a breath from me. My skin yearned for more contact.

"I'm sorry," he said, but the squawk of a walkie-talkie interrupted the rest of his apology.

"Get them out of here," a pissed, staticky voice commanded. "We can't film with all this fucking noise!"

Another voice responded, one that was deeper and closer. "On it."

Before I could blink, Danny yanked me up the trail and we became wanted fugitives. If I weren't in stupid heels, we would've made it much farther. But the dirt-covered slope was too slippery. I face-planted on the ground, and because of our joined hands, Danny fell too, right into a bed of cacti.

Danny yelped frantically as he jumped back onto his feet. If I hadn't seen it with my own eyes, I wouldn't have believed that he had the athletic ability to bounce back up so quickly. Then again, humans have the miraculous ability to summon strength when faced with adversity. Like getting poked with spindly needles right in the butt.

I winced as I tried to pull myself up. My palm had a scrape, but the cream suit took a worse beating. It was ashen from the dirt. Nat was going to be pissed. "Are you okay?" I asked Danny.

"What do you think?" he screeched. When Danny tried to dust the short needles off his pants, they only got stuck to his hand. "Oh fucking hell."

I'd barely gotten myself into a push-up position before I was pulled up by two security guards. Our time on the run was up.

 *Chapter Six*

I PACED OUTSIDE OF THE TENT WHERE THE ON-SET MEDIC WAS treating Danny. I wanted to see how he was doing, especially when he grumbled or hissed in pain, but the security guards let me go only as far as they could see me.

The medic pulled off her gloves as she stepped out to give us the final prognosis. "He'll be fine. The cactus he landed on had short, soft spines. They mostly stuck to his clothes, but there'll be some minor irritation."

My hand pressed on my chest, relieved that Danny was okay, but something didn't add up. "It sounded like he was in pain, though."

The medic smirked. "He's suffering from a prickled butt and a bruised ego."

Danny emerged from the tent, limping with his suit jacket folded over his arm. "Thank you for your help," he said to the medic, adding under his breath, "and for telling the whole world."

"You should thank Natalie," the security guard said, as he escorted us to a golf cart. "She insisted that someone take a look at you."

Danny wasn't exactly the picture of gratitude as the security guard zoomed through the botanical garden, taking us on a bumpy ride with little regard to Danny's injury. Danny's mouth formed a tight line, his jaw clenching with every sharp turn.

"I'm sorry," I whispered between us. "This was my fault."

"It's fine," Danny said through gritted teeth as the cart took a sharp turn. "It was an accident."

That might have been true, but it didn't make me feel better. In a show of solidarity, I reached out and covered his hand with mine. The medic might have classified Danny's injury as minor, but his discomfort was evident. Danny drew a sharp breath, furrowing his brows at the sight of our hands. He stared at my hand like it was a nuisance, so I withdrew it. Nothing I did seemed to be right, so I gave him as much space as I could until we got into my car.

"I'm so, so sorry," I squeaked out as I drove out of the parking lot. I had to run over a speed bump, causing Danny to wince. At this rate, I wasn't sure if he was going to last the ride to my apartment. What were the odds that Danny believed in third chances?

"Just"—Danny held his breath as the car dipped and transitioned onto the curvy, tree-lined road that took us through the affluent San Marino neighborhood—"drive gently." The poor guy was leaning so as to put all his weight on one butt cheek.

"Do you need a . . ." I didn't have much to offer. There were some extra napkins in my glove box, but that didn't seem helpful. "You look uncomfortable."

"Well, a cactus gave me acupuncture on my ass, so I'm just feeling a little vulnerable right now."

It was hard to be mad at his snappy tone when he put it that way. "What can I do to help?"

"It's okay. I'm fine. I can make it to your place." As if to prove it, Danny sat up straight in his seat, squarely on his whole ass. He played the part of a perfectly healthy man for a hot second, but when the car rolled over a few reflectors dividing the lanes, he whimpered with a sad puppy face.

"Danny. Stop being macho." That was a sentence I never thought

I'd say. "Tell me what's wrong," I implored. Danny shook his stubborn little head. "Fine." I signaled to change lanes. "I'm going to take you home, then."

"No," he insisted, growing more frustrated. "I don't want us to waste time."

How could he think about keeping on schedule when he was injured? "Forget about the reunion. You're hurt."

"I'm not hurt per se."

What was that supposed to mean? "If you're not hurt, then what is it? What's bothering you?"

"It's that . . ." Danny sighed and after some time he mumbled, "It still feels like there's something . . . poking me there." The tips of Danny's ears turned hot pink.

"Let me pull over," I said, ignoring Danny's protests. There was a row of cute shops on the next block, and Danny could use the restroom at any of those establishments. I found a parking spot along the curb.

Danny ducked and looked out of the windshield. "You brought me to Noodle World?"

"What?" I looked above my steering wheel at the building ahead. "Huh. I had no idea there was a location here." I'd only been to the one in Alhambra. It was the ideal place for cheap late-night eats after a night of partying (so I've heard). I never imagined anyone from San Marino trekking out of their mansion to eat pan-Asian noodles. "Do you think they have spicy spaghetti?"

Judging by the expression on Danny's face, he didn't seem to care about the possible differences in their menu. It was a fair question, since this location didn't have a random gigantic Bob's Big Boy statue at the entrance like the one in our hometown. That alone made this establishment classy by comparison.

I opened the center console and dug under some old CDs I'd forgotten about. When I bought the car, the salesperson had thrown in a first-aid kit and other small accessories to "sweeten" the deal. Who knew that kit would come in handy? "Here. There are some bandages in here."

I was in the driver's seat, so there wasn't much Danny could do. Plus, it was unrealistic of him to sit in that uncomfortable position for too long. He was bound to get a cramp.

Danny begrudgingly relented and took the first-aid kit. "I'll be back."

After he disappeared into the restaurant, I texted Nat to apologize for disrupting the shoot.

> Rachel: sorry about earlier

> Nat: me too. I should've told you about the passes

> Nat: They might be in my desk

> Nat: Or check in the fridge

Nat wasn't the most organized person in the world, but she wasn't the type to put random things inside the refrigerator. They had to be around somewhere.

> Rachel: k

> Nat: I might wrap up soon here. I think I can still make it.

Rachel: To what?

Nat: The reunion

She still wanted to go?

Nat: Can you bring me an outfit?

That didn't narrow anything down. Nat's closet was bursting at the seams with clothes. She liked to show up to auditions dressed for the part, so she had pieces for characters of all walks of life. I'd bring five outfits for her to pick from to give her some options.

Rachel: Will do

Nat: See you soon

Not too soon, I hoped. I wasn't even halfway to our place yet.

Rachel: Text me when you're on the way

What was keeping Danny so long? I was about to text him, but we hadn't exchanged numbers. I got out of my car and went into the restaurant, crossing the dining room full of chatty patrons.

I knocked on the restroom door. "Danny?"

"Rachel?" Danny asked, his voice muffled through the door.

"Yeah. Everything okay in there?" Danny grumbled something, but I couldn't make it out. "What was that?"

The door opened a sliver, enough for me to catch the profile of his face. "I need some help."

"Okay." I swallowed. I had a feeling about where this was going. "What do you need?"

Danny sighed his deep suffering. "I can't really see behind me. Can you take a look for me?"

I read between the lines to gather what Danny couldn't muster to say. He wanted me to check out his ass. This would've been more exciting under different circumstances, but my answer would've been the same nonetheless. "Yeah."

Without warning, Danny yanked me inside and shut the door.

"You have to stop doing that," I hissed. "I'm not some rag doll you can throw around." I instantly forgot about my arm, though, when I caught a whiff. Men's restrooms were the pits. Not that I frequented them often, but whenever I mistakenly walked into one, the overwhelming chemical smell of urinal cakes made my head spin. I pinched my nose. It wasn't the time or place to faint.

Danny locked the door and turned around. My eyes darted to his unbuckled pants, and I tried miserably to think of unsexy things like taxes and the blister that was forming on my toe.

"All right," Danny said, snapping me out of any inappropriate thoughts, "let's make this quick."

"We got this," I said, sounding dumb to my ears, but the smell in the bathroom was potent. It was killing my brain cells with every passing second. I washed and dried my hands before taking a look. "You're lucky I'm not squeamish. Remember when we had to dissect a frog for bio? I aced that shit."

Danny wasn't listening to me. He paused for a second, like he needed to gather himself before he unzipped his pants and let them fall to the floor. I knelt down until I was eye level with his scientifically round butt. It was covered by black boxer briefs, which helped me narrow my field of vision to his wound. There was a pink patch about the size of a golf ball, located south of his butt on his thick, muscular thigh.

Focus, Rachel.

Someone pulled on the locked door from the outside and knocked, reminding me that I had to act fast. But the medic had done a good job of treating the wound, and I wasn't sure what I was looking for.

"I don't see anything," I whispered. I tilted my head and leaned closer. There was a glint of something that looked like a blond hair. I shined my phone flashlight on it to get a better look. "Wait. There are"—I counted in my head—"three little spines still stuck on you."

"Can you pull them out?" Danny asked like a prayer.

I assessed the wound again. I had to tackle this strategically before I made things worse. The spines were too short to pull out with my hands. I searched my purse for the small makeup bag I always carried for touch-ups. Luckily, I found my tweezers. I cleaned them with an alcohol wipe, scrubbing them like I was about to go in for surgery. "I'm going to need you to stay still."

"Okay." Danny shut his eyes. "Do it."

I went in a few times and clipped nothing but air. It was hard to see while staying at a respectable distance.

"Um." I swallowed. "I have to get closer. I might have to hold your leg. The, uh"—I cleared my throat—"inside of your leg."

Danny mumbled some curse words. "Just do what you need to do."

"Okay," I said, praying that he didn't hear the crack in my voice. I palmed the side of his thigh, ignoring the way his muscles flexed from my touch. He was probably bracing himself for some pain. Was Danny afraid of needles?

When I was a kid, the nurse would talk to me, asking me about my favorite color or food to distract me while she administered shots. It was pretty effective, so I gave it a try. "Hey, Danny," I said, as I positioned the tweezer over a cactus spine. "What's your favorite animal?"

"What?"

I didn't think the question was that hard, but apparently it confused Danny enough that he twisted his body around to look at me, putting my face and his right butt cheek on a collision course.

Danny's ears brightened to his signature hot pink. "I-I didn't mean to do that. Are you all right?"

"I'm fine," I said, trying to be cool about it. The last thing I needed him to do was panic. "We're both adults here."

And one day we would laugh about the whiplash I experienced after my face bounced off his ass, but for now, I had to get these damn needles out. I gripped his thigh harder this time, reminding him not to move. "Now, answer the question. Favorite animal."

Danny groaned as he contemplated his answer. "I don't know? A parakeet?"

His favorite animal is a bird? I plucked a needle. One down, two to go. "That's oddly specific."

"That's the first one that came to mind."

"A bird, though? Not a cat or dog?"

"What's wrong with birds? I had one as a kid."

"I don't think you ever mentioned that," I said as I plucked the second needle. "What do you like about them?"

"You don't think they're cute?"

I held my tongue because, no, I didn't think birds were all that adorable. Also, if I opened my mouth, I was afraid I'd say what—or who rather—I did think was cute. After I removed the last bit of cactus from Danny's leg, I wiped the small wound with an alcohol wipe and delicately affixed the biggest bandage I could find. "All done."

"That's it?" Danny glanced behind him to review my work. "That wasn't so bad."

Our eyes met briefly, and awkwardness settled in. I was still on my knees, intimately close to his ass. I scrambled to my feet. "If you still feel something, I can double-check at my place."

"I think we're good," Danny replied, his voice sounding a little strangled. He pulled his pants back up. I turned away to give him as much privacy as I could, but I couldn't help but notice his pink cheeks. This must have been humiliating for him.

"If I haven't said it enough, I'm sorry. For lying and for this."

"Stop apologizing." Hearing his frustration made me want to say sorry again, but I held it back. Danny hastily opened the door and almost walked into an older patron standing in the hallway. The man grunted, annoyed from the wait, but his jaw dropped when I followed Danny out.

I couldn't give much thought to a judgmental uncle when Danny couldn't even look me in the eyes. How were we going to recover from this? When I'd decided to attend the reunion, I didn't think it'd be this hard to make amends. Wasn't time supposed to be on our side? It had been so long that I didn't even remember exactly what we said to each other. The thing I couldn't forget was the hurt and defeat in Danny's face when I said I never wanted to speak to him again. He knew as well as I did that I'd make good on that promise.

We were about to exit the restaurant when Danny took a detour to the front counter. The hostess handed Danny a to-go bag.

"You bought something?" I asked as I held the door open for him. The telltale aroma of Thai basil gave away the spicy spaghetti inside. I wasn't hungry before, but I was now.

"The restroom was for customers only." Danny opened the passenger door. "Might as well get something you like."

I couldn't believe that Danny would do something nice for me after everything that had transpired. I made sure to drive to my apartment as carefully as I could.

April 2003

Danny was online, but his screen name had been idle for a long time. His away message had some lovesick lyrics from a Dashboard Confessional song.

Did he like someone?

I blinked away the temporary surprise. It was stupid, really. In the years that we'd chatted online, we talked about crushes. That was before I knew who he was and where he went to school. It was normal to be curious about the kind of person that could catch Danny's eye. What if it was someone in our class? I should ask him. He'd tell me. I started typing, but then backspaced.

What if he just really liked that song?

Ugh. Even when he left clues, it was hard to know what was going on in Danny's head.

> **xxaznxbbxgrlxx:** can you burn me a copy of the dashboard album?

Five agonizing minutes later, he replied.

> **SuperxSaiyan85:** you got it

Chapter Seven

I STOPPED SHORT OF OPENING THE DOOR TO MY FIRST-FLOOR apartment. "I wasn't expecting a guest, so—"

Danny tilted his head, leveling his half smile. "I'm not going to judge."

He said that now, but he had no idea what he was about to walk into. If the arched doorway hadn't clued him in, he'd soon see the apartment complex was literally a hundred years old. My apartment was less than six hundred square feet and had an air-conditioning unit protruding from the wall that worked when it wanted to.

I unlocked the door and flipped on the lights. Nat's clothes were strewn across our couch. The most probable scenario was that she had tried to pack early for South by Southwest but stopped at some point because she couldn't decide what to bring. Since I wasn't there to help her talk through her options, she had ditched the clothes until I came home. This would've all been fine if Danny wasn't behind me.

"Make yourself comfortable," I said as I swooped up as many of Nat's clothes as I could hold. "The restroom is down the hall if you need it."

Danny nodded as he crossed the threshold into my space and placed the food on the kitchen counter. Like most of our guests, Danny was drawn to the living room, which Nat had decorated with props she'd stolen from every set she'd been on. I left Danny there while I ducked into Nat's room. I dropped her clothes on her bed and searched her desk. There was nothing but an assortment of pens and notes she wrote to herself. I wasn't trying to be nosy but couldn't help noticing that the note right on top, ironically enough, had "Don't forget passes and clothes" scribbled on it. What would she do without me?

As Nat had requested, I picked out a few tops and pants for her to change into. I sent her a quick text asking for her ETA and let her know we were on the way back. She reacted to the message with a heart, which told me nothing other than that she was probably in between takes if she responded that quickly.

When I reentered the living room, Danny was flipping through the playbill from a small play Nat had performed in with East West Players. Seeing that he still mouthed words as he read had me feeling some sort of way. I wasn't sure what way, but then Danny's face revealed a guilty smile, like I'd discovered him snooping when I was the one who'd been caught red-handed.

"I went to the opening night. Nothing like live theater, right?" I wasn't sure why I said that. I'd suddenly been overcome with restless energy that had nowhere to go. I hung Nat's clothes over the back of the couch and dabbed my forehead.

Danny slid the playbill back onto our bookshelf and picked up the earpiece that Nat wore in the *Beyond the Dark* pilot. It was the only episode in which her character wore it because someone realized how impractical it was for a scientist to wear such ornate jewelry during space missions. "Interesting things you've got lying around."

"Yeah. Never a dull day around here." I took the earpiece from Danny and returned it to its rightful place, trying not to think too much about the brush of our fingers during our exchange. "Sorry. This one's very special to Nat."

"These too?" Danny pointed at a pair of red Solo cups, the same ones Nat and I were holding in *The Summer Before Last.*

"Don't tell me you've seen it."

Danny replied with a cheeky smile. "I had to. How often do you see someone you know act in a movie?"

"Yeah, but you could tell it was going to be bad." The movie centered on a bunch of dudes renting a beach house to have one last great summer together before college. It was ninety minutes of horny bros trying to get laid. It wasn't cutting-edge material.

Danny shrugged. "Your cameo made it worth it."

I had no idea what to say to that. I cleared my throat. "It's only a cameo when the part is played by a celebrity."

My explanation seemed to make the awkwardness worse. Confusion flashed in Danny's eyes. God, why couldn't I accept the compliment? Before I could rectify it, Danny changed the subject. "Did you find the passes?"

Right. The passes. "Let me check the kitchen."

This was the perfect distraction to keep me from fixating on how I fumbled our conversation. I didn't need to go very far to see that the passes weren't in the fridge. Nat had been wrong on both of her guesses. The passes were under our fruit bowl. She must've left them there after her morning banana. I stuffed them in my jacket pocket and was about to fetch Danny when the spicy spaghetti reminded me of its presence. Damn, it smelled so good. I opened the bag and twisted noodles onto a fork before I put the rest in the fridge. I managed to steal a delicious bite without accidentally giving myself a tomato stain. It was a small win, not adding injury to my dirty suit. I contemplated changing my clothes, but I caught the time on our microwave. We had to go.

"Found 'em," I announced. "Let's go—"

As I stepped back into the living room, Danny was picking up the plexiglass diamond-shaped award I'd received from FreeStream earlier that year to recognize my ten years of service. It was an oversized paperweight now.

"See? I did work there," I said to plead my case for my little white lie. I removed the clear plaque from Danny's hands and ran my fingers over my etched name. "I should have tossed it in the trash."

"It's impressive that you stayed that long," Danny said.

"And look where it got me. In the end, it didn't count for anything." I put the award back in its place on the bookshelf. "Sorry. I don't mean to be a downer. I try to be positive. Sometimes I'm relieved that I don't have to go back to that job, but I'm also scared. I don't know what's next."

"It's okay to have conflicting feelings about it." Danny's face softened with sympathy. There was something precious about his face that made me want to hold it close. People talk about looks that could kill, but Danny's could soothe. "You experienced a loss. It's okay to grieve."

"Is that what this is?" I'd experienced setbacks before, but they hadn't felt like this. Getting laid off felt like having PMS-grade mood swings every day. I didn't know whether to be happy or sad. "It doesn't feel like it."

The one feeling I was certain of was that I was tired. I'd spent the beginning of my career delivering mail, answering phones, doing anything to please my bosses in hopes of getting the slightest chance of moving up. I molded myself into whatever other people wanted me to be. I played the game and it worked. I wouldn't have gotten the referral to FreeStream if my old bosses hadn't liked me. But if I tried really hard to look at this unemployment phase as an opportunity to pivot into something else, didn't that mean I'd have to work my way up from the bottom again? My body felt heavy at the thought. I'd already paid my dues.

"If it's not grief, then maybe you're having a midlife crisis," he mused.

"I'm not in a position to get a sports car at the moment."

Danny made a clicking sound as his mouth pulled into an awkward smile. "Probably a good idea, given your driving record."

"Oh shut up," I said with a laugh. "You have to come up with new material. I'm telling you, I've changed."

"So you say."

I narrowed my eyes at him, though there was no heat behind them. It was a verbal poke in the ribs I was used to getting from Danny. I missed the way we used to bicker. It used to all feel so easy. "I swear. I'm different now."

I waited for Danny to retort or smile this conversation off, which he'd do if he didn't have a comeback ready. But instead, he rested one hand on his hip and the other on the bookshelf behind me, creating a semicircle around me. "Not too different, I hope."

He said this with a light and airy huff, transparent in its sincerity.

Nostalgia was doing a number on me, because the first thing I thought about was another time when we stood this close, slow-dancing at the Spring Fling. We hadn't planned to go together. I didn't dress up, opting for jeans with a nice top. Danny gave me a hard time for working at a dance, and when I wouldn't leave my post, he sat and hung out with me.

"But you have to dance at least once," he'd said. "You can't come to a dance and not dance."

When I finally agreed, the next song happened to be a slow song. Danny didn't even have a reaction to it but just held out his arms. We'd always have that one dance together.

My heart raced from the unbidden memory. Even though it happened decades ago, the same overwhelming mix of confusion and excitement took over my senses.

"Why did you invite me tonight?" I blurted. I had to know. I had too many memories that blurred the lines of our friendship, that had made me think he cared about me, only for us to go our separate ways. It took a lot of time and effort to keep those memories at bay, to put them far enough away to fade. I didn't have enough bandwidth to relive adolescent feelings. It was hard enough the first time.

"Why did you come?" Danny asked, more curious than accusatory. I rolled my eyes at this blatant attempt to dodge the question, but then he added, "I thought you'd never come back."

I'd really dug my own grave when I shouted that for the whole school to hear. But it wasn't like I'd had some master plan to give him the silent treatment for twenty years. Did he forget that he left town after graduation without telling me? "So you didn't think I'd show up?"

"No. That's not it." Danny's dark brown eyes sank into mine, inadvertently starting a staring contest. I could've looked away, but then I'd have to contend with the soft hair that framed his unfairly handsome face. My hands itched to reach for him and see if he'd lean into my touch. But I kept them at my sides because I had to stay strong. I needed answers first.

"Can't I come and see an old friend?"

Danny leaned in, giving me a close-up of the tick in his jaw. I braced myself for another fight, but his eyes lowered like a surrender until all I saw was the fan of his long lashes. "Is that all we were?"

The sliver of vulnerability, that hope in his voice utterly disarmed me.

"No." That simple little word took all of the air out of me. Now that it was out in the open, I remembered why I never talked about my feelings for Danny. I couldn't take them back if I had been wrong. I hated being wrong.

Danny's eyes flicked up, searching mine like he had to make sure he heard me correctly. I was almost offended how surprising this was to him. Friends didn't usually go around kissing each other, for one thing. But I couldn't completely fault him. Back then, we couldn't wrangle our emotions. We kept them right beneath the surface until they exploded out of us like a cannon set to destroy everything in its path. If we'd learned anything from our mistakes, it didn't have to be that way this time.

"Is that what you thought?" I asked. If we were finally going to ask the questions, we might as well be thorough.

Danny shook his head, paying special attention to my mouth.

I pressed my hand firmly on his chest before I lost myself to my baser instincts. I wanted so badly to kiss him and pour everything into it. Years of regret and wonder and missed chances. I wanted him to feel it all. But kissing Danny had dismantled years of friendship in a matter of months. I couldn't let it cloud my judgment when I was trying to get to know the person he was now.

"We should go," I said. Disappointment washed over Danny's face. His lips parted like he was about to say something, but then his phone pinged. I couldn't read the message since it was upside down from my view, but I caught Mariana's name. It was enough to snap me out of this haze.

I patted my pockets, making sure I had everything I needed and fished out my car keys. "Come on." I nudged him out of my apartment. "We don't want to keep anyone waiting."

"Rachel."

I got in my car and turned on the ignition. Seeing Danny again was more than I had bargained for. I wanted to get some closure, not reopen old feelings.

"Rachel," he repeated after he sat down and buckled his seat belt. "Can you stop?"

"We're going to be late," I said and put the car in reverse.

"Let them wait. I didn't come for them."

I stepped on the brakes, leaving the car halfway in the street. This direct side of Danny was new, and it was like my brain couldn't handle it while driving at the same time. It was a jolt to the system, injecting new life into something I thought was gone. Sounds were coming in louder and lights were brighter.

I realized a second too late that these sensations weren't all in my head. A car racing down my street had crashed into the back of my car, sending it spinning. I couldn't tell what was left or right. By the time the airbags deployed, the only thing grounding me was my seat belt, cutting into my skin, and Danny's hand gripping mine.

 *Chapter Eight*

IT TOOK ABOUT TWENTY MINUTES FOR A POLICE OFFICER TO AR-rive and take down a report of the hit-and-run. He walked around my crunched-up car to assess the damage, taking notes along the way. "We pulled over the driver a mile away for speeding."

"Can I get him to pay for the damages?" I asked, unable to shake off the tremor in my voice.

"That's unlikely, given the nature of the collision," the police officer said, not bothering to look up from his notepad. "The other driver had the right of way."

"But he wasn't supposed to be driving so fast," I argued, desper-ate to say my piece. I didn't even see the other car when I backed out. Didn't that count for something?

The officer's face showed no emotion, like he was immune to my plea. "Be grateful that no one got hurt."

Sure. I'd agree that it was nothing short of miraculous that Danny and I came out of this crash physically unharmed. But had the police officer considered the pain of having to live in LA with-out a car?

I looked up, desperate to conjure any kind of hope, only to be boxed in by the LA night sky, which suffered from so much pollu-tion that very few stars shined through. The police officer spoke as he shoved a report in my hands, but it registered as muffled noise.

It wasn't until the officer left that the shock waned and I regained the part of my consciousness that was flipping out.

"Fuck." I lost the strength to stand and crouched on the edge of the sidewalk, ducking my head in between my knees. Just what I needed. Now I was jobless *and* carless. My car was basically my second home, and it was now unrecognizable.

"Here." Danny held out one of the reusable shopping bags that I kept in my trunk. "I collected as many personal items from your car as I could. There wasn't much I could salvage."

"You didn't have to do that," I said, touched that he tried to get into the wreckage, though maybe it wasn't too hard since half of my windows had shattered. Then the tow truck arrived. Watching my car get taken away triggered big fat tears. I couldn't hold back the ugly crying.

"Hey, hey." Danny sidled next to me, letting me lean on him. "It's going to be okay."

"No, it's n—" I hiccupped. Damn it. I couldn't get out another word without choking on it.

"You're right. I shouldn't have said that. It sucks." Danny wrapped his arm around my shoulders, resting his head on top of mine, locking me into a side hug. It was dangerous, how quickly his warmth comforted me. It was a balm, alleviating the pulsing anger and worry holding my body hostage. "Don't feel bad. It was an accident."

"But now we're stranded." Goddamn these narrow streets and reckless drivers. Without a car, I was stuck. I hated LA sometimes.

"Oh." Danny checked his watch. "Well, the reunion is well underway. We'll have to be fashionably late, then."

"It's not fair," I said, wiping away the last of my tears with the back of my hand. "I was thirty minutes early, remember?"

"Don't worry. You'll still get extra credit for your punctuality." There was a smile in his voice that I wished I could see, but I didn't want to leave this Danny bubble. It was safe and cozy in his arms, like being wrapped in linen that had dried in the summer sun. I wished I could've stayed in the moment longer, but unfinished business left me restless.

"How do we get back, though?" Since I usually had a car, I never used a rideshare service. I didn't have any of the apps on my phone.

"You still want to go?" Danny ducked his head and met my eyes, seeking confirmation. I had to wonder if my question was so unreasonable.

"Yeah." The thought of staying home alone while my life was in shambles made me more depressed. "I need to get out and blow off some steam."

I thought Danny would try to talk me out of it, but then he started texting someone with his free hand. "I know someone who can drive fast. He can be here in ten minutes."

"Who?"

Danny wouldn't say, but I found out soon enough when a gigantic SUV pulled up, driven by none other than Tao Sun, the notorious, larger-than-life thrower of parties. Back then, he always had people over because he wanted to be everyone's friend. The feeling wasn't mutual. Personally, he was too loud for my taste, and it didn't help that he wore too much Acqua di Gio. I mean, he was fine, but only in small doses. If I spent more than ten minutes with Tao, my face would curdle like it did when I sucked on a lemon wedge.

Since that was likely to happen, I sat in the backseat while Danny took the passenger seat up front. I didn't want to offend Tao when he was doing us a huge favor.

"Hey hey! Yo, Danny!" He greeted Danny with a hard clap on the back and a wave to me. "And freakin' Rachel! Long time no see!" Tao was as excitable as ever. His look had evolved into a confused hypebeast, wearing more brands than a NASCAR racer.

"Thanks for picking us up," I said as I buckled up. "How did you get here so fast?"

"I live in Los Feliz," Tao said as he drove off. "We should hang out more, Rach. We're practically neighbors. You can stop by and borrow a cup of sugar anytime, you feel me?"

"No." It shot out of my mouth as easy as breathing.

Tao laughed, taking it in stride. "Classic Rachel. If you ever change your mind, let me know."

"Will do."

Danny swung his head back, and he gave me a look that I couldn't interpret. If he was checking on me because Tao was being annoying, then he must not have remembered how Tao hit on every girl in our class, hoping for one yes. Rejections were so meaningless to Tao that he kept chitchatting. "How about you, Danny? Where've you been? I haven't seen you lately."

"You know. Work." Danny said this dismissively, apparently uninterested in elaborating. "What about you?"

"Ah, you know, I've been dabbling in a little bit of this and a little bit of that. I sell some stuff on eBay. Have some money invested in a little bit of this and that. Can't put all your eggs in one basket, if you know what I mean."

"Whatever you gotta do, right?" Danny said. If he understood anything Tao said, he'd have to explain it to me later.

"You know how it is," Tao said, reaching over for a quick fist bump. "You were always hustling back then. Same with you, Rach, except your hustle was for As and shit."

"Guilty," I replied.

"What were you two doing tonight?" Tao said with an obvious *wink-wink* in his voice. "I remember the two of you spending a lot of time together back in the day."

"In the library," I reminded him. I didn't want to go down this road, but old memories were the only thing that connected us.

"Our high school reunion's tonight," Danny said, effectively changing the subject. "I sent you an invite."

Oh. I guess I wasn't the only one who received a personalized invite from Danny. It didn't feel good to be on the same level as Tao.

"Oh right, right, right," Tao said. "Sorry. I have plans tonight."

"You . . . do?" It was hard to believe when he had appeared out of thin air to drive us back home.

"I wear a lot of hats, so I'm not tied down to any schedule." Tao merged onto the freeway. "But hey, this is a reunion right here. What have *you* been up to, Rach?" Tao sneaked a glance at me through the rearview mirror. "Busy taking over the world?"

"Uh . . ." Danny didn't turn around, but I got the sense that he was waiting to see how I'd respond. I could lie. Tao wouldn't know any different. He didn't seem like someone who followed entertainment news. But after losing my car, I didn't have much else to lose by being truthful. "I'm jobless actually. I got laid off a week ago."

"Oh. Sorry to hear that. But you'll land on your feet. You always do." That was nice of Tao to say. I wished I could bring myself to believe it. "What about your fam? You married? Kids?"

Maybe it was just me, but I could've sworn the temperature shot up in the car. I should have been used to these questions by then. I heard it ad nauseam from my parents and older relatives, and I heard it whenever I had new coworkers. What was it about being a single, childless, middle-aged woman that made people treat me like I was a carnival sideshow? I was painted as either a ruthless career woman or a sad, lonely, little lady. I wasn't either. I worked hard to be an independent woman, but I had other wants and needs outside of work. Things just hadn't worked out the way I thought they would. With as much confidence as I could muster, I replied, "No husband, no kids."

I couldn't see Danny's reaction, if he had one at all. I wondered what his situation was. I was so focused on getting us back on good terms, I hadn't even thought to ask. I didn't see a ring on his finger earlier, but he could be dating someone.

I didn't come for them.

He'd said that earlier, hadn't he? That meant he came for me, right? Was he looking for closure too?

Tao was still watching me through the mirror, waiting for me to add more. I'd forgotten to answer his other question. "My family's good. My parents are retired. My sister's good. My niece is graduating high school next year."

"Oh, you're a real auntie," he replied.

"I am, I am." It hurt to get called an auntie by a stranger in public the first time, worse than the first time I was called "ma'am." But after sixteen years as Hailey's aunt, I accepted it. I might not be a mother, but I was a real, bona-fide Asian auntie. A cool auntie, if I said so myself. "What about you?" I asked, turning the tables on Tao. "Are you married?"

"Nah. Life's too short to settle down, you know what I mean?" I did, but perhaps not in this context. "But we should hang out more," he insisted. When I made an agreeable but noncommittal noise, he added, "What if I threw a kickback tonight?"

"A kickback?" Danny asked. "I thought you said you had plans."

Tao exited the freeway, bringing us back to Alhambra. "Yeah. My plan was to party!"

I scoffed at the idea at first, but why the hell not? I never went to any of Tao's legendary parties before, and it seemed like something I should experience at least once. When would another opportunity present itself? "Sure. I'll go."

Tao punched his horn. "That's what I'm talking about!"

"Do you need me to bring anything? Wine?" I suggested.

"Wine? Pfft." Tao threw out a dismissive hand. "You just gotta bring yourself, Rach. But you," he said to Danny, "can bring some beer."

"Where's this party going to be?" I asked.

"You've never been to my parents' house?" Before I could say no, Tao kept talking. "Danny's been there. He'll tell you."

My mind was blindsided by a memory of Danny drunk-dialing me after one of Tao's parties. He'd said all kinds of nonsense. That was what I thought at the time. He must have been really drunk because we never spoke of it.

"Your parents' house?" Danny asked. "They don't mind?"

"Dude, they can hang all night."

Tao pulled into a shopping plaza across the street from the oldest location of The Hat. The car windows were closed, but I swear I could smell their pastrami from where I sat.

"All right," Tao said, putting the car in park. "We're here."

"What do you mean we're here?" I said. Clearly, this wasn't our high school.

Tao tapped on the sticker on his windshield, which looked like a cute onigiri. "I have to pick up food for delivery. It'll be a quick stop."

"Are you being serious right now?" He was delivering food? Was this the "this" or "that" he referenced earlier? Good for him for having a side hustle, but it was already past eight. The reunion was half over. "We're like five minutes away. You can't take us there first?"

"Come on, Rach. I gotta make that cash, you feel me?"

"No, I don't freaking feel— You know what?" I unbuckled my seat belt. "Thank you for the ride. I'm going to walk the rest of the way."

"Rach!" Tao called out. "It'll be fast. I'll drop you off after I make the delivery. The customer is only in . . ." Tao squinted at his phone and then faced the screen toward Danny. "Hey. I don't have my reading glasses on. Does this say San Gabriel or San Manuel?"

One of those cities would make us lose time and the other would make us lose time *and* money. Neither option was acceptable. "Bye, Tao."

"Kickback later! Don't forget!" he shouted as I stepped out of the car.

We'll see about that. If he was out making deliveries, I doubted this party would come to fruition. "Danny. You coming?"

Before Danny got out, he gave Tao one of those goodbye nods that made me wonder when they became so chummy. We headed east toward Commonwealth. I walked slowly, not wanting to rush Danny when he was still limping. The sky was black, but the street was buzzing with life. Rows and rows of cars were zooming in both directions, passing the bright restaurant storefront lights. My stomach grumbled for food so loud even Danny heard it over the traffic.

"Do you want to stop and eat?" he asked. By that point, we were too far away from The Hat to go back for pastrami.

"No." We'd come this far and we were beyond fashionably late. We were capital L Late.

"No one's going to care if we're late," he said, as if he read my mind. "Over a hundred people RSVP'd. Mariana hasn't texted me since we left your apartment. She's got things handled."

Probably because Mariana used to throw every school assembly, including a choreographed dance number to whatever song was popular that week. A hundred RSVPs was a cakewalk for her.

"I don't care what Mariana thinks." Danny side-eyed me, not believing a single word I said. "I don't!"

"You want me to believe that after all the trouble we went through to get those passes?"

"It wasn't supposed to be this way," I reminded him. Leaving to go get the passes was supposed to be a quick trip. "We just had bad luck."

"Yeah." Danny's steps dragged on the concrete. "Tell me about it."

March 2003

I couldn't sleep after the Spring Fling. Every time I closed my eyes, my brain replayed the moment Danny's arms circled my waist. Since we were the same height, our faces were inches apart, as close as we'd ever been. Close enough to notice things I hadn't before, like the small silver scar that ran parallel to the corner of his forehead. He also had a defined Cupid's bow, which pointed a big arrow at his lips. I had to look over his shoulder to stop myself from staring. It wasn't like I could help it. His face was right there.

What was most perplexing about the whole thing was that

it didn't feel weird. At least, it didn't when it was happening. Everything about the casual way Danny asked me to dance felt like a natural extension of our friendship. So why was I still thinking about it so much?

I had to stop or I'd go out of my mind. I had to remind myself that our dance ended as fast as it started. Once the song was over, Danny left with his friends for Tao's party. I could've gone, since Tao's parties weren't exclusive. Everyone had an open invitation. But I'd told my parents that I'd come home by eleven, so I went home to spend time with my AP prep books. I wasn't sure why I bothered with them. The words looked like gibberish because my mind was broken, filled with thoughts about Danny's warm body and how he smelled like nothing except for the faintest scent of soap.

The phone rang, interrupting my hormonal state. It had to be a prank call. No one ever called this late.

"Hello?" No one replied, so I tried one more time before hanging up. "Hello?"

"Did I wake you?" It was Danny. He sounded tired or drunk. Probably both. Before I could answer, a third party joined the call.

"Who's this?" my dad mumbled, sounding barely conscious.

"I got it, Ba." I waited until I heard the phone click off before I spoke again. My parents were used to boys calling when Angela still lived here, but not in the middle of the night. "No, you didn't wake me. How did you get my number?"

"Nat gave it to me." I should have known. "What? I can't call you?"

"Not at one in the morning."

"Why didn't you come to the partyyyyy?" Okay. He was

drunk. His voice lowered to a whisper. "Do you wanna know a secret?"

He was acting like such an idiot. It was kind of funny, so I played along. I whispered back, "What?"

"Nat kissed Mariana."

"So?" Nat had come out as bi the year before. Everyone and their mother knew about it. It was all people could talk about for weeks because there were only a few other kids out at school.

"On the mouth!" Danny continued. "In front of everyone!"

"Good for her," I said. Nat was fearless in that way. Not much embarrassed her.

"Have you ever kissed anyone?"

Forget the hormones. My entire body was malfunctioning. I couldn't get my mouth to produce any words. Danny and I had chatted a lot over the years online, but we'd never really talked on the phone like this before. What if Danny heard the panic in my voice?

"Why do you want to know?" I hedged. Was he trying to make fun of me? "Have *you* kissed anyone?"

"I asked you first." This was so childish.

"No, I haven't, okay?" It was embarrassing to say out loud. It felt like everyone else had experienced at least their first kiss by now.

"There's nothing wrong with that," he replied. "My first kiss was with a girl in middle school, and she did it on a dare. It meant nothing to her or me."

Danny was trying to console me, but even his sad first kiss sounded better than being a late bloomer. "Sometimes I won-der if I should kiss someone and get it over with."

"Like who?"

"I don't know." It didn't matter at this point. It could be anyone who'd be willing. "I don't think Nat would mind."

"Nah. Not Nat."

"Why not? Whenever I ask someone about it, no one seems to have had a good experience." At least Nat knew what she was doing. She'd kissed plenty of people.

"Yeah, but... it doesn't mean you shouldn't waste it either."

He might not have said the words, but I heard the judgment. Why did I say all of that? I probably sounded pathetic. "Don't tell anyone."

"Who would I tell?"

"I know how guys talk." It didn't take much to overhear guys talking about girls they'd supposedly hooked up with or objectifying girls they wanted to be with. Sometimes when I felt down about my single status, I'd wish I was one of the girls guys talked about. But then I'd hear them talk about getting a piece of ass and wonder why I had the misfortune of being attracted to boys at all. "You guys pretend like you don't gossip, but you do."

"Don't look at me," he said, his words blurring into a yawn. "I can keep a secret. I keep lots of secrets."

"Like what?"

Danny stayed quiet, proving his point. Or so I thought. When he spoke again, his tone had shifted to something more serious. "I've been working with my brother." I was going to tell him that I knew that already, but then he added, "He's, um... he's gotten into a lot of trouble."

"What kind of trouble?"

"Money troubles. He keeps trying to get rich quick, but

then he keeps losing money. His booth at the mall is the most legit thing he's ever tried. I want to make sure he sticks with it."

So that was why he'd been working so much. It was pretty sweet of him to do that. "You're a good brother."

Danny didn't seem to take the compliment well because he responded with a grunt. "I want to be good at other things."

"Like what?"

"Like . . . like . . ." Danny finished his sentence with a quiet snore. Right when he was opening up, the idiot fell asleep. Danny knew how to leave a girl wanting more.

Chapter Nine

"IT USED TO BE THERE."

Danny stopped in the middle of the sidewalk and pointed across the street to a little corner plaza that was too small to be a strip mall. There were two storefronts, but from where we stood I couldn't make out what kind of businesses they were.

"The internet café," Danny supplied when I didn't say anything. "It used to be there, where the boba shop is."

I did a double take. I couldn't tell it was a boba shop. There was a pergola that hadn't been there before, covering the outdoor seating with twinkling lights. And unlike chain boba shops, the place didn't have a big flashy sign.

"It looks so different now," I commented. The shop was cute and romantic. Nothing like the teen hangout spot it once was.

"Yeah," Danny said wistfully, making me wonder how much time he'd spent there. "Do you remember the day we met?"

How could I forget? "You ran me over."

"Well, I think we're even now."

"That"—I pointed at his butt—"was an accident."

"So was mine." Danny laughed for the first time that evening. While it was one of those disbelieving I-can't-believe-I-had-to-say-it kind of laughs, seeing him smile made me smile. "Let's go check it out."

"But the reunion," I reminded him. We didn't come this far to make a boba pit stop.

"It's only a drink," Danny said, with an inexplicable lightness, given how delayed we were. If I wasn't mistaken, he even seemed downright giddy. "It's not going to take long."

I begged to differ, but then Danny took my hand and escorted me across the street. Any protests I had died on my lips. This was something I never understood. As human beings, we use our hands for everything. They're at the ends of our arms, openly doing the most benign tasks. But the simple contact of two hands, holding on to one another, feels so deeply personal. Danny's fingers firmly intertwined with mine, his knuckles gnarled like the rings of a tree while his palm provided a soft landing place for mine. I didn't want to let go.

I had to let go, though, when Danny held the door open to let me into the modern and blindingly white shop. My hands now held a sticky, laminated menu with way too many options to choose from. Cheese foam? Crème brûlée? How were people coming up with so many new flavors and toppings? Milk tea was so complicated now. "I don't know what to get."

Danny diligently read each of the unique combinations while he bopped his head along to the lo-fi music playing overhead. "I might get a plain milk tea with boba. I'm trying to cut back on sugar."

The sound of blenders mixing up smoothies must have messed up my hearing. Danny used to eat and drink anything that was put before him. "I've seen you eat an entire full-size Snickers bar in five seconds."

Danny patted his stomach. "Doctor's orders. I'm prediabetic. I even had to cut back on rice."

One would think someone had died by the way I gasped. How do you take rice away from an Asian person?

"I'm fine," he continued. "I'm taking precautions since diabetes runs in my family."

Danny ordered an unsweetened boba milk tea for himself. I ordered the same in solidarity and because I couldn't decide. We sat at a nearby table while we waited for our drinks. It was unbearably normal for two people who'd had the most hectic evening.

"So what do you do these days?" I asked, immediately self-conscious for starting a conversation with small talk. I'd seen him without his pants on. "I imagine work keeps you busy."

"Yeah. Many of my clients request remote meetings, so I don't travel as much as I used to." Danny fiddled with the receipt that had our order number on it. "It made my mom happy."

"How is your family, by the way?"

"They're good, they're good." Danny's voice pitched higher as he repeated himself. "My mom remarried around fourteen, fifteen years ago. She's retired now." He took out his phone and showed me pictures of his smiling mom and her partner. Things seemed fine on that front.

"And how's Jimmy?"

A wave of emotions swept over Danny's face. There was a quick angry eyebrow scrunch, followed by a sour twist in his lips. The grand finale was an anticlimactic shrug. "I don't know."

"What do you mean you don't know?" I said, surprising even myself. His family had always been a touchy subject that I never pressed too hard on. Not knowing where our relationship stood, I couldn't risk saying or doing anything that could push him away.

"Last I heard, he moved to Seattle." Danny stood to retrieve our drinks. He was stalling. He had to be because when he sat back down he took a long sip. Long enough for six boba pearls to travel up his straw.

"It's okay," I said, backtracking. My curiosity wasn't helping. "You don't have to say. It's none of my business." I scooted my chair back. We had our drinks, so we should make our way back to the school.

Danny put down his cup with a thunk, stopping me from getting up. "Actually, it is."

This I had to hear. I sat back down. "What do you mean?"

"Where do I start?" he said under his breath. "After Jimmy was released from jail, I lost track of him." He shrugged again when my eyes threatened to pop out of my face.

I didn't see that coming. I'd followed Danny's advice. I steered clear of Jimmy whenever I went to the mall. Sometimes I'd stay on the second floor and go down the escalator on the opposite side to avoid him. "When did he go to jail?"

Danny looked off to the side as he thought. To an outsider, he'd have looked like he was browsing the bookshelf, choosing from a collection of board games and manga stacked there. Belying his soft, pensive expression were the angled lines of his profile, especially his sharp eyebrows pointing at the worry lines on his forehead.

"Do you remember how I moved a lot?" he asked finally. I nodded. "My parents used to make up all kinds of excuses, like our landlord raised the rent. But I knew it was because of Jimmy. He owed a lot of people money, and they didn't mess around. We didn't know how bad it was until they'd show up out of the blue to collect and, you know . . . they weren't friendly about it."

Danny mindlessly rubbed his temple, inching closer to that silver scar underneath his hairline. "Around graduation, these guys were showing up at my house every few days. It was hard to leave the house sometimes. That's why I was late to Awards Night."

"Oh." All roads kept leading back to Awards Night. I didn't know what to do with this new information. An explanation should've been a balm, but it only made the wound sting more. I'd known that his family situation wasn't the best. He'd said little about it, but enough that I knew how distracting it had been. Danny used to work every day to support his family, even helping his brother when it had caused him a lot of grief. I'd selfishly thought that Danny didn't show up because of our fight, like being a no-show was his version of revenge. After I went home that night, I'd decided to shut him out and pretend he was merely a blip in my senior year. Even if he'd tried to explain all of this back then, I wouldn't have let him because I was hotheaded and emotionally stupid.

"Danny, I'm so sorry. I had no idea it was that bad."

Danny shook his head as he swirled his drink. "It's not like I told you any of this. I should've told you. I should've done a lot of things differently."

Danny's eyes lifted until they locked on mine, and kicking in like muscle memory, I held my breath. This was the game we'd played countless times. We'd flirt at the edge of honesty then back away, left with having to guess the rest. It had never occurred to me that I'd gotten things so wrong.

"I wish I'd known. I wouldn't have—" But I couldn't blame Danny for not telling me. I wasn't exactly nice to him toward the end. It was too late to defend my choices, especially now that I knew what had been going on with him, but maybe explaining them would help him understand. "You know why I wanted you to be there, right?"

"Because you wanted me to witness you beating Mariana?"

Danny said, probably to annoy me. He knew the reason. "You told me you weren't sure if your family would make it."

That was what I told him, but it wasn't the entire story. "My parents never came to any of my school events, so inviting them to Awards Night was a long shot. But then my dad's print shop went out of business and he had a short window to move his stuff out. My mom went to help him, and they totally forgot about Awards Night."

It was stupid that I still felt disappointed about it, especially when I didn't win anything. Had my parents come, it would've been a complete waste of their time. "Business hadn't been going so well for a while, but when my dad decided to close, it started to hit me that he wasn't going to be able to help me pay for college. I needed the awards. I thought it would help me get more scholarships."

Danny didn't say anything. He didn't have to. We both knew how things turned out. The only recognition I received was the one printed on my name tag. Most Likely to Succeed. What a joke.

"I was stressed out and I took it out on you," I said. "I'm sorry."

This conversation was long overdue, but it was good that we finally cleared things up. Danny seemed to think so too. He fixed a smile on his face that didn't really match his melancholy eyes.

"I don't want this night to be about regrets. We're starting over, remember?" Danny tapped his boba cup into mine. "To new memories."

It was tempting to return the gesture and knock his cup back and pretend everything was okay. I could've replied with something like, "We'll make it a night to remember," or some other sentimental cliché that could have doubled as our prom theme. But my cynicism had sharp claws. Danny's rosy outlook felt more like smoke and mirrors. There was a nagging feeling in my gut telling me to dig a little deeper. As much as Danny had just shared, I knew he dealt with things by keeping it light. In the past, we'd sweep our fights under the rug and pretend they never happened. Maybe if I hadn't had tunnel vision when we were younger, I would have noticed that pattern sooner. I wasn't about to let history repeat itself.

"Why didn't you tell me about your brother before? We used to talk all the time."

This was one of the times I wished we were having this conversation over text, so he wouldn't hear the vulnerability in my sandpaper voice. I didn't want Danny to think I was still hung up on this, but there was no denying at this point that I was. I needed to know where things went wrong.

"I didn't know how. My own parents wouldn't even talk to me about it. There was this unspoken expectation that whatever happened in our house stayed in our house." Danny shrugged. "It's hard to talk about the things that you're taught to hide."

"Like us?" My body flushed with the heat of embarrassment. I'd said the silent part out loud.

"What are you talking about?"

If Danny needed to jog his memory, then we were at the right place. "You never talked to me at school, even after we found out we'd been chatting online. It was like you didn't want anyone to know we were friends."

"You need to look in the mirror, Rach." For a second, I thought he meant that I had something on my face, until he said, "It goes both ways."

"What's that supposed to mean?" I asked. Danny shook his head like he didn't want to touch this topic with a ten-foot pole. "I can handle it." Danny gave me a look like he wasn't convinced. If he needed proof, I had plenty to give him. "An asshole producer once told me that he could see me in a movie if I shed a few pounds. He went as far as to say I'd look less bloated if I cut back on the soy sauce." It was a racist and misogynistic double whammy. "Working in Hollywood," I continued, "made me grow a thick skin quick. I can take it."

Danny ruminated for a bit, wariness apparent on his face as he raked his hair. I rested my arms on the table like we were sitting in a boardroom. Whatever he had to say, I wanted to hear it. Eventually, he relented and dropped his answer quickly, like he was running away from a grenade. "You always cared too much about what other people thought."

I wished my drink had some sugar to make this feedback go down easier. "What are you talking about?"

Danny shook his head, unwilling to elaborate, but I egged him on. "If you don't tell me, I'm never going to know."

"Fine," he said, though he avoided my eyes. "Your clothes, for one."

Is he being for real right now? He was going to start with something superficial?

"What about it?" I patted away a dusty spot on my elbow, a souvenir from my fall. "I can't look nice for the reunion?"

"Yeah, but this"—he waved his hand up and down at my clothes—"it's a little much for the high school gym, don't you think?"

I scoffed as I buttoned up my blazer. I failed to see what was so scandalous about this camisole. A little cleavage never hurt anybody. "You need to get out more."

"You asked for this," he reminded me.

"What else? It can't be the outfit," I said. We'd gotten this far. He might as well tell me everything. "I've always been this way, apparently. How so? Was it because I wanted to be the best? Collect awards?" I didn't see how that was a bad thing.

"You lied to people about your job," he said, as if I'd forgotten.

"Were you planning on coming clean, or were you going to wait until you were officially inducted into the Alumni Hall of Fame?"

I crossed my arms over my chest. None of my answers to my class-mates' questions were anything to be proud of, but I must've done something to get selected in the first place. "Is it so bad? Haven't you ever wanted to people to think you were worthy of recognition?"

Danny squared his shoulders as a blistering heat ignited in his eyes. "You have no idea," he said. "But at what cost, Rach? Your in-tegrity?"

"Since when did you become the moral police? It's just an award from school."

Danny dug his hands into his hair, causing it to stand on end. "Who are you? Do you hear yourself right now?"

I did. But I couldn't stop myself from saying whatever it took to win this argument. At my ripe middle age, I was aware of my pat-terns. I'd gotten into enough hot water in relationships to know that much about myself. But knowing about my bad habits and doing something about them were two separate things.

"Sorry it's not the Grammy Awards, Rachel, but it's a big deal to some people who appreciate the honor."

"The Grammy Awards are for music," I corrected him, practi-cally shouting. It wasn't the sharp comeback I'd heard in my head. Danny was still mostly right.

Danny's chair scraped the floor as he rose from his chair. "Let's revisit when we can talk more calmly."

"I'm calm!" That earned me a "get real" look from Danny. Ad-mittedly, I deserved it, but damn, it pissed me off.

"Why are you asking me, then?" He threw his empty boba cup into the trash can on his way out. "You seem to have it all figured out."

If that were true, why did I feel like I just lost?

 *Chapter Ten*

I WALKED AHEAD OF DANNY DURING OUR SHORT TRIP TO THE school to prove that I didn't care what he thought about my plan. It wasn't my fault that nobody confirmed my employment status before I was selected. Had Danny considered that before accusing me of being a liar?

I wanted to share this tidbit with Danny, but when I turned around, he was half a block behind me. I had enough awareness not to yell in a quiet, dark neighborhood. I could barely make out his face, but I recognized the clop of his steps and the shadow of his sagging shoulders from the faint reach of the streetlights. Here I was thinking that I was giving Danny the silent treatment, but he was doing the same to me.

What was I doing? Talking things out should've brought us closer to a resolution, but we weren't any better now than we used to be. Instead of reconciling, talking had been like pressing on a bruise, checking to see if it still hurt. I had to rethink this. It wasn't like there was a recipe to follow for apologizing, forgiving, and forgetting. I had to handle this with more care.

"Danny." We were nearing the entrance of the school gym and I wanted to smooth things over before we got swept up by other people.

Danny ignored my attempt to restart our conversation. As we reentered the gym, he swiped the backstage passes from my jacket pocket. "I'll put these on the donation table."

Well, this was going great. Danny wasn't on my side, and Nat wasn't here. I'd have to sit through this reunion on my own. But first, I made a pit stop at the restroom. Between the heels that were not made for walking and the large cup of milk tea, I needed to hide there to collect myself.

The gym restroom was utilitarian by design. The same decades-old fixtures and sterile subway tiles still made the point that this place wasn't for gussying up. The only thing in the bathroom from this century was the automatic soap dispenser, but even that was half empty.

I wet a paper towel under running water and dabbed it against the sides of my neck. The coolness of the water permeated my hot and sticky skin. I could blame being overheated on the walk to the school, but I'd been simmering ever since the tiff with Danny. I couldn't tell if coming back here had made me regress or if it was Danny's presence that made my emotions run rampant, unfiltered and oversaturated, in a way that didn't seem real.

"Get it together, Rach," I mumbled to myself.

A door from one of the bathroom stalls swung open as I was touching up my makeup.

"You're back." Only Viv could step out of a bathroom stall like she was strutting through New York Fashion Week. She still had that X factor that drew everyone's attention. She turned on the squeaky faucet to wash her hands. "I wasn't sure if I was going to see you again."

"It took longer than expected. It's a long story," I said, hoping I wouldn't have to explain. Viv and I never had the type of relationship where we'd confide in one another. We weren't from the same social circle and acknowledged each other only when we had the same classes together. "I hope Mariana's not upset that we took awhile to get back."

"Oh, don't worry about that. Mariana was busy putting out other fires." Viv tore off a paper towel and dried her hands. "Some people who RSVP'd never showed up. I'm not sure there'll be enough money to cover the event. Mariana was trying to cut costs by having it here, but I don't know if that'll be enough."

That was shocking. Some Commonwealth alums lived out of state now, but a significant number of us had stayed local. They might not all be in Alhambra, but they were scattered around LA and Orange County. It couldn't have been too hard for folks to attend.

Viv swiped her lips with fire engine red lipstick. "And then someone brought booze. We didn't notice until people started dancing kinda sloppy." She chuckled. "It was funny, but you know. It's against the rules." Her eyelashes fluttered as she rolled her eyes.

"How are we still sneaking booze at our age?" I mused.

"I know, right?" Viv shot me a smile through the mirror. "Well, I'll let you get back to your speech."

I froze. "My what?"

"Weren't you practicing your speech right now?" Viv scrunched her nose when I didn't reply. "Mariana wanted the honorees to say a few words. I thought she emailed everyone about it."

I would've seen it if that was the case. I still checked my email regularly, even though the only messages I was receiving these days were requests to rate my recent online purchases. Maybe the message was sent to my old email. "I RSVP'd late," I said, thinking out loud. "It probably fell through the cracks."

A chill ran down my spine. It wasn't like Mariana to forget details like that. I was sure she would've told me to prepare some remarks. Had I known, I would've declined. What could I really say about my career now that it had come to a sudden halt? My last memory of having a job was leaving the FreeStream building with a security escort. That wasn't the kind of uplifting anecdote anyone wanted to hear. I had to come up with something fast, but I wasn't good at improvising.

"It'll be fine. It doesn't have to be long," Viv reassured me as she gave herself one final once-over in the mirror. She must've seen the panic on my face because she said, "I have some rosemary essential oils. That helps with anxiety."

"No thanks." I didn't want to smell like a roast chicken for the rest of the night.

"Maybe Danny could help you," Viv suggested.

My ears perked at the *wink-wink* in her voice. "What are you getting at?"

"What?" Viv said innocently. "I noticed you two hanging out again. It's not a secret that you two broke up on Awards Night. Everyone heard you," she said easily, oblivious to how horrifying it was for me to learn that there was a collective memory of that incident. So horrifying that I didn't bother to clarify that Danny and I never dated. It was our friendship that broke up, and that hurt worse. "He's single. So are you, aren't you? I sort of noticed that the pictures of your engagement disappeared."

I didn't even question Viv's eagle eyes. I might not have posted much on social media, but Josh did when we were together. Our engagement announcement drew lots of responses, mostly from his college friends and coworkers from his accounting firm. It wouldn't have been too hard for some of my high school friends to see it then. The announcement was splashier than the news that we called things off. In lieu of a joint statement, all posts about us quietly disappeared from Josh's Instagram in a matter of days.

"Danny and I are just getting reacquainted," I said.

"Okay," Viv said, making her way out. "Whatever you say."

I didn't like Viv's extra coy tone one bit, but I didn't have the time or capacity to worry about rumors when I had to come up with something positive to say about my nonexistent career. Leaving the restroom, I looked for a quiet place to think but somehow got caught up in a mob of people traveling down the hallway like a school of fish. Mariana was at the forefront, leading the group to turn the corner, past the athletic trophy cases.

"Thanks to the passing of local bonds back in 2017, some facilities have been updated over the years. But it wasn't enough to keep up with budget cuts," Mariana recited while walking backward like it wasn't the first time she'd said this that night. "This means—" Mariana looked over her shoulder and spotted me. "Rachel! Glad you could join us," she said, similar to a teacher when a student shows up late. The callout had heads turning to me. "We're going to see one of the smart rooms on campus."

"Rachel?"

"Daaaang! Rachel Dang!"

I'd recognize those voices anywhere. They belonged to Nelson Kwan and Felix Guzman, who were part of Danny's clique. I hung back and found them at the tail end of the tour group with Danny, who averted his eyes after an acknowledging glance. The silent treatment was still on.

Nelson looked about the same, except he'd traded in his ironic graphic tees for a button-down and tie. Felix was still tall and lanky but was now rocking a bald head.

I must have been staring at his missing hair a little too hard, because Felix rubbed the top of his head, giving it a shine.

"I shaved it off on purpose," he said, looking more sheepish than I'd ever seen him.

"Yeah, because it was almost gone," Nelson chimed in with a full-body snicker. That earned us a few shushes from the folks up front. Felix, the quiet one of their group, gave Nelson a friendly shove in the shoulders.

"Sorry. I—" I shook my head. How could I be so rude? "Hi," I said, trying to start the conversation over. "It's been a long time."

I tried to go in for a hug, but both of them gave me a wave instead. I didn't think anything of it. It wasn't like we were close friends. They were always off in their own world, hanging by the same table in the quad near the cafeteria or getting an earful from teachers whenever they skated through the walkways. They caught me up with what they'd been up to as quietly as they could. Felix was a city planner in Fullerton and was married with three kids. Nelson was single and taught kids how to play guitar since a back injury forced him to end his general contractor career early.

"The pay isn't as good, and I have to hear 'Mary Had a Little Lamb' a hundred times a day, but it's low stress and flexible, so I can help out my parents now that they're older," he explained rather articulately. I wondered if he said this often.

"That sounds nice," I said, unsure why Nelson had a chip on his shoulder. I remembered him bringing his guitar to school and garnering the adoration of many girls who wanted to be serenaded. But Nelson shrugged it off and split off when we entered the classroom where I once took a Spanish class. The classroom now resembled a computer lab. Each desk had its own laptop, and the wall had what appeared to be a digital whiteboard with "Welcome Class of 2003" scrawled across it.

"You are all standing in a math classroom," Mariana announced once everyone was inside. "It's outfitted with the most current technology. Hopefully, we'll raise enough money tonight to transform a few more rooms like this one."

"Wow, this is amazing, Mari," said a man who might've been on the water polo team. I wasn't sure because I wasn't accustomed to seeing any of the water polo team with clothes on. "This is so different from when we went to school."

"Dude, if we'd had this when we were in school, we would've surfed the internet during class," Nelson said from across the room, where he'd been keeping close to Danny. I'd taken a few steps to regroup with them, but then Nelson pulled Danny into the far corner, to do what, I wasn't sure. Reminisce about matrices?

"There's software on each laptop to make sure it's only used for educational purposes," Mariana said.

"There's always a workaround," Nelson replied. "Kids are smart. They find a way."

"That's true," I said. "My assistant could get past any paywall or firewall to get what she needed. She actually figured out which Netflix series was getting canceled days before the news hit." I probably should have asked Zoe how she did that, but I didn't want to get implicated in any secretive things she was up to.

Nelson didn't appreciate me adding my two cents. I was only trying to back him up, but he didn't seem to take it that way. He all but ignored me as he approached the whiteboard and popped the cap off a red marker to draw a smiley face.

"Don't let Nelson bother you," Felix said when I returned to my corner of the room. I must've made a face. I'd been told that I made a long, stony face whenever I didn't get the result I wanted.

"What did I do to him?" I already had one person mad at me. I didn't need another.

"Nothing. He's being protective of Danny."

I assumed that meant that they were still close. "Why?"

"Because you really messed him up back then," Felix stated, like it was a well-known fact. "He didn't want to talk. He wouldn't come hang out. He moped around up until he moved. You broke the man."

I'd expected Felix to accept Danny's version of events, which probably painted me as a villain. But it landed like a blow to learn that I'd ruined Danny somehow. I hadn't thought about Danny's feelings in those terms. Back then, Danny never gave the impression that he cared enough about things long enough to let them bother him. It was becoming more and more obvious that I'd been wrong.

Felix popped his head up to make sure there was no one nearby before he said, lowering his voice, "We don't want to see him get hurt again, especially after his divorce."

Divorce?

Everything that had happened before this conversation evaporated from my consciousness. Why did the fact that Danny had been married affect me at all? Our lives had moved in different directions and I'd had my own fair share of relationships. Of course the same would go for him. I guess I hadn't fathomed that Danny might have one relationship that he thought at the time could last forever.

I had to know who this person was. How did they meet? Did they meet online? Or did they have a meet-cute like something out of the movies? Was she out walking her dog when the leash tangled Danny and her together? Or was it one of those situations where they had to marry or else she'd forfeit a large inheritance? I had to know.

Felix must've registered the surprise on my face because he quickly backtracked. "Damn it. I thought you knew. Everyone seems to know everything these days with social media." He rubbed the top of his head again, giving it a good buff. "Forget I said anything. You didn't hear anything from me."

This night was getting really confusing. Viv was rooting for me, and Nelson wanted me to scram. What a homecoming this was turning out to be. LA might not always love me back, but at least I didn't have to deal with people having opinions about my personal life, past or present. The worst part was that Danny was right. Why did I care so much about what people thought?

As the group made its way back to the gym, I overheard someone go on and on about their 401(k) and someone else about the rental property they were fixing up. Somewhere in the mix, Mariana referred someone to her chiropractor. It was a lot of grown-up talk coming from people who used to recap the latest *Smallville* episode during passing period. I didn't have anything in common with anyone here anymore. I should've followed through on my promise and forgotten about high school. If I left now, I could pretend this night never happened and go back to my messed-up life. My real life.

With not much light from the half-moon, it was dark in the quad. I could slip out of the group and leave the school without anyone noticing. I gradually slowed my pace and fell behind everyone. Once I was a few feet away from them, I made a break for it, turning sharply to cross the next quad, the one that faced the school entrance. My parents' house was a short five blocks away. I would be home in no time. For a second there I thought I was going to make it, but soon I heard footsteps catching up to me.

"Rachel," Danny whispered as if classes were in session. "Where are you going?"

What was I doing? Standing in the middle of the hallway, facing the entrance of Commonwealth, I was reminded of the person I used to be. I used to roam these halls like I owned them. There wasn't anything that could have knocked me down. I'd look at a roadblock as a challenge to overcome. If it required hard work, I'd give it 110 percent. If I was stuck, I'd retrace my steps and take a different route. If there wasn't a path, I'd forge one.

But that was then. Life had knocked me down, and somehow I was coming back to Commonwealth neither smarter nor better. I didn't know who I was anymore.

"You were right. I shouldn't have misled everyone tonight." I cleared my throat, hoping my voice was coming out calm, even if it wavered. "Coming here was a bad idea."

"So that's it?" he asked, stepping around me until he stood between me and the exit. "You were going to bail and disappear for another twenty years?"

It looked that way, didn't it?

"What do you want me to say? I just had a shitty day on top of an already shitty year. I'm going through a tough time, if you couldn't tell."

I struggled to keep my voice down. Emotions were rioting in my body, confusing my fight-or-flight response.

"I can," Danny said, matching my frustration. "But I can't talk to you when you're being like this."

"Like what?"

Danny held up his hands, surrendering. "I can't have a normal conversation with you. I have no idea how you're going to react."

"Well, I'm sorry if I don't have it all together all the time!" A tear escaped from my eye. What a time to not have tissues on me. I wiped my face indelicately with the back of my hand. "I'm kind of in the middle of a personal crisis. I'm sorry I'm not making the best decisions!"

"That's not what I'm saying, Rachel." Danny ran his hand through his hair. His chest heaved with deep breaths, like he'd been running. "You just—you just—" Danny, honest to goodness, growled so loud, I jumped back. "I can't even think straight. That's how much you frustrate me!"

"Same to you!" I paced a few steps to work off some steam. As much as we tried, we were still the same, weren't we? We always riled each other up. "Why are we doing this to ourselves?" I asked when I was calmer. "I shouldn't have come."

Danny closed his eyes as he tilted his head left and right, like he was trying to relieve the tension in his body. Everything about him was tight, from his suit to his stony face. Danny dug a finger into the knot of his tie, loosening it as he swallowed hard. "Then why did you?"

I didn't want to admit that I only came because I thought Danny wanted to be friends again. In my fantasy, Danny would've apologized profusely for complicating things when he kissed me, leading me to believe we were something we weren't. But I was the one who had ended things in spectacular fashion. At this point, it didn't matter so much who apologized first and for what. If I held on to this grudge, we'd stay stuck, forever still images from each other's past.

"Because I'm sorry that I hurt you. I'm sorry I 'messed you up.'"

"Where's this coming from?" Danny asked, crossing his arms and holding them protectively over his chest.

"I talked to Felix."

"I'm going to kill him," Danny said under his breath. He ran a hand through his hair, ruffling the waves. "So Felix told you that and now you're suddenly sorry? I had no idea you held his opinion so highly."

"No, that's not it," I insisted. I waited until the sound of my pounding heart receded enough to be able to hear my own thoughts. "I'm sorry I was too selfish to be a good friend. I said some shitty things to you, and I regret it deeply. And I'm so sorry I pushed you away when you were one of the most important people in my life."

I hadn't planned on being that honest, but the words spilled out. Danny stared, mouth slack, devastating me with his dark brown eyes. I wished he'd say something instead of making me wait. Silence is the worst answer after you've poured your heart out.

"I'm gonna—" I tried to sidestep around Danny, but he blocked my way.

"You were going to leave after saying that to me?" Danny's eye twitched. He was annoyed with me. We couldn't get anything right tonight. It was too much to hope that a single night would magically make everything better.

"Why are you yelling at me?" I desperately wanted to know, because we'd gone through too much shit tonight to turn on each other.

"Because that's the first time you've ever said that to me, and I felt that way about you too! Goddamn it, Rachel. Do you know how many nights I stayed by my computer, waiting for you to sign on? Or stared at the back of your head in class, hoping for a glimpse of your face when you turned around to pass papers back?"

An overwhelming swell of emotion wiped my mind of any

words. I had no idea what to say when all I wanted was for Danny to repeat what he'd just said, over and over, until it healed the teenage part of my heart.

"Hey!" a deep voice shouted from the distance. The person had a flashlight and waved it in our direction. "What's going on over there?"

Naturally, I did what every rule-abiding and former top student did at the hint of trouble. I grabbed Danny's hand and made a run for it.

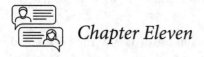 *Chapter Eleven*

WE TURNED A CORNER AND HID AGAINST A PAIR OF DOORS LO-
cated between a bank of lockers. Danny audibly swallowed as he
collected himself. "Are you out of your mind?"

Yeah, quite possibly. What did he expect after dropping his
confession twenty years too late? I wasn't sure whether I should
kiss him or cry.

"Why did you run?" he asked, snapping me back to the present.
"We weren't doing anything wrong."

"I don't know," I said lamely. I wasn't going to tell him that
there was still a part of me that worried about my permanent
record. It was impeccable, and it was going to remain that way.

"Running makes it seem like we were up to something."

Okay, I handled it poorly. He didn't need to rub it in. I lifted
my finger to my lips to remind Danny to keep quiet. I didn't hear
anything, so I thought we were in the clear, but a faint flash of
light came from our right. I pressed my back flat against the door,
hoping the lockers would hide me. "How do we get out of this?" I
whispered as quietly as possible.

Danny tapped my shoulder and directed me to look at his face.
He mouthed something I couldn't make out. The footsteps were
approaching us, so we didn't have much time. Danny put his lips
to my ear and spoke as quietly as a gentle breeze.

"Take. Off. Your. Shoes. They're. Loud."

The adrenaline pulsing through my veins made me extra at-
tuned to the tickle of Danny's breath on my skin. If it had been a
different time and place, I would've taken off more than my shoes.
One by one, I stepped out of my heels and slid down to pick them
up. Danny turned the doorknob to the door he'd been leaning
against, but no such luck. It was locked. I got ready to run again
when Danny darted in front of me, caging me in.

"Sorry," he muttered as he pressed his chest against mine, trying the door behind me. I didn't dare to respond when the slightest movement would've had my lips brushing his. I didn't have
the chance to anyway because we stumbled into a dark room not
a second later.

Danny cleared his throat as he straightened up and turned on
the flashlight on his phone. We were in the front office, where visi-
tors had to stop by before they could enter the campus. Surrounding the lobby were administrators' offices.

"What's our plan?" I whispered, trying not to think about the
cold tile floor on my bare feet.

"Uh, hide?" Danny tested the door to the vice principal's office.
It was locked. "Something you're good at." He said this jokingly,
but we both knew there was truth behind it.

"I can't help it if I excel at everything."

"Rach." Danny stopped his search and turned off his flashlight.
It took a second for my eyes to readjust to the darkness. "What do
you want from me? Did you come tonight just to rehash old shit?"

"No, I—" It was too embarrassing to admit that I wanted to
relive a time when I knew what I was doing. In the last twenty
years, it had seemed like the rules of the game we were all playing were constantly changing. Like life was a game of blackjack
and suddenly the way to win was to get twenty-five instead of

twenty-one. But even then, getting twenty-five didn't matter because the house always won. I guess I hadn't figured out this adulting shit yet, and I wanted to go back to a simpler time when I was the master of my own destiny. "I was feeling lost and . . . I don't know. This was the last place where things made sense. And I wanted to see you . . ."

"And . . . ?" he asked, sweeping a hand across himself, as if to say he was right there to be seen. He was egging me for an assessment.

My eyes roamed Danny's body, stopping to linger on my favorite spots, like his face, which could send me spinning for days with a single, soft look from him. Then there were his shoulders, where I found shelter. But if I had to choose, the feature I loved most were his strong hands with those slender fingers that looked like they were meant to play an instrument, though he never did, to my recollection. "Like a piece of art, okay?"

Danny coughed into his fist at my snark, but he couldn't hide the curl of his satisfied smile. His eyes dropped with a reciprocating glance. "You're not so bad yourself."

Thank god it was dark. My skin must have been cotton-candy pink.

"You could have reached out earlier," he added.

"Do you know how many Danny Phans there are?" I was too anxious and turned around to search for a way to get past the front counter. Our best bet was to find cover underneath it. "And what about you? I don't suppose you were looking for me."

"You made that impossible," he replied. I couldn't argue with that. I wasn't active on social media. Even when I'd had a profile, I never updated it or checked it. "But it's nice knowing you didn't forget about me."

As if I could ever forget him.

Something fluttered in my chest as it sank in that we'd both looked for each other at some point, but it was outweighed by the fact that the search led us here, hiding from the powers that be.

"Hold that thought." I placed my hands flat on the front desk and attempted to hop onto it. If I could hold myself up long enough, I could swing my legs over and get to the other side. After a couple of attempts, it was apparent that I was neither tall enough nor strong enough to pull it off. Danny stood to the side, doing a poor job of holding in his laughter.

I huffed as I leaned against the counter. "You could make yourself more useful and give me a lift."

"I have a better idea." Danny unlatched a swinging door at the opposite end of the counter and let himself in.

I dusted my hands as I crossed the room. "That would've been helpful five seconds ago."

"And deprive myself of seeing how you'd pommel-horse your way over? Never." Danny stopped and pointed his flashlight on the wall. "Hey. Look at this."

I scurried over to Danny with my shoes dangling on my fingers. He narrowed his eyes to read the big plaque on the wall, but I didn't need to look closer to know what it was. The Student of the Year plaque once haunted my dreams. It hung right outside a back door to the principal's office. Covered with names etched in gold, it went back to 1965, when the school was first built. I'd never known there was a back door there because only people who were called into the principal's office went through that way.

Danny ran his finger down the list until he found our graduation year. "Does it still piss you off that Mariana won for our class?"

Was it something I thought about on a daily basis? No.

But did seeing my reflection in the backdrop of Mariana's glittering name grind my gears? A little bit.

"It's whatever," I said, realizing that sounded like bitter grapes. It was my only loss to Mariana that stung.

"'Whatever'?" Danny mocked. "Didn't you call it your Wimbledon Trophy?"

Damn it. Was he dead set on making me cringe at myself all night?

"It's the most prestigious of the Grand Slam tournaments," I asserted.

That is, according to me it was. One could argue that Wimbledon was pretentious, with the all-white attire, but personally I thought it was elegant as fuck. I always looked forward to watching the tournament every year. "It's—"

"Your favorite," Danny chimed in, taking the words out of my mouth. "I know."

The corners of his lips tipped upward, and I knew exactly what he was thinking. Once, I had made the error of professing my love of Wimbledon with my own rendition of the NBC Breakfast at Wimbledon theme song, air-drumming to the march of trumpets. Some things weren't meant to be expressed out loud.

Danny started to hum some version of it that sounded unrecognizable through his snickering. He was being an ass, which made it all the worse that I found it endearing. He was having so much fun crowing his off-tune imitation of fanfare, it was hard not to smile back.

"Are you done yet? Did you forget we're basically fugitives?"

"To *fug-* is 'to flee,'" Danny said. "You taught me that."

A spark of pride flickered in me. "Nice to know you remembered your prefixes. Can you focus here?"

Danny laughed but went silent when the lobby doorknob jiggled. I would have stood there frozen if Danny hadn't swept me into the nearest room, wrapping his arms around me like he was shielding me. The door closed behind us, leaving us in the dark, but the smell of paper and sharpened pencils gave away the supply closet.

"Hello?" a voice shouted. Though it sounded muffled from where Danny and I stood, I recognized the voice. It was the same voice we'd heard in the quad. Light appeared at the bottom of the door as the sound of footsteps grew louder. If it wasn't already weird that I was clutching Danny, the light made things ten times more awkward. I could see where I'd been breathing into his neck and the smattering of goose bumps on his skin. It wouldn't take much to press my lips on every single one.

Danny tucked his head over my shoulder, whispering just a breath above silence, "Sorry for dragging you in here." Sorry was the last thing I was feeling at the moment. "We'll be out of here soon."

I wasn't in any rush to disentangle. I steadied my breathing as I took in his faint cologne. It was some combination of a fresh linen scent and his salty skin that, if we weren't literally hiding, I'd have inhaled all for myself.

"It's not like we've never done this before. I don't mind," I whispered back. Danny didn't reply right away, making me wonder if I'd revealed too much in my hazy lust. I let go a little to put a sliver of space between us, as much as Danny's tight hold allowed. "Can I say that?"

"What?"

Doors were being opened and shut as the person outside searched the other offices. My racing pulse kicked up a notch. Given our predicament, I kept things concise. "Because . . . I 'messed you up'?"

He exhaled slowly, his body deflating with his sigh. Danny didn't deny it, which made me want to crawl into the ground. But then he whispered something back. Something that sounded a lot like, "Missed you too."

He missed me too, or he messed me up too? I pulled back so I could see his face. I needed confirmation of his exact words. I wouldn't survive this if it turned out to be a bad case of telephone. "Say that again."

Danny swept his tongue between his lips before he mouthed the words more slowly. "I. Missed. You. Too. I didn't know how much until I saw you again."

I didn't care to correct him—after all, he did mess me up too— because the feeling was mutual. I had held on to good memories during our time apart, but being in Danny's presence again gave them a new dimension. His hands, once nervous and shaky, caressed my face as his fingers slid into my hair. His bright eyes had a new touch of sadness, conveying some unspoken apology that I wanted to hear. Instead, the only sound was his uneven breath mirroring the desperate strain of my own.

"Can I . . . ?" Danny asked, but I was already on my way there. Kissing had made our friendship murky, but we were older now. We could redefine what it meant to us now . . . couldn't we?

The first achingly soft press of our lips said *I'm sorry* as memories of golden light flickered in my mind. But regret and longing soon emerged, spreading a dull, persistent ache from my heart.

Danny kissed me again, with growing urgency, the taste of his tongue beginning to ward off bad memories. I was getting lost in my desire when he broke away.

"There's so much I want to say . . ." Danny paused when light swung in our direction, and waited until it shifted away. "But not here."

"Why not?" There was nowhere else we could go. It seemed to me we might as well hash things out here, unless this was his twisted way of letting me down gently after getting some closure. That could wait until the buttons on his shirt weren't digging into my chest.

"Because"—his lips brushed against mine—"I don't want to whisper like it's a secret."

If that was the case, then I could be patient. I gave him a peck, intending it to be one last kiss for the road, but then it evolved into something not so innocent. We managed to be quiet until Danny's leg stepped in between my legs. The delicious friction had me gasping before Danny's hand covered my mouth.

"Anyone there?" a voice announced, the same one from the courtyard.

Footsteps approached in our direction. I held my breath, for no good reason except in the hope that, in the best-case scenario, not breathing made me invisible.

Then another voice responded, and the footsteps retreated.

"Winston?" It was Mariana. Hearing her voice threw a bucket of ice over my mood. "Everything okay?"

"Yeah," the man replied. "I thought I saw someone here."

Wait. Winston? As in class clown Winston Lin? How did he get access to the office? Was he the security guard here or something?

"Was it Danny? I've been looking for him." Mariana's voice was steeped in exasperation. "He's supposed to help me with the auction. We're running behind schedule."

"No, I haven't seen him," Winston replied.

Danny peered over his shoulder and back at me, mouthing, *Wanna get out of here?*

I shook my head. I wasn't going to give myself up now. Danny was right. Running made us look suspicious. I couldn't imagine what Mariana and Winston would think if they discovered Danny and me hiding in the supply closet in a compromised position, all because I got spooked. I had too much pride to present Mariana with gossip on a silver platter.

The footsteps came toward us again. Danny walked me backward to the very back of the closet, though it didn't provide any more cover. I shut my eyes, waiting for our time to run out, but then the footsteps sounded like they were veering to the side.

"Sorry," Winston said as the door to a different office opened. "I need to get my other set of keys to lock up when the reunion wraps up."

"Sorry to make you stay late," Mariana replied.

"Eh, it's okay. All in a day's work as principal."

Principal? This was the same guy who attempted *Jackass* pranks at school, giving all the administrators headaches? What kind of parallel universe were we living in right now?

"Besides," Winston said, "you're helping me with the fundraising."

"It's nothing. We were going to put all this work into the reunion anyway. We might as well let some of that effort go to some good use." Mariana's heels clacked against the floor, bringing her closer. "Wow, I haven't seen that in a long time."

"What?" Winston's voice gradually grew louder as he moved around the office. "The Student of the Year plaque?"

"Yeah."

"Sorry to tell you, Mari, but it's rigged."

What?!

Danny covered my mouth before the word burst forth from the depths of my wrath, then offered a silent apology for the sudden contact. The move stunned me, but it was probably for the best given that I'd have given our presence away otherwise. Fortunately, Mariana was louder.

"What?!" she exclaimed. For once, Mariana and I were on the same page.

"The administrators say the teachers voted on it, but the deciding vote always came down to the principal. So really, it was favoritism." Winston relayed this information as the sound of their footsteps began to recede as they walked farther away. "And whoever gets the second highest number of votes gets 'Most Likely to Succeed.'"

They shut off the lights, leaving Danny and me alone in darkness once again. The sound of the back door being locked followed. It was about five seconds before Danny let go of me to check if it was safe to leave the closet. He peeked out the door and then opened it wider, giving me an all-clear nod.

The bitterness I'd buried long ago over this stupid loss resurfaced. The biggest aspiration of my teenage life was built on a lie. The Student of the Year Award wasn't determined by merit, and my peers didn't choose me to be Most Likely to Succeed. Teachers gave it to me as an arbitrary consolation prize.

"Shit. We're not locked in, are we?" Danny asked as we reentered the front office.

"We can still open it from the inside," I said as I zoomed past the plaque. I couldn't look at it anymore.

"How do you know that?"

"Some of us stayed late after school and got accidentally locked in." I wasn't sure why I said that like it was a flex. "That doesn't matter. None of it ever mattered."

Danny caught up to me. "Rach . . . you don't care about that, do you?"

How could I? Apparently, it was all a sham. The school had dangled a fake carrot in front of me. For the better part of my life, I'd thought I was the girl most likely to succeed. It wouldn't hurt so much if I had still come out of school above it all, but now, after getting laid off, I was back at square one. I couldn't help but feel like I'd pushed myself through late nights, offering to go above and beyond, keeping my head down until I got to the other side, only to get nothing. None of it ever mattered.

Danny's phone lit up from a text. "Shit."

He swiped the notification away with a little more force than necessary. "I have to get back to the gym. The auction is starting. I'm supposed to run it." He searched my face. Whatever he was looking for, he didn't find it. The moment we'd had was lost. It was in the trash, along with my career and my car. "Hey, Rach."

I blinked until I saw him more clearly.

Danny gripped my arms and held me at a distance, like he was examining me. "You're going to be okay, right?" My head bobbed in a lopsided nod. Apparently, that was enough to convince Danny. "Good, because don't think I'm forgetting about what you said earlier. If you want to make things right, then stay until the end of the reunion. Can you at least do that?"

I had to snap out of it. I couldn't let old high school grudges distract me from the real reason I was here. "Yeah. I'll be here."

"Good." Danny planted a kiss on my forehead. "Because we're not finished yet."

April 2003

SuperxSaiyan85: meet you at the library tomorrow

Danny was a mystery. After the drunk phone call, he avoided me. He gave the usual excuses about his jobs, but he wouldn't make eye contact with me at school. Worse, he hadn't been online either. If he had, he was ghosting. Did this out-of-the-blue message mean we were okay? Were we moving on, business as usual?

I checked his AIM profile for any illuminating details, but all I gleaned was that he was currently listening to "The Middle" by Jimmy Eat World.

xxaznxbbxgrlxx: why

He had never showed up before, and he had less reason to once I offered to share my notes.

SuperxSaiyan85: Mrs. Chang found me during passing period and told me she better see me studying

Well, if the principal had threatened me, I'd do the same.

xxaznxbbxgrlxx: Is she really your aunt?

SuperxSaiyan85: do people still think that? She's a family friend.

xxaznxbbxgrlxx: ok. Be there at 3

The school library practically became my second home. With AP tests only weeks away, assignments were piling up. Some study groups decided to divvy up the work and share answers because there was simply no time to do everything on top of sports and clubs. Nat and I exchanged some assignments, but she wasn't in all the same classes as me, so I was on my own for the rest.

I put my pencil down and laid my head on top of my history textbook. At the table on my right, Josh Wu was working steadily through each of his physics problems like he was writing letters of the alphabet. He didn't stop and second-guess himself like I did. I would have loved to barter homework with him, but despite having a few classes together, we didn't speak to each other. He kept to himself, staying in his lane the way I stayed in mine. Josh flipped the page to his homework packet, not even noticing that I'd been watching him the whole time. I closed my eyes, listening to the soothing sound of his pencil scribbling on paper.

A backpack slammed next to me, interrupting my peace. My eyes popped opened in time to see Danny waving apologetically to our librarian. "Hey," he whispered as he took the seat next to me. "No sleeping in the library."

"You're late," I said, smoothing my hair as I sat up. I pointed at the clock above the front counter. It was three forty-five.

"I had to take care of something."

At this point, I thought, Danny should trademark his vague excuses. "You could've told me during fifth period if you were going to be late."

"It's only forty-five minutes. What's the big deal?"

"The big deal is that I'm helping you and you could at least do me the courtesy of telling me if you're going to be late," I said, sounding snippy rather than assertive as I'd intended. I had my reasons lined up in case he called me out on it. I was stressed from the extra work, and college acceptance letters were coming any day now. Anyone who applied to private schools would receive their admission decisions this week. Mariana had already accepted her early admission to Georgetown. The UCs were lagging. Exams were looming. The direction of my life was going to be determined in a matter of weeks, maybe days, and I had no idea where it was going to take me.

With all of that on my mind, somehow my thoughts circled back to Danny. Why did I revolve my schedule around him? If he was late, that was on him. If he didn't log into AIM, then I'd actually finish my homework before midnight. Why was I so concerned about him? Why did I care so much if he said hi to me in class, or wonder if he got enough sleep? Why did I want to spend more time with him when I already saw him five days out of the week?

Danny opened his backpack and took out the stack of flash cards I let him borrow. "Test me."

I glared at him for the demanding tone, but I reluctantly took the cards. I was still his tutor after all. I worked out my frustration as I shuffled the cards.

To my pleasant surprise, Danny recited every detail I'd written on each card with startling precision. We went through every American and British author and their celebrated works. At times he answered with his eyes closed and sometimes while doodling on the margins of his notebook, like he was showing off. When Mrs. Chang popped into the library, as she had promised, he didn't even stumble, only smiled as he waved to her. As quickly as she appeared, Mrs. Chang departed once she saw Danny being productive.

"Do you have a photographic memory or something?" I couldn't recite my own flash cards that well.

"I've been studying when it's slow at work or when I get home," he explained.

"Oh." Was I allowed to feel proud that I helped in some way?

"That's why I haven't been online."

Now I felt dumb for taking his absence personally. He had more responsibilities than me. Of course he had more important things to do than chat on AIM. "Does that mean you'll show up tomorrow?"

It was a fair question since he hadn't shown up consistently, but Danny was looking at me as if I asked him if the sky was blue.

Danny warpped a rubber band around my flash cards. "I thought it was an open invitation."

"It is. You're always welcome."

Someone across the library shushed us. I wasn't sure

where it came from, but enough people looked in our direction to confirm that the admonition was meant for us.

"Um," I said, lowering my voice, "do you want to meet at my house instead?"

I wasn't sure why I was holding my breath. I'd had friends over for projects all the time. And technically speaking, Danny was one of my oldest friends. There wasn't any reason to feel nervous about being alone with him in my house while my parents were at work.

Danny's face was starting to look like a pufferfish as he thought about his answer. My mind started to fill with all the ways I'd made things awkward when his mouth popped open.

"Uh, yeah. I just need to tell Jimmy I won't be going in for my shift."

Again, I had worried for nothing. He had to adjust his schedule. That was all.

"Okay. It's a d—" I coughed. I almost said it was a date! Which it totally wasn't! It was totally normal to confirm a meeting by saying it was a date . . . right? "It's a dead-end street . . . my house." This would've been a good save, but my house wasn't on a dead-end street and Danny would see that when he came over. "I mean, you pass one on the way there." I waved my hand in the air. Hopefully, he'd get the hint to disregard everything I'd said in the last ten seconds. "Meet me in the parking lot and you can follow me there."

I opened my book and pretended to study before this conversation could become a bigger disaster. What was going on with me? Why was I getting so worked up over studying?

Chapter Twelve

COMING TO THE REUNION WAS SUPPOSED TO BE LIKE TAKING PE for an easy A. I wanted an effortless ego boost, but everywhere I looked, there was a reminder of how much I'd gotten things wrong. For instance, I thought I'd be able to convince Danny to skip the auction so that our lips could have a reunion of their own. But Danny took his responsibility seriously, and given that we'd already caused enough delays, he went forward with fulfilling his duties. While he went to catch up with Mariana, I was left alone to mingle with people who'd already found their former friend groups. Across the gym, cliques claimed their own tables. It was high school lunchtime all over again. I was an interloper, dropping in during the middle of festivities. I'd always wanted to stand out, but not like this.

I picked up a clear plastic cup of sparkling cider off the table of refreshments and sipped on it as I checked out my dinner option. There was a pasta buffet and salad bar that I assumed was meant to make this event feel like a sit-down occasion. That probably would have worked in a corporate environment, where a pasta and salad spread was considered a neutral choice. But it hadn't whetted the palates of the mostly Asian and Latine crowd at Commonwealth. There was still a lot of food left.

I drifted into the sea of round tables in search of a place to sit when someone grabbed my arm.

"Rachel fucking Dang! Where have you been?" Belinda shrieked. I was speechless. Belinda was a sweet and down-to-earth friend who always had a sketchbook in her hands. I'd never heard her go feral like that before. She tapped her husband's shoulder. "Oscar! Scoot over!"

Oscar dutifully did as he was told and freed up his seat, giving way for Belinda to pull me down. I greeted the other people at the table. The man next to Tina was her actual husband this time, and the bespectacled man next to him was Arnold Li. In high school, Arnold was on another level of nerd-dom. By senior year, he was doing independent study because he'd completed the highest-level courses Commonwealth offered. No wonder he was working at JPL. I was sitting among the who's who of Commonwealth High School.

"We thought you disappeared," Belinda said. "Mariana didn't want to induct any of us into the Hall of Fame until you came back. We've been waiting for you forever."

"I had no idea." Mariana really put me in a bind. She didn't say any of this before I left. "I'm sorry."

Tina, who was sitting on the other side of me, embraced me gently, but accidentally knocked her head against mine as she tried to hug me tighter. "It's okay. We're a little sloshed," she said. That was my interpretation of her slurred words. It sounded more like "Izokay. Wur a lil slush."

"How can I get in on that action?" I asked. I could use some of what they had and was happy to catch up to them.

Bo flashed his flask from the inside of his blazer. "I have some mushrooms too, if you want."

"Are you a drug dealer?" I asked, unsure if it was a good idea to pass my cup over to him. His expensive suit and slicked hair could be a deceiving cover.

Bo threw back his beautiful head as he laughed, revealing his shiny veneers. "No, but I know one." He splashed some brown liquor into my cup and handed it back to me. "I made some smart investments, so I don't need to do the nine-to-five. Why work harder when you can work smarter?"

Good for Bo, not having a desire or need for work, but I wasn't built that way. I liked having a strong work ethic and seeing the product of my efforts. I'd never once seen work as a bad thing until I was laid off. What was I busting my ass for? It couldn't be for a job that didn't love me back and it couldn't be for awards that I didn't earn.

I sipped my drink and checked out the rest of our table. Belinda hadn't blinked in an awfully long time and Arnold was tearing his dinner roll into tiny little pieces. "Is everyone high?"

"Don't judge." Tina frowned and pointed a finger at Belinda that was probably meant for me. "I hired a babysitter to be here, and damn it, I'm gonna live it up tonight!"

Arnold finally noticed my presence and put his bread down. "Oh my god. Rachel? How are you? What are you up to?"

If I'd run into them hours ago, I would have tried to save face, but life was slowly taking everything away from me, so why pretend? They were all so gone, they weren't going to remember this conversation tomorrow anyway. To hell with it. I gulped down my entire drink. "I'm unemployed. Got laid off last week."

Belinda's eyes were wide as saucers. As her hands landed on my shoulders, I braced myself for the positive consolation. My bets were on "Whoever hires you next will be so lucky to have you."

"You're. So. Lucky!"

Hold on. She was happy for me?

"God, I'd love not to work right now," she said, slumping into her seat. "The grind never ends."

"Well, it wasn't my choice—" I started to say, but then Tina interrupted me.

"Me too! Enjoy your time off," she said as if I were taking a vacation. "Bake some sourdough bread or some shit."

"I could use some bread," Arnold said, somehow forgetting the dinner roll he'd just destroyed. He directed his glassy puppy eyes at me, like he was begging for another treat.

"Do you want more—" I shook my head. Why was I trying to talk sense into someone who was as high as a kite? "I'm taking a break before I jump into my next job. I need to figure some things out first."

"I hear you," Oscar chimed in. "Life's too short. We're not meant to spend all our life clocking in and out of our jobs. What is the purpose in doing that?" At least he understood. "You know what helped me?"

Nothing I'd tried so far had helped, so I was open to hearing his advice. After all, he was the most reasonable and least inebriated person at the table. Oscar leaned in to let me in on his secret.

"One word. Ayahuasca," he said, spreading his arm as if the word had magically appeared in a rainbow above us. I laughed, but Oscar was 100 percent serious. "You will see life in a whole new way," he implored. "My first retreat was in Peru. It was led by two experts, and it was eye-opening, Rachel. I became a hummingbird, going around from flower to flower to drink sweet nectar. Everything was in bright colors." Oscar snapped his fingers as he tried to come up with the right words. "Like, like, pinks and purples, like those folders you girls used to have."

"Lisa Frank?" I supplied.

"Yes!" Oscar's eyes were wild with enthusiasm. "And then at some point—because there's no telling between time and space—I became a blank page that was being drawn on. It was like the ink was my blood. I've never been more connected with my inner self."

"And then what?"

"And then I threw up everywhere," he concluded.

I sat there, befuddled, as Oscar, a medical professional, continued to evangelize traveling to a remote area and leaving my mental state in the hands of unknown and unlicensed "experts," as he called them. Good for him for finding something that worked for him, but I'd rather figure out my life without turning into an A-ha music video.

Belinda rolled her eyes as she pushed Oscar aside. She had probably heard about his psychedelic escapades more than once. "A break is good. I'm sure you'll land on your feet in no time. You got this."

I'd heard this type of encouragement whenever I faced a setback. Having a reputation for getting things done meant people had a lot of confidence in my reliable success. But today such words gave little reassurance. I'd spent my whole life working for the next big thing, thinking that I would eventually reach a level of success that promised a rich and beautiful life. But running the rat race had led me nowhere. And even if it had landed me somewhere, that would have been no guarantee that I'd be happy, as my peers were making evident. They were successful, sure, but they were also looking for ways to temporarily escape their lives. So believing in myself seemed pointless.

I needed more answers, not more questions.

"Thanks," I said, even though I would've liked for someone to tell me it was okay to not be okay. Where could a sad person go to mope around without feeling pressured to power through life with a smile?

"There you are." Mariana was frazzled and out of breath as she skidded to a stop. "You're all finally here. I told the crowd that we had to postpone the award ceremony until all the recipients were present." It was obvious she was referring to me, but she clutched my shoulders anyway in case I wasn't sure before. "Do you know if Nat's close?"

I shook my head. "I'm sure she's on the way."

Mariana's smile fought to look pleasant. "Well, sit tight. Don't go anywhere."

I was trapped. I had no idea what I was going to say in my speech. Disclosing my unemployed status to my inebriated friends wasn't the same as broadcasting to a captive audience that my supposedly glitzy career in entertainment was a thing of the past. Such a confession was going to leave people more confused than inspired.

Danny tapped on a microphone, prompting the DJ to turn down the music. "Is this thing on?" he asked. The crowd hushed as he introduced the auction. "I hope all of you had a chance to go on the tour of the classrooms with Mariana. All of the proceeds from tonight's auction will go back to the school, so please show your generosity! We have some great items up for bid."

As Danny went through all the prizes, Bo dropped an elbow on the table and propped his head up, blocking my view of the stage. "So, Rachel. You're looking good these days."

"Uh . . ." I wasn't sure what Bo was angling at, but he was making me uncomfortable. Bo and I had only exchanged polite small talk about classes back in high school. "You too. You look great."

"I know. I saw the way your jaw dropped before." I'd only meant to repay his compliment, but his smarmy smile made me want to take it back. Bo's glow-up gave him some confidence, something he'd seemed to lack in high school, but there was a difference between confidence and being full of it.

"So, what? You came to show off?" I asked. I stretched my neck to look over his big head.

"What's wrong with that? Isn't that what you're doing?" I hated the way Bo's eyes dipped from my face to my suit and lingered long enough to make me want to crawl out of my skin.

"No. This is how I dress for work." For the one or two premieres I'd go to a year, but he didn't need to know that. I pointed at Danny to remind Bo that the auction was going on, but he ignored me.

"I think you know better than anyone that looking the part is half the battle. You can be smart and have the best ideas, but if no one's paying attention to you, no one's going to see it."

"You don't think that's shallow?" I asked.

Bo sniffed as he rearranged his bangs so they fell evenly across his forehead. "I forgot how judgmental you are." I held my tongue, mostly from shock. I had no idea he thought that of me. "No, I don't care. Let people look. That's the whole point. I'd rather be noticed than ignored."

Bo misunderstood me. I wasn't being critical. I was trying to clarify his stance, but the way Bo was manspreading, swirling his liquor in one hand like he was modeling, made it easy to see the image he was projecting. If he wanted people to fawn over him, I wasn't going to get in his way. But I wasn't going to participate in it either.

Onstage, Danny welcomed Viv, who brought up the first item: a gift basket with three bottles of wine. "There are paddles on the tables. Please use them to bid. I'm going to open this wine basket at fifty—"

"Three hundred!" Bo bellowed, ignoring all the protocols. Instead of using a paddle, he circled his arm like he was buying a round for everyone. "You've been holding out on us, Dan Man!"

The heckling stunned Danny, and he struggled to move on. "Uh . . . do we have three-fifty?" No one held up their paddle. "The basket goes to Bo! You can pay and collect your prize—"

"Fuck that." Bo stood, withdrew a wad of cash from his pocket, and threw a few bills in the air. Gasps and whispers grew louder as he grabbed the basket from Viv. "I believe this is mine."

Before the situation could escalate, Winston whisked Bo away. "All right, buddy. Let's go for a walk."

I could've sworn Winston did a double take when he walked past our table, but if he recognized me, he didn't show it. He kept dragging Bo toward the exit.

"That wasn't part of our program," Danny said, garnering a few chuckles. He checked in with Viv, making sure she was okay before moving on. Viv regrouped quickly, even rolling her eyes when Danny offered to emcee the rest of the auction alone. He managed to get through the next few items without incident. The auction became heated when everyone at my table kept outbidding each other for the time-share weekend getaway, but ultimately Belinda was the victor. I thought about bidding, but in the end she paid a pretty penny for it. She kept saying how much she needed the time off, so I sat it out.

"Now here's something special." Danny gave his best game-show host impression and directed everyone's attention to Viv, who fanned herself with the backstage passes. Danny quickly checked his notes. "The winning bidder and their guest will get the red-carpet treatment at the *Beyond the Dark* wrap party, held at the FreeStream studio lot. The evening will start with a tour of the set, guided by Commonwealth's own Natalie Huang. Then they'll meet the cast before dancing the night away. I'll open the bidding at a hundred dollars."

There was one taker, but no one else raised their paddles.

"Come on." Danny's microphone went limp as he showed his disappointment at the low offers. "This is your chance to get your intergalactic groove on. Stay up late with celebs beyond the dark." Danny's punny plea was enough to get a bid for a hundred and fifty bucks and then another for three hundred. A small bidding war erupted, and after some back and forth, the backstage passes ended up going for eight hundred dollars.

The most captivating part was watching Danny from afar as he worked the crowd through the rest of the auction. When he called on folks, begging for more money, he gave them his full attention, even if just for a moment. That time, however long, was theirs. It was a small gesture that made people feel big. That was how he made me feel, and now he was sharing that gift with others.

He was a star, piercing the night shadows. I was just a hapless person, staring at the sky, waiting to make a wish.

"Sold for five hundred dollars!" Danny pointed at the lucky winner of a new TV, some guy I think had a locker near mine. "If you have a winning bid, pay Viv to receive your prize." She stood and waved from behind the check-in table. "Viv, how much did we raise?"

Viv counted with her fingers and whispered to herself as she tabulated the final amount. "Including those who donated directly to the fund, we have a total of five thousand, four hundred, and seventy dollars!"

Danny applauded along with the crowd. "And now I'll turn it over to Mariana to begin the Commonwealth Hall of Fame ceremony." After he gave Mariana the microphone, he glanced at me with a look of concern. The time had come and I had a choice to make. There was no escaping now.

I typed hasty bullet points about my career in my phone, but I was thwarted by a text from Nat.

Nat: Still on set. Can you cover for me?

The lies kept piling on. Pretending my career was alive and well wouldn't hurt anybody, but there was no way I could stand in for Nat. People wanted to see someone famous, and that I certainly was not, unless we counted my memorable senior year outburst.

There was no time to spin Nat's absence because Mariana was already beginning introductions.

"It is my pleasure to induct members of our class to the Commonwealth Alumni Hall of Fame. This award recognizes their achievements in their professions and communities following graduation. Our first inductee is Dr. Arnold Li. After graduating from Commonwealth, Dr. Li went on to earn his PhD in planetary science from CalTech. His research was used to develop the latest Mars rover, advancing our knowledge of the Red Planet. In his off time, Dr. Li volunteers with his local animal shelter. Dr. Li, would you like to say a few words?"

Arnold wobbled onstage to collect his award, a framed certificate. He cleared his throat right into the microphone, causing some feedback. "Do you know where I can get more bread?"

Mariana laughed nervously. "Um, thank you, Arnold. So humble, that man," she said, directing him to stand at the far end of the stage before he could say more. "Our next honoree is another member of the academy. This time in the fine arts. Dr. Belinda Kang graduated with her PhD in art history from Columbia. She's currently a professor at UC Irvine, where she continues her research on modern Asian American art and photography. Dr. Kang, would you like to share a few words?"

I had to give it to Belinda. She crossed the stage with the grace of a royal. No one could tell she was drunk, until she burped.

"Excuse me," she began, laughing off her faux pas. "First and foremost, thank you for this honor. Commonwealth holds a special place in my heart, mostly because I met my Oscar over there." She gave him an excited wave, the kind you might give when you hadn't seen someone in a long time. "You're a work of art to me, honey!"

"Okay!" Mariana's smile pushed the limits of her face as she sent Belinda to take her spot next to Arnold. "Our next inductee needs no introduction. Commonwealth's most famous alumna, Natalie Huang, has worked in TV and film for the last twenty years. You may remember her from *The Summer Before Last* or her memorable dancing in the background of a popular Gap commercial. She currently stars as Commander Justina Tan on FreeStream's *Beyond the Dark* series. Welcome back, Natalie!"

A rousing applause erupted. It was the loudest the crowd had been all night.

I checked my phone. No word from Nat. Damn. I tried to come up with a PR statement, but only breakup announcements came to mind. It wasn't applicable to ask the audience to respect Nat's privacy at this time. Mariana threw a "WTF is going on?" look at me. It was my cue that the show must go on.

The cheers tapered off once they saw that I was the one coming up to accept the award. Someone shouted, *"Who are you?"* from the back, which was just what my ego needed. Mariana's smile was strained as she reluctantly handed me the award to keep the ceremony moving along.

"Hi. I'm Rachel Dang. Natalie regrets that she couldn't be here to accept the award, so I'll be accepting it on her behalf," I said, taking a page from Academy Award speeches. "The theater bug bit her here at Commonwealth, and for that she'll be forever grateful."

Mariana rushed to the mic before I walked off. "Not so fast, Rachel. Rachel is our final honoree of the evening." She flipped the program to my bio. "Rachel has spent over a decade in the entertainment industry, climbing the ranks at FreeStream, where she oversees business development strategy and global partnerships, consistently increasing revenue for the streamer. It's no wonder why Rachel was voted Most Likely To Succeed." Mariana clapped, leading the audience into applause. "Would you like to share what this award means to you?"

Way to leave the loaded question for me. Mariana gave me my award, a small wooden plaque that wasn't as big as the ones I had sitting on my bookshelf. Still, the guilt felt heavy in my hands now that I was juggling two plaques. The liquor caught up to me as I struggled to remember the bullet points I'd written down. "I-I did do that," I said, fumbling my words. "What Mariana said. TV and film were my home away from home, in a way. It's what I did in between the late nights of studying. I . . ."

I lost my train of thought. Faces were becoming fuzzy. I could've used this to my advantage. It would've made it easier to stand up there and pretend my life was wonderful. I blinked to clear my vision, and the first person I saw was Danny. He was off to the side, standing behind the donation table, nodding a silent encouragement to keep going.

I knew, no matter what I said, that Danny would look at me with that kind face and support me, even if he disagreed with me. But, as much as I hated to admit this, he knew me too well. Even though I craved the validation that I'd done something right with my life, the recognition meant something to me because I believed in the integrity of the process. Accepting this award under false pretenses didn't represent the person I wanted to be, and Danny knew it.

"I don't work at FreeStream anymore, though. I was laid off. I'm actually Nat's assistant, picking up dry cleaning and awards"—I held up Nat's plaque—"and anything else she wants me to do. But if you let me keep this"—I thumbed over my engraved name above the Commonwealth crest—"I'd be incredibly honored. I spent all my time at Commonwealth working my ass off, and it would mean a lot to me to receive this award from my peers."

It was painfully quiet for five excruciating seconds. Nobody wanted to applaud at that depressing speech. There was such a thing as being too honest.

A clap broke the silence and then another, building momentum. It was coming from Danny, standing proudly in the middle of the basketball court. It was like a scene out of a movie, except this time I wasn't the spectator. It was happening to me. What I wouldn't have done to have a sweeping soundtrack to underscore this as a triumphant moment, but Danny was alone in his mission. I experienced so much secondhand embarrassment watching Danny clap harder, trying his damnedest to get people to put their hands together, but fuck if I didn't fall for him a little bit.

Mariana finally asked Danny to stop and had the inductees pose together for a group photo. She retrieved the microphone for closing remarks. "That's it for us tonight. Thank you, Class of 2003, for showing up for Commonwealth High. Please get home safe, but if you have one last dance in you, here's your chance. Good night!"

The group of inductees cleared the stage as the DJ turned up "One More Time" by Daft Punk. Tina met her husband on the dance floor, while Belinda returned to the table to pick up her purse and her husband.

"You outta here, Rach?" she asked, as she opened her wallet.

"Um." I searched for Danny. He was hanging around the back table to help Viv close out the auction. "I'm going to stick around for a while."

"Are you sure?" Oscar shrugged on his jacket. "Some of us are going to Tao's. Did you hear he's throwing another party?"

"How did you find out?" I asked.

Oscar showed me his phone. "There's a text going around. Everyone here probably got it too."

"You should come." Belinda pointed a finger at me and drew circles around my face. "Take your mind off whatever is happening there."

"Okay." I did wonder what Tao's epic parties were like when I was in high school. Maybe it was time to finally see what the hype was about. Besides, I wasn't ready for the night to end yet.

After Belinda and Oscar took off, I felt my phone vibrating in my purse. It was Nat, finally.

Nat: Is the reunion over?

Nat: Did you get me a change of clothes?

I smacked my forehead. I'd forgotten all about that. Nat would forgive me when I told her about my car getting smashed. It was too much to explain over text, though.

Rachel: Reunion is wrapping up.
No on the clothes. Sorry.

Before Nat could complain I was a bad assistant, I typed my next message.

Rachel: Tao's having a party. Everyone's going

As far as I knew, everyone was going.

Nat: Same address?

Rachel: I think so? I'll confirm

Nat: Text me. See you soon

Rachel: okay boss

Nat usually went straight to bed after a long shoot, so she must have been in a good mood if she still had the energy to party. Thank goodness. The way this night was going, I needed Nat to keep me grounded in case more shit happened.

People were stoked about Tao's after-party. It came up in every conversation I passed as I made my way out of the gym. I found

Danny almost in the same way I'd found him when the evening started—stacking chairs and returning them to the storage room.

"Do you need a hand?" I asked. "Or two?" I slow-clapped to a crescendo, though I almost lost the beat when Danny released a grunt as he folded a table.

"I could've used that ten minutes ago."

"I wasn't going to clap for myself." I bit my lip to suppress my smile. I didn't want Danny to think I was making fun of him when it was brave of him to publicly support my cringey speech. "Thanks for doing that, though."

"You did good up there."

I basked in the pride in his eyes. It left me feeling positively electric, like that was all it took to recharge my battery.

"See you at Tao's!" Belinda shouted as she passed by, disrupting the moment Danny and I were having.

"Tao's? You're going?" It didn't seem to be Danny's top preference, judging from the hesitation in his voice.

"I kinda promised Nat I'd meet her there," I replied, deploying the big, innocent eyes that had gotten me out of trouble during the first half of my life.

Danny propped his hands on his hips and stared directly into my eyes, making sure I was sure. "I hate it when you do this."

"What do you mean?" I batted my eyes. "Do what?"

"This." He rolled his hand like he couldn't find the right word. "Resort to whatever this is to get what you want. It's beneath you."

The booze was sinking its teeth into me because I wanted to say I'd rather have a certain someone beneath me, but I managed to keep that thought in my head. "Let's drop by and say hi."

I was saved by Danny's phone, which lit up with notifications. I snuck a peek as Danny read his message.

Tao: WHAT: BYOB KICKBACK

Tao: WHERE: TAO'S OG PALACE

Tao: WHEN: NOW TIL????

"Come on. When will there be another chance to hang out with everyone?" I found myself saying.

"Hopefully not today," he said, but he couldn't really believe that. After all their planning, the reunion had brought in only half of our class. This really could be the last time this group of people were together for a long time. Why not go all out while we were at it?

"I stayed until the end of the reunion. I kept my promise." I tugged on his sleeve. "Let's keep the night going. We can talk at the party."

Danny sighed, more wistful than disappointed. I almost backtracked because I would've hated for us to go our separate ways like this, but then he fished his car keys from his pocket. "We have to make a stop first."

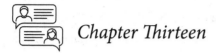

Chapter Thirteen

April 2003

Danny showed up at my house with his skateboard under his arm. He was a few minutes late, but I used the time to tidy up the house and pretend it was totally normal to be alone with a boy in my house. I wasn't worried about Danny. It wasn't like anything would happen, since we were just friends. I was worried because, if my parents knew, they'd disapprove. They always warned Angela and me to be careful around boys.

"School first, boys later."

"Boys only want one thing."

I'd always brushed off their warnings, but now I couldn't get them out of my head. It was annoying when their nagging worked.

"Come in," I said.

Danny leaned his skateboard against the wall, leaving the collage of stickers facing out. It was so beat up, it was hard to tell what was what. "I found this in the library." He reached into his backpack and brought out a new test prep book. "It came with a CD. I thought you'd want to check it out."

That was thoughtful. If only my parents could witness that there were boys who had more than one thing on their minds. "Let's go to my room."

Heat crept up my face as soon as I said it. I was the one with only one thing on her mind. I pointed Danny to my room while I grabbed another chair. My original plan was to study at the dining table, where there was more space to spread out, but the only computer in the house was the one in my room. It took up most of my desk, which left enough room for me to do my homework. It wasn't set up for two. "I'll be right back. You can start up the computer."

I scurried back out to the dining table and stole a chair. By the time I came back to my room, Danny had made himself comfortable on my computer chair and was staring at the computer screen, except the CD was still in its sleeve. What was he doing? I slid the chair next to him and looked at my computer screen, which had a wallpaper of Keanu Reeves in the scene from *Speed* where he's standing behind Sandra Bullock as she drives the bus.

"You have a thing for Keanu Reeves?"

"What's with the judgment?" I said as I sat down next to him, painfully aware of the one inch that separated our thighs.

"No judgment." Danny chuckled as he pressed the button to eject the CD-ROM tray. "I didn't know you liked older men."

"He's thirty-eight," I blurted out in my defense. Danny seemed less amazed that I knew that off the top of my head, given how his eyes bugged out.

"He's like twenty years older than us."

"And?"

"And?" Danny laughed. "Wow. Okay. So not even *The Matrix* Keanu?"

"He was older in *The Matrix*," I retorted.

"But Neo can do this." Danny's arms flailed as he leaned back in slow motion. Once he was done dodging imaginary bullets, he sat back up and tapped his finger on the screen. "You like *this guy*?"

I could've written an essay about how Jack Traven was superior to Neo, though my top five reasons revolved around Keanu's arms in the movie. I could've said how *Speed* was my favorite movie because I'd watched it so many times. It was always on TV whenever I channel-surfed. That probably would've stopped Danny's teasing, but I couldn't hear my thoughts over my heartbeat. Danny was sitting in the very spot where I'd spent years chatting with him, smiling like he'd discovered a secret he wasn't meant to find. But he had things all wrong. The secret I'd been hiding wasn't about the person on the screen, but about the person behind it who stayed up with me until one in the morning, talking about everything and nothing at the same time.

"Yeah. I like him." I couldn't pinpoint when I started to feel that way about Danny, but I knew my days were better with him in it. I could be myself around him, and I couldn't say that about a lot of people.

Danny shook his head and we got to studying. For once, he was the one thoughtfully going through the material. I was going through the motions. It was hard to focus when our knees knocked every time he swiveled his chair to ask me a question. I was second-guessing everything. I didn't put on deodorant because the scent was too strong, but now I wished I had. Why did I tie my hair into a ponytail? Yes, I always did that so I could look down at my test and not have hair falling over my face. But having my hair back made my face look severe and intimidating. At least, that was what my teammates said during tennis practice. I never minded projecting that image when facing opponents.

Why was I getting self-conscious about it? This was Danny. He had seen me like this before. It was all the same to him, so I had to stop acting like something was different. Except, I couldn't stop staring at him. Did he always have freckles? They were sprinkled across his cheeks and nose, like a finishing touch on his cute face.

"The answers aren't over there, Miss Dang," he said, pointing over his shoulder, imitating what our teacher Mr. Jackson would say to him when he caught Danny spacing out. He glanced up after he finished another question. "Is everything okay?"

"Do you want to watch a movie?" I blurted. I needed something more interesting than US history to keep my eyes forward.

Danny didn't need much convincing. He dropped his pencil and pointed at my DVD tower in the corner of my room. "Can I pick?"

"Yeah." It didn't matter. I'd seen them all before.

Danny scanned my DVD tower. "Surprised I don't see *Speed 2* in here."

I snorted. "Keanu's not in it. Besides, sequels are rarely better than the original."

I went back to the kitchen for some refreshments. When I came back, Danny revealed his pick—*28 Days Later*. Nothing like a virus-induced zombie apocalypse to set the mood.

"What would you do if you woke up and the entire city was empty?" he asked when I passed him a bag of potato chips.

"I'd freak out like a normal person," I said. I set down a box of chrysanthemum tea in front of him. "Hope you're okay with this. It's all I have."

"What are you talking about? I love this." Danny happily pierced his juice box with the attached straw like a little kid. I had to turn back to my computer screen before I was attacked with more cuteness. "Okay, but after freaking out, I think you'd be the kind of person who'd gather supplies. Rally other survivors."

"Maybe," I said, even though I didn't believe it. I couldn't even keep my eyes open during a gory scene.

"It's true. People really look to you." Danny pointed at the shelf above my monitor where I displayed my awards and trophies. I must not have reacted the way he expected because he said, "Wow. I can't tell if you're being humble or if this is a walk in the park for you. Do you wipe your tears with these certificates?"

I laughed as I returned to my seat. "Neither," I said, but it was a little of both. None of these awards felt big enough to brag about.

"If you don't even care, why bother collecting them? Spread the wealth." Danny picked up my "Most Improved" trophy from my last tennis season. I was proud of that one. I had practiced my backhand all summer until I could consistently hit the ball down the line.

"I care." I cared enough not to let Danny take one of my trophies, even if it was in jest. Deep down, I did care a lot about succeeding. I always have. My mom loved to tell the story about how I'd climb the refrigerator to get my own milk because I wanted to do it myself. She told that story with a sense of pride, mainly because it helped that I wasn't clingy when she was busy working and taking care of our family. Doing things myself was an asset, though it wasn't always easy.

It bothered me when teachers and sometimes my peers would write off my accomplishments because I happened to be Asian. I put in too much work to have my success explained away by a lazy stereotype. I liked the challenge. I liked having my name associated with glittery words like *success* and *achievement*. Winning awards fueled my ambition and gave me the same rush of adrenaline as hitting a winning forehand. My confidence was earned. "I wouldn't put these out if they didn't mean something to me."

"I don't know how you do it."

Danny wasn't inviting me to explain. He'd seen my weekly planner, which was scheduled to the minute. If there was time to kill, it could be used to be productive. But the awe in his voice disappointed me because even though I had a reputation of being a well-oiled machine, I was still a person.

"I could say the same to you. You're juggling two jobs. My only job is to bring in good grades."

"It's not the same," he said, visibly uncomfortable with the compliment. "I wouldn't do it if I didn't have to."

"Why do you have to?"

"To make money and help my family," he said, like I was being oblivious. There had to be more to it than that, though. There was a weariness in his voice that his nonchalance couldn't mask. I waited for him to elaborate, but he said, "You wouldn't understand."

"Are you serious?" Did he think I was rolling in dough? Our situations weren't that different. All of our parents were refugees. We came from working-class families, and we lived on the same side of the city, trying to do our best. He was talking like I was from another planet or something. "Last night, after dinner, I overheard my parents talking about how business has slowed at the print shop."

"Oh?" Danny sat up in his chair. "How come?"

"Business has been slowing now that everyone has digital cameras. Now there's camera phones." Whoever thought it was a good idea to put those two things together?

"But camera phones can't even take good pictures." Danny showed me the pixelated photos on his Nokia to prove his point.

"Yeah, but still, no one's printing as much as before." I shrugged. I wasn't an expert on the business, but from what I'd gleaned from my parents' conversation, it didn't sound good. I knew I should look into getting a summer job. "So I understand if you're going through money trouble."

We hadn't talked about it since that night he called me drunk. I wondered if he'd forgotten all about it, because my naked attempt to find common ground flopped. Danny stared emptily at the movie, as if he were numb to the terror playing out on the screen.

"Sorry to hear about your dad," he said after some time.

I shrugged, disappointed that Danny didn't say more. I read between the lines. He'd said before that he was good with secrets. I hadn't considered that he meant he was keeping stuff from me. "My parents sounded more sad than worried. It makes me nervous, though. I've never been good with change."

"I'm not worried about you," Danny said. "I know you can handle yourself."

"Thanks." Danny meant well, but at that moment I kind of wished someone would worry about me from time to time. The problem with appearing to do well on my own was that I attracted people who wanted something from me. It'd be nice to get help without having to ask for it every time.

I mulled this over as my mind drifted away from the movie. I shut my eyes during a violent scene, but when I reopened them, the credits were rolling. I'd fallen asleep.

It was getting dark. My room was streaked by the last orange remnants of sunlight. My neck hurt from sleeping at a weird angle in my chair, and I couldn't lift my head. Danny had fallen asleep too, and somehow I'd tucked myself into his shoulder. I tried to slip out, but my sudden movement sent Danny's arm around my waist, to keep me like a crutch for his very warm body. I suppressed a gasp.

"The movie's over," I said, shaking him to wake him up. "We should get up."

Danny grumbled as he shifted. The guy was like a log. I needed him to get off me before I expired from the heat. "Hey." I tipped my mouth to his ear. "Wake up."

Danny's eyes finally cracked open and his head lifted. It took him a second to come to awareness. First, he looked at the screen and then back to me.

"Hi," he said, like it was completely normal that our bodies were entwined and that our faces were so close. I could see the faint pink patch on his cheek where his face had rested on my forehead like it was a pillow.

"Hi," I repeated. I'd memorized hundreds of SAT words and the best I could come up with was *hi*. My brain was useless since I was hyperfixated on Danny's hand, which hadn't moved from my waist. "Did you like the—"

Danny dropped his soft mouth on mine in the same out-of-the-blue way he'd entered my life. I didn't want to move, afraid that any movement would cause us to knock our teeth and ruin this honey-sweet kiss. But I followed his lead and parted my lips. It was better than anything I'd ever experienced in my life. Like every ounce of joy concentrated into one lingering kiss. I wanted it to last forever, but a rumbling sound stopped me cold.

Someone was opening the garage door. My parents were home! There was no time for more kisses. I had to get Danny out of my house before my parents found us and lectured me to oblivion. "You need to go."

I dragged Danny up to his feet and pushed him out of my room, all the way to the front door. I didn't mean to treat him like a rag doll, but time was of the essence. The entrance from the garage led into our kitchen, so if we acted fast, there was a chance I could get Danny out of the house without being seen. I unlocked the front door and listened out for the garage door to close.

Danny hopped on one foot as he tried to put his shoes back on. "So, tonight?"

I didn't register his question until he acted out typing. He wanted to chat later.

"Okay, yeah." I picked up his skateboard and shoved it in his arms, pushing him out of my house as the garage door descended. "Cut across the yard to the right, so they can't see you."

"Have you done this before?" he whispered back. There wasn't any time to explain that I'd seen Angela's boyfriends do the same.

"Get out!" I bellowed with fiery urgency, sending Danny off on a panicked jog across the lawn, seconds before my parents entered the house.

"Rachel! See bai!" Ma shouted, commanding me to eat as she set plastic bags of takeout on our dining table.

I never ate so fast in my life.

As soon as I could, I jumped on AIM and idly waited for Danny's screen name to appear. I couldn't focus on home-work. All I could think about was the kiss. It was as if I were in one of those time-lapse videos of racing clouds and bloom-ing flowers. Experiencing something magical made me lose all sense of time and space.

I rubbed my chest. I had heartburn from all the food I ate. I cleaned my desk twice as I waited. I almost smashed my keyboard after the second notification that a different friend had signed on. But at long last, at a quarter past nine, Danny signed on.

SuperxSaiyan85: hi

Again with the "hi."

SuperxSaiyan85: have you been on for a while?

Yes.

xxaznxbbxgrlxx: No. Just logged on

SuperxSaiyan85: I can't stay long

SuperxSaiyan85: I haven't started that essay due tomorrow

Shit. I forgot about that too. The prompt was stuffed somewhere in my backpack. It was going to be another all-nighter for me.

SuperxSaiyan85: but I wanted to say sorry about the kiss. I didn't mean to

I had no idea my heart was made of glass until it shattered. What was Danny trying to say? Was the kiss an accident? It didn't feel like one.

SuperxSaiyan85: Can we forget about it?

How was I supposed to respond to that? That I'd rather jump into a black hole first? Was the kiss so bad for him that we had to erase it from our memory? Impossible. This pain was unforgettable, but ending our friendship over this would only make the ache worse. So I did something I never thought I'd do. I lied to Danny.

xxaznxbbxgrlxx: yeah lol it's all good

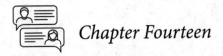 *Chapter Fourteen*

"WE NEED TO BRING SOMETHING TO TAO'S." DANNY GRABBED A shopping cart and strolled into the produce section of a supermarket across town.

"Why did we come to this market?"

Danny ripped off a plastic produce bag. "As opposed to . . . ?"

"An Asian market?" We'd passed by at least three on the way to this store.

"This is closer to Tao's house."

"Or do you mean it's closer to Fosselman's?" I asked. I'd caught his longing gaze at the ice cream shop when we drove by. Too bad they were closed. If I recalled correctly, Danny liked their lychee ice cream. "Don't lie."

He replied with a sheepish, albeit guilty smile.

"I thought you were supposed to cut back on sugar."

"It doesn't hurt to look," he said, picking out some oranges. I would've just tossed the most orange-colored ones into a bag, but Danny took the time to check for ripeness, and he weighed them before bagging the ones he wanted. There was something sweet about watching him do such a simple task. Danny pushed the cart toward the refrigerated aisle. "What are you doing next weekend?"

I tried to ignore the uptick in my heart rate. It was nice of him to ask instead of assuming I had no life now that my career had tanked. "I'm going out of town with Nat. She's doing press at South by Southwest."

"Nat gets to bring an entourage?" Danny whistled, impressed. "That's some A-list shit."

I laughed because Nat would disagree, but she was on her way there. According to the Nielsen ratings, *Beyond the Dark* was hardly a household name, but through the power of its small but mighty fan base, it had caught enough of Hollywood's attention that Nat was turning away projects for the first time in her life. "She's getting her due. So are you."

Danny lifted a shoulder. "You could say that."

"Come on. You don't have to be humble. I saw all the testimonials on your website."

"That's to attract business. I don't really care about it. It's just work."

I wish I knew how to adopt that philosophy. I used to come home from the office and immediately fire up my laptop on the kitchen table. The line between my professional and personal life blurred, and it was hard to distinguish where one ended and the other began.

"Do you mind if I pick up a few things for myself while we're here?" Danny asked as he compared bunches of bananas before settling on one.

"Yeah, sure." I really couldn't get over this domesticated version of Danny. I couldn't remember the last time I had roamed in a supermarket. I used to get so busy with work that I'd pick up any kind of fast food on the way home or leech off my parents. I never kicked the habit, even after dating Josh. He worked long hours, especially during tax season, and we spent most of our time together eating out because it was convenient and frankly better than anything we could've made ourselves. These days Nat did most of the shopping, choosing farmers markets over our local store. "Do you do this a lot?"

"What? Feed myself?" Danny chuckled at the absurdity of my question. "It beats the alternative."

"I—" It was silly to be so fascinated by it when he put it that way. "I've only ever seen you at school. I'm not used to seeing you do this," I said, as he bagged green onions. "Did you always cook for yourself?"

"Here and there, when my parents had to work late. You know, easy stuff like spam and rice. I started again after my divorce, but I try to eat healthier." Danny side-eyed me when I missed my cue to act surprised. "You knew about my divorce, huh?"

"Kind of," I said sheepishly. "Felix told me."

"Just like high school." Danny didn't seem to be bothered by the gossip, though. "I thought you would've found out from Facebook or something."

"I don't really use social media."

"I should've known. You didn't reply to my invite for months."

Had he been waiting for my response? I put the thought aside because I had bigger questions. "How come it didn't work out? If you don't mind me asking."

Danny shrugged. "We met in college and dated a couple years. After we married and started living together, we realized we were very different people. It was as amicable as it could be. We didn't have many assets to divvy up, so it was quick. But that's the way I see it. If you asked my ex-wife, she'd probably say that I didn't communicate well."

"Hmm, *interesting*."

"What about you?" Danny said, giving me a friendly jab in the arm. "How come you're not married yet?"

"Are you my mother?" I laughed, but I knew Danny wanted a real answer. "I came close. I was engaged."

"Yeah, I heard."

Since Danny knew how that led nowhere, I kept it short. "But," I began, bracing myself for Danny's reaction, "we both put our careers first and we couldn't find a compromise."

"Hmm, *interesting*," he said, giving me a taste of my own medicine.

"Whatever." I rolled my eyes. "We are who we are. At least we know that much."

We strolled through the market, passing every aisle. There weren't any other shoppers at this hour, so some employees were using the downtime to restock shelves. I wasn't sure if it was the bright lights or the eerie quiet as we went about this mundane task, but shopping with Danny was sobering. My life before wasn't normal. Even though I'd barely had any time to do basic things for myself, it didn't bother me. I never had a reason to change my career because it had been this big, often celebrated part of my life. But how rewarding could it have been if it left me looking in the opposite direction, searching for meaning?

Danny stopped and turned around when he noticed I was no longer beside him. "Do you need something? A lucky charm?"

I didn't understand Danny's question until I noticed the four-leaf clover Mylar balloons floating down the seasonal aisle where I'd stationed myself. "I wouldn't turn one down," I said. "Or a pot of gold. You wouldn't happen to have one of those, would you?"

"What's going on?" Danny leaned his elbow on the shopping cart handle. "You were ready to go to a rager a minute ago."

Yeah, well. That had been the liquor talking. Now reality was like an alarm clock trying to wake me up while I kept hitting the snooze button every ten minutes. "I don't know if I should tell you. It's kind of a bummer."

Danny walked back to me, dragging his cart behind him. "We literally talked about my divorce in the produce section, Rach."

He had a point.

"I was thinking about how disconnected I am. I can't tell you the last time I came to a supermarket. What kind of life is that?" I shook my head, embarrassed by what I'd admitted.

"That's nothing to feel bad about. Everyone's busy."

"But why does it have to be that way? Like, what was all of this for? I put in so much time to reach the next step, always wanting more, when it turns out it was all meaningless. The awards were fake. The stable job was a lie. At this point, I thought I'd be at the prime of my career and my life, but I'm back to where I started, doing someone else's grunt work." I huffed. "What am I supposed to do? I'm too old to start over. I don't want to go back to revolving my life around work, until I'm starving for a break, looking up trips to Peru so I can get stoned out of my mind."

Danny had been nodding encouragingly up until the last part. "Sorry? I'm not following. Are you going on vacation?"

"No." What was I doing? This was a pathetic midlife crisis. I couldn't have just pampered myself or splurged on a new lifestyle like a normal person. I had to go and unload my insecurities next to a refrigerator piled with corned beef to the tune of some Kelly Clarkson song. "I keep feeling like I should know better by now, but I don't know anything at all."

I clutched my arms, trying to comfort myself after exposing my vulnerability. Danny didn't say anything right away. He stood still as another shopper walked around us. At first, I thought I'd scared him, but as the seconds ticked by he remained present, waiting until calm settled between us. Finally he spoke.

"I get it," he said gently as he reached for me. His hand was warm on my arm. "It's scary when we don't know what's next, but don't let fear distort the truth. You wouldn't have gotten this far if you didn't do something right. Be gentler on yourself."

"Thanks," I muttered. Danny was right, but it was still hard to hear. I was used to having answers. I stretched out my hand until it covered his to show my gratitude. "I didn't mean to turn into an emo drunk and dump all that on you."

"It's not my first time at this rodeo," he said, wrapping me in a hug that ended too soon. "Every time you've felt overwhelmed, you've 'dumped' your feelings on me."

"How did you put up with the melodrama?" I groaned, thinking about all the stupid stuff I complained about when we were teenagers.

"I didn't put up with anything. I listened because it mattered to you."

My face flushed with heat, and I was certain it wasn't from alcohol. This version of Danny had all the right words, it seemed.

"But what about you?" I'd learned more about him this night than I did back then. "I wished you would tell me everything that was going on with you. I would've listened." It would've mattered to me too.

Before Danny and I discovered each other's real identity, I was the one who tried to work out my messy adolescent thoughts and insecurities in our chats, because he'd respond objectively and without judgment. Once we met in person, the air of mystery disappeared, since we knew each other from school. I knew who his friends were and where he worked. I thought I knew enough about him that I didn't press him to tell me more than he was willing to give. Looking back on it now, I see how lopsided our relationship was. If I'd dug a little deeper, things wouldn't have ended in a misunderstanding.

"It's always easier to look at someone else's problems than face your own." Danny shrugged as if his blazer wasn't fitting properly. "I'm trying to get better at it, though."

He pushed the cart around the corner to the aisle of wine and spirits. I should have felt grateful to shift the conversation away from my existential crisis, but I didn't want Danny to stop talking. I sped up until I was in front of the cart and then grabbed the edge with both hands to bring it to a stop. "So, tell me," I said, ignoring the puzzled look on his face. "What problems does Danny Phan have nowadays?"

"There's a woman blocking my shopping cart. Does that count?" He nudged the cart forward to shake me off, but it was going to take more than that. After a short standoff, he walked around me and with one hand picked up a case of Blue Moon. "You're so direct."

He didn't have to say it like it was a bad thing. What was wrong with getting straight to the point? "You said you want to improve your communication skills. I'm giving you an open floor," I said, sweeping my arms widely. "You don't have a single problem? Is life going swimmingly? You can say so if that's the case."

Danny side-eyed me. "Did you forget that I got poked in the butt tonight?"

He meant for that remark to stay between us, but his voice carried in the empty store. He probably would've rephrased it if he'd known there was an old lady behind him. Her jaw dropped before she backed away, but not without checking out his otherwise fine-looking ass.

Danny tried to salvage the situation. "It's not what you think!"

he called out, but the lady was gone. He turned around with a glare. "You've caused me plenty of problems tonight. How about that?"

I bit the inside of my cheek to stop myself from snickering. "I'm sorry."

"Oh, you sound sorry." Danny tried for sarcasm, but I heard the hint of laughter. "You really sound like someone who was begging for forgiveness"—he checked his watch—"an hour ago."

"How am I doing so far?"

"Terrible." Danny held the palm of his hand level to the floor next to his hip. "You're like down here."

I sucked my teeth. "I better try harder."

"Please don't." Danny twisted at the waist to stretch. "My body can't handle any more chases or long walks."

What could his body handle?

Mine warmed as thoughts of our rendezvous in the supply closet returned, but I tamped them down. We had kissed hours ago. Maybe that was all the closure I was going to get. I didn't want to break this new camaraderie we were building. Besides, the timing couldn't have been worse. I had no business starting any relationship, especially not one with Danny, when I was feeling this lost. If we were going to restart whatever this was, then I wanted to give it the best chance possible.

I stepped out of the cart's way and walked slowly beside it. "So, is there anything I should know before we get to Tao's?" I'd heard plenty of things on the Mondays after his parties. The reactions ranged from "You had to be there" to "Oh, it was sick!" I wasn't sure what I was in for.

Danny's face remained neutral, giving nothing away. "Don't go in with a game plan. Tao's parties are unpredictable."

Chapter Fifteen

TAO'S PARENTS' HOUSE WAS ON A COMPOUND AND FLANKED BY two identical-looking two-story homes, both of which were occupied by his extended family. There was always someone around who claimed to be a cousin of Tao's, but it was hard to know if they were first cousins, second cousins, or cousins in name only. Needless to say, this family rolled deep. Which meant, by the time Danny and I arrived at the house, the long driveway was filled with cars.

"They should have their own valet," I mused as we passed by.

Danny drove around until he found a space conveniently across the street, in another driveway.

"Danny. You can't park here."

"Yes, I can," he said as he pulled up the brake. His confidence was alarming. Who parked at strangers' houses?

"Do you know who lives here?"

"Yeah. Me." Danny turned off the engine. "Why do you think I have Tao's number? I see him every time his family has a party, which is about every other weekend."

I peered out of the windshield. It was dark, so I couldn't see much of the bungalow. "It's nice. When did you move in?"

"Last year, after the divorce. I thought it would be nice to move back to Alhambra. I always liked living here." Danny's voice was wistful, making me wonder if I played any part in his nostalgia.

I wasn't sure what I was hoping for when I glanced over at him. Some sort of confirmation that it was good before it went bad?

With his head rested back, Danny met my eyes and held my gaze with a gentle intensity, stretching this moment. It warped my sense of time, as if it wasn't that long ago when we used to sit this close together in the library.

Bass boomed from Tao's, breaking our spell. "Sounds like the party's getting started." I unbuckled my seat belt. "We should—"

"Wait," Danny covered my hand, stopping me from jumping out of the car. "Do you mind if I change really quick? Ever since the cactus incident, my suit feels itchy. I want to wash up a little."

"Yeah, of course. It's your house!" I announced as if he didn't know. It was like the light physical contact made all the blood in my body rush to my hand and left nothing for my brain.

Danny's place was nice and cozy. The smell of a fresh coat of paint hung in the air. It must've been renovated recently. The finishes made it look like a new house, but the creak of the hardwood floors gave away its age.

"Have a seat," Danny said. "I'll be right out."

"Take your time," I said as Danny disappeared into the hallway. I took off my jacket and slung it over my arm as I browsed around.

Hanging over the fireplace were three skateboard decks without wheels, like panels to display an image of the anime *Cowboy Bebop*. Danny was such a fan of the show that he had burned a copy of the series for me. I'd only gotten around to watching three or four episodes before we graduated. When the live-action version came out, I wondered if he'd seen it.

Picture frames perched on the mantel. One was of his mom and his stepdad holding a big jackfruit in a Vietnamese outdoor market. In another, more recent photo, Danny was surrounded by a group of friends, all of them holding snowboards on a mountain. There were a couple more pictures with these same people—one at a group dinner and another at the wedding of one of the couples.

"What are you doing?" Danny's voice startled me. I was so shocked that my hand gripped the frame and I couldn't put it down. I stood there, frozen and useless, watching Danny, who'd changed into a casual pair of slacks and a shirt that was tragically in the process of getting buttoned. "Snooping around?"

"Uh-huh," I said, momentarily dumbstruck with lust.

A small, amused smile appeared on Danny's face as he crossed the room to look at the picture in my hand. "Those are my cousins. We went to Mammoth last year."

"You guys are close," I stated. It was apparent by the grins on their faces.

"We grew up together before I came to California."

Before California? "Where did you live before?"

"Houston."

Right. He mentioned that his mom relocated there to be near family. I repeated this fact a few more times in my head before I filed it away with the other new things I was learning about Danny.

He pushed his sleeves up before he took the frame from me and placed it back at its original spot. "We try to see each other once a year, usually around the holidays."

"That's nice." I willed my eyes not to follow his forearms, though his face wasn't helping my hormones either. "You've done well for yourself. You should be proud."

"I learned from the best." I pointed at myself to confirm he was referring to me. Danny smirked. "Who else would I be thinking of?"

"You don't need to flatter me while I'm complimenting you,"

I said. "Don't lie either. You slept through most of our tutoring sessions."

"I was listening. I liked the sound of your voice. I still do."

My ears perked up. They were surely red by now.

"I watched how you pushed yourself to keep going, and I emulated that, except for the planner. I never remembered to write in mine."

"All right. That was very nice to hear," I admitted, "but if you feel bad for me—"

Danny turned, facing me with his clear eyes. "Why would I feel bad for you? All I ever wanted was for you to notice me."

That was the most wonderful and infuriating thing he'd ever said to me. I hit both of my hands against his chest. "Why didn't you ever say so?"

"Because I was stupid?" Danny grabbed both of my hands and pressed a kiss on my palms, sending heat through my body. "And I assumed if you wanted me, you'd tell me. When you wanted something, you went after it."

That applied to assignments, not crushes. "But what about the time you kissed me and then you asked me to forget about it?"

Elevens appeared between Danny's eyebrows as he thought. "You pushed me away and ran me out of your house, Rachel. I thought you hated me for taking your first kiss."

I couldn't help laughing at our tragic misunderstanding. It was stunning, really. "My parents had come home! We were about to get caught."

Danny's face scrunched up even more. "I don't remember that. I was probably too worried about kissing you and not fucking things up." Danny slipped my jacket from my arm and draped it over the armrest of his couch. Then he placed my arms over his shoulders, bringing us together until his temple met mine. "Did I mention I'm stupid?"

"No, you're not." Danny knew exactly what he was doing when he ran his hand down the nape of my neck, then followed the shiver down my spine. My skin grew hot to the touch like I'd been basking in the sun. "You didn't fuck up the kiss either. It made my heart sick when you took it back."

"Can I make it up to you?" Danny asked, leaning dangerously close.

"How do you plan to do that?"

"How about 'I'm sorry' to start? Can you forgive me for getting tongue-tied if I tell you I had a hopeless crush on you? Because I did. And if that's not enough"—Danny dropped a kiss on my shoulder—"I have other ideas."

"I'm listening." I didn't need to be persuaded, but Danny could have the floor. The couch or the dining table too, if he wanted.

Danny held my face as we kissed like he was making sure I never forgot how good this felt. His desire was apparent, and it was tempting to run my palm over the bulge in his pants. His arms circled around my waist as he dropped a kiss on my collarbone. His mouth traveled lower, pressing another kiss close to the lace trim of my camisole. If he was going to keep making his way down, my jelly legs weren't going to cooperate.

"Do you want to take this somewhere else?" Danny asked, his eyes dark and wild. "Somewhere with no pictures of my family staring at me?"

I couldn't help belly-laughing as he dragged me into the hallway. Before I could ask which room was his bedroom, Danny had my back against a wall and was kissing me, fierce and at times impatient. I held his face to try to slow him down when his hand slipped under my camisole. I moaned as his thumb circled my nipple.

"You've gotten better at this," I said, arching into his touch.

Danny buried his head in the crook of my neck, pressing a smile into my skin. "Do I get a 'Most Improved' Award?"

I was happy to give him validation in other ways, but my phone rudely interrupted us.

"Ignore it." I reached into my pocket and haphazardly pressed buttons until the trilling stopped. I desperately kissed Danny, trying to regain the lost momentum.

"Uh, Rachel?" It was Nat's voice, coming from my pants pocket. I broke away from Danny, pushing him until we were an arm's length apart. "What am I hearing?"

To Danny's dismay, I whipped out my phone and put it under my ear. "Hey!" I blew past Nat's question and pretended I didn't hear it. "What's up?"

"I'm in front of Tao's," she replied, slow and skeptical. "Are you here?"

I winced as I palmed my forehead. "I'm on my way," I forced myself to say. I couldn't look Danny in the eye as his face fell. "Two minutes."

"Okay, I'll wait for you."

I ended the call and made sure to lock my screen before I slipped it back in my pocket. Danny's head lolled back as he stared at the ceiling. "You couldn't tell her there was a change in plans?"

"I can't leave her hanging." I straightened my clothes and went back to the living room. "She's technically my boss, and she knows when I lie." As much as I hated to admit it, it was probably best to pause and think about this. It was so tempting to forget everything for a second and let myself feel good (because damn, it felt good), but I had no idea what this was leading to. My life was in shambles, and I didn't know how Danny fit in the mix.

I shuffled on my blazer as Danny fixed his clothes and hair. I grabbed his face, angling it until he looked me in the eye.

"To be continued, okay?" I planted a kiss on his lips as a promise. "We'll make a quick appearance."

Danny pouted as he grabbed his jacket. "Whatever you say."

April 2003

Danny didn't make it easy for me to apologize. It had been a few days since we argued over our essay grades. He brushed me off at school and he wasn't online. I thought it'd be odd if I showed up at the mall out of the blue, so I resorted to writing a note.

"Sorry for being a dick. I'm happy that you got an A. I really am. Forgive me?"

I tore the sheet from my notebook and ran my thumbnail across the creased edges, folding it into a neat rectangle. For a final touch, I drew an arrow on the pull tab with my gel pen and waited until passing period to drop it in Danny's locker.

I turned the corner and stopped. Danny was behind his locker door, putting his books away. I couldn't leave this note when he was there. I hid it in my backpack seconds before his locker door slammed shut.

"Rach." Danny stood there, totally cool. Well, I could do that too.

"Oh hey. Didn't see you there." I fixed my glasses, acting natural, as one does after they've kissed their friend and then had a big fight.

"I was about to find you."

"You were?" Could my voice get any higher?

"Yeah." Danny waved me over. "Let's, uh, walk and talk."

I had no idea where we were going. Danny was leading us to the science quad by the back of the campus, but his fourth-period class was economics. "What did you want to talk about?"

I swallowed to keep down the pressure building in my chest. I still liked Danny, but I'd blown my chances when I started that fight. How would I begin to explain all of that? Maybe I should read him the note.

Danny's head turned left, then right. "Do you trust me?"

"Yeah," I answered as swift as the breeze. Our relationship wasn't perfect, but I knew that deep down Danny was a good person.

"Good. Just follow my directions."

"O . . . kay . . . ," I said, as we passed the last classroom. Where was he taking me? No one ever came to this side of campus, except for the kids who smoked during lunch.

Danny grabbed my wrist. "Run!"

I tried to keep up. I was athletic, but Danny ran fast. "What the fuck, Danny? You're making me ditch class?!" *There goes my perfect attendance record!*

Danny shushed me. "Your grades are so high, Rach. You can spare a day off."

We piled into his car. I buckled my seat belt and then ducked my head. "Where are we going?"

Danny had a mischievous smile as he turned on the engine. "Anywhere you want."

Chapter Sixteen

I SHOULD'VE THOUGHT ABOUT AN EXPLANATION FOR NAT AS I crossed the street. I couldn't imagine what was going through her mind, watching Danny and me come out of his house together. But I also had questions for her.

"What are you wearing?"

This wasn't an Oscars red carpet question because Nat was certainly not in a designer gown. She was fully covered in a black catsuit and electric blue wig, which made her either a terrible burglar or an obscure *X-Men* character. I couldn't decide which.

Nat pursed her lips. "Since you didn't bring my clothes, I walked off set in costume."

"What about what you wore to set? You couldn't wear that?"

Nat flipped her blue hair over her shoulder. "I wasn't going to show up in sweatpants."

Ah. Nat wanted to look hot. Well, mission accomplished.

She nudged me aside. "Excuse me, but is that you, Danny?"

"Hi, Nat." Danny offered her a wave, rather than a hug. They weren't close back in high school, but I wondered if Nat looking like a naked shadow also played a part in his cool response. Either way, Nat didn't seem to mind. She was preoccupied with checking him out, raising her (blue) eyebrows in her assessment. "Congrats on your show. I see the billboards on the freeway."

When Nat turned her attention back to me, she was smirking. It was the kind of smirk that let me know that she figured out what she'd overheard a few minutes earlier. Instead of saying anything, she threw her leather jacket around her shoulders, showing me some mercy. "Shall we go inside?"

Danny led us through the side gate, which took us directly into the bustling backyard.

"Whoa." The place was packed. "There's more people here than at the actual reunion."

"Don't tell Mariana that," Danny said.

I didn't have to. Mariana was sipping from a red Solo cup with a bunch of water polo folks on the other side of the pool. She could see it for herself.

"Hey! You made it!" Tao came over to greet us with open arms. I'd managed to avoid those arms when he picked us up earlier, but since he was the host here I let him wrangle Danny and me into a bear hug. "And this is . . . ?" It took Tao a second to see beneath the wig, but once he figured out it was Nat, he did something unimaginable. He gave her a bow. "Famous actress Nat Huang! Someone bring this woman a drink!"

"Oh, stop it." I hadn't seen worse acting from Nat since she tried to fake cramps for a birth control commercial. You'd think someone who'd walked their own red carpet would be used to this kind of attention by now. Nat was practically preening.

Tao cleared the path for our group and led us to the center of the party. "I can't believe the turnout. Everyone's back in town!"

"Yeah, it's like there was a reunion tonight or something," Danny commented, only loud enough for me to hear. Tao's goldfish memory was the least bizarre thing about the party. While our former classmates danced to the Vengaboys, a collection of Tao's relatives, young and old, were barbecuing by the patio, having their own gathering. It was hard to tell who was intruding on whom.

"Oh yeah. Don't forget to wish my mom a happy birthday," Tao said as he left to check in with other guests. "Drinks in the kitchen."

"I'll go put this away," Danny said, hefting his beer. "Do you want anything?"

"Whatever you're having," I replied, sending him on his way.

"I can't wait to hear all about that," Nat said once Danny went into the house. "I know you're not on the clock right now, but heads up. After South by Southwest, my schedule's going to pick up. I'm flying back to wrap up the last episode of the season. And then there's that indie family dramedy I signed on to do in New York."

I thought back to Nat's calendar. I'd seen it so often, I had it memorized. "Isn't that a couple months away?"

"Well, a friend of mine texted me about doing a digital short in April. I'll be out all summer, so can you look into subletting the apartment?" We'd done this before when Nat was getting paid peanuts to film some small movie that no one's ever heard of, but that was before she had thirty thousand Instagram followers.

"Why are you doing a digital short? You're the lead of your own show! Aren't you afraid some fan is going to post about where you live and what your room looks like?" Nat stopped to think about this, possibly—probably—for the first time. "Can't you cover rent for a few months?"

Nat chewed on her lip. An awkward silence fell between us, making me wonder if I needed to find Nat a financial adviser too. "You're not the only one FreeStream axed."

"Is the show getting"—I could barely get the word out—"canceled?"

"It's going to hit the news tomorrow." Nat's face fell, and I felt her sadness instantaneously. That was me a week ago. I searched for a quiet place to talk. Maybe there was something we could work out that didn't have me rooming with a stranger for the summer. I was too old for this shit.

"There are scripts sitting in your inbox right now. You're going to be okay, Nat."

"That doesn't mean anything, Rach. I'd have to go through the audition process. It could be months before I find out if I was selected or not."

The fear of rejection still loomed over Nat. When there was no guarantee that you were going to work in this town again, it was hard to turn down a sure thing. Wasn't I doing the same? "But what does your agent—"

A group of clamoring women emerged out of nowhere and effectively pushed me out of my own conversation.

"OMG, Natalie!" some woman shrieked. "We weren't sure if it was you, but then we saw the Commander's badge on your costume!"

Really? The badge gave Nat away? Not the Marge Simpson blue wig?

"Can we take a selfie?" the woman asked, already holding up her phone to their faces.

"Sure!" Nat put on her winning smile and threw up a peace sign. After posing for a few pictures, Nat picked up some shots off a tray Tao's cousin was parading around. "I need to let loose for tonight," she said to me, "and we'll talk business tomorrow, okay?" She handed me a glass and clinked it with her own. "Fuck FreeStream."

Hear, hear. I threw back my glass. Ugh. It was like drinking fire. When I regained my senses, Nat had already been whisked away by her old drama friends, who peppered her with all kinds of questions about her acting life. Without Nat, I didn't know where to go, but if she needed a fawning audience to lick her wounds, then I wasn't going to get in her way.

"You need a chaser?" Mariana handed me a red cup with an orange slice floating in it. "It's beer. If Tao catches you drinking water, he'll pour you a shot."

"Thanks." I swirled my cup, unsure if I wanted to drink it. The shot Nat gave me was more than enough. "Thanks for putting on the reunion."

"Yeah, right," she said before she took a sip. "It was a shitshow."

"Sorry," I said, remembering my own contributions to her headaches. "For what it's worth, I thought it went well."

"Not as well as this party." Somewhere on the lawn, Tao had set up a table for beer pong, which drew a rowdy crowd. "I should've thrown a kegger," Mariana lamented. "This was easier when we were younger. The committee took months to plan the reunion, and yet we still couldn't make anyone happy. Stuff kept falling through the cracks. People wanted to keep ticket prices low, but then people complained about the refreshments. There's only so much I can do with a shoestring budget. Meanwhile, my wife is texting me all night, asking if I made goodie bags for my kid's class. Like damn, it never ends."

So Mariana wasn't invincible. I thought I'd be happier about this revelation, but I related to the feeling hard. I knew better than anyone that we all had our limits. "Well, you have one less thing on your plate now."

"There is one last detail I need to close out." Mariana placed her hand on my shoulder like we were about to have a heart-to-heart.

"Rach, I can't let you keep the award. We had other people under consideration who are . . . how do I say this?"

"Who are what? Employed, therefore more deserving?"

"Yes," she said, so visibly relieved that I was afraid she might hug me. "You get it. It wouldn't be a good look. How would we be able to explain it to the students or the school board that we awarded someone who was essentially unemployed? What kind of message would that send?"

"Sure. We wouldn't want anyone to think that you can bust your ass your whole life and still get let go. That's not aspirational." For a second there, I thought I could empathize with Mariana, but I was never going to forget this. This conversation had cemented her as the enemy. I handed her my beer. "Wait here. It's in the car."

"It's not personal, Rachel. We want to be fair."

"Oh totally. We don't want people to think that awards are rigged, right?"

Mariana gaped, and I accepted that as a win. It was a small win, but I wasn't choosy these days. I pushed through the crowd to find Danny. I ran into a few old tennis teammates, sitting around a fire pit. I promised to come back and hang out when I wasn't burning with resentment. I finally spotted Danny mingling with Tao's family.

"Hey," I said, waving him away from their dinner party. An auntie shoved a plate of birthday cake in his hands before letting him go. "Can I get your car keys?"

"What do you need them for?" Danny's eyebrows arched with fake suspicion. It was terribly cute. "I can't have you going joyriding."

"Mariana wants the award back," I muttered.

"Damn, that's cold. Let her wait. It's not urgent."

Throughout our friendship, I had respected Danny's neutral

stance on Mariana despite my one-sided rivalry. However, it was nice to have him siding with me this time.

Danny stuck his fork in a square piece of cake, which had two layers of vanilla sponge cake divided by a layer of whipped cream frosting and yummy crunchy pastry. He tipped the plate at me. "Do you want it?"

I wasn't one to say no to cake, but this wasn't a regular offer. *He's watching what he's eating,* I recalled. *Can't have too much sugar.*

"You don't want it," I stated as I took the plate. Danny shook his head. "Because you can't have it."

He replied with an innocent smile that could let him get away with murder. At the very least, it let him get away with my heart. It was scary how effortlessly we were falling back into our old ways. Him leaving me to decipher what he really meant. Me seizing the challenge like it was a game I wanted to win. I used to feel so special, as if I cracked Danny's code or something. Now that I was older, I didn't look at it through the same rosy lens. I'd been around too many sweet-talking, bullshitting Hollywood types. I just wanted people to say what they meant.

I dug into the cake and people-watched from our little corner. A swell of hollers came from different corners of the party.

"Come on, Winnie!" some guy shouted from the diving board. "Get the pool party going! We know how much you love to skinny-dip!"

Winston took a bow, but declined, instead smoothing his tie as if to show people he was a serious adult now. It didn't stop a group of guys from chanting, "Take it off! Take it off!" Near the dance floor, a group of former cheerleaders huddled together to put the record straight on some hookups. Everyone had an agenda that night.

There was something I'd been curious about, and the alcohol had loosened my limbs and my lips. "Do you remember calling me one night after one of these parties?"

"Vaguely," he said, averting his eyes. He was a bad liar.

I pointed my fork at him. "You were drunk."

"I might've been." His voice echoed in his cup as he sipped his drink.

"You asked me if I ever kissed anyone." I kept my tone casual because that wasn't the point I was trying to make. "You said you wanted to be good at other things, but you never said what. I always wondered what you meant by that."

Danny pulled a longer sip, buying himself some time. "I felt like I was pulled in a lot of directions back then, trying to make everyone happy. I wanted to help my brother stay out of trouble. I wanted to help my parents by supporting myself. I wanted to be better at school. I wanted to be a better friend." He held on to his cup like it was his security blanket. "I wanted to be with you, but . . ."

That "but" made my heart fall to the floor with a thud.

Danny shrugged in a pathetic way, like he didn't want to finish his sentence, but he did. "But you know. You were you and I was me."

I honestly had no fucking clue what that meant. "What? Like you couldn't imagine being seen with me?"

Danny stepped back like he'd been punched in the face. "W-what? No! The opposite. You were so driven that I didn't think you'd give a guy like me a chance. You had every minute of your day planned, Rach. It was impossible to see you outside of the hour you blocked off to tutor me."

I took Danny's cup, but it was empty. I had nothing to chase the burn. Everything Danny said was true. I had a one-track mind back then, and it was scary to think how little attention I paid to anything outside of school. I knew better now, but it had been a hard habit to shake.

Danny reached for my face. I thought I had frosting on my chin, but he was thumbing away a tear. I didn't know why I was getting emotional about it all of a sudden. As horrifying as it was to cry at a party, I had some answers now. This was progress.

"That's fair." I was proud of how diplomatic I sounded. I blinked away any remaining moisture from my eyes before anyone else noticed. "I didn't really know how to be anyone's girlfriend back then." Or now, for that matter.

Danny's eyebrow arched, confused. "It wouldn't have been that hard, Rach. I would've been on cloud nine if you walked me to class like this." He held my hand, firmly, lulling me closer with every swing of our joined hands, making my heart skip.

Some people around us took notice. It was hard to ignore their eyes, waiting and wanting for something to happen. Anxiety crept up the back of my neck. I considered letting go of Danny's hand, but I didn't want that either.

"People are looking at us," I whispered.

Danny glanced side to side, tipping his chin when he made eye contact with some of the onlookers. He was remarkably fine with being gawked at like a circus act. My reputation hadn't made me popular, but at least it had shielded me from distracting gossip. I wasn't strong enough back then to withstand being talked about, whether the speculation was true or not.

"Let them look," Danny said, challenging me with an irritating calmness.

"Danny," I warned. Fortunately, a rousing game of beer pong

took the spotlight away from us. A belligerent Belinda shouted at Nat to chug. "Some of us weren't built to be the center of attention."

"Says the person who collected awards for fun."

"That was different." Awards were based on merit, or at least I thought so at the time. "I didn't want people asking me if we were hooking up during tutoring."

"Well, we kinda were," he pointed out. My face heated at the drop in his voice. "So what? It's no one's business but ours."

Danny and I had different memories of high school, when everyone had made it their business to know other people's business. But he also had a point. Why did I care what my high school friends thought? They had no bearing on my life anymore. Besides my own, there was only one person's opinion that mattered right now, and he was looking at me with the same playful smile on his face as on the day we ditched school.

Before I thought too hard about the people around us, I kissed his cheek. As we broke apart, Danny stole a kiss from me, catching the corner of my mouth. Somewhere in the distance someone—someone who sounded like Nat—cheered. "Was that so bad?" he asked.

"No," I admitted, despite some embarrassment.

"We don't have to stay," he reminded me. The arch in his eyebrow told me where his mind was going. I looked around. It was kind of hard to sneak out now that we had made our presence known.

Tao walked over and handed me a shot, just as Mariana warned me he would. "Cheers," he said, smirking as he waited for me to drink up. I threw the glass back just to get it over with. I think it was tequila. Everything was starting to taste the same. Seeing that his job was done, Tao turned around and moved away to mingle with others.

Danny seized the opportunity and made a break for it. I yelped as he grabbed my wrist and dragged me toward the side gate. "Let's go before he sees us."

Refreshing cool air filled my lungs as we escaped. We said hi and bye to a blur of faces. For a second, I thought that things were finally turning around. I freed myself from caring about this party and everyone in it. I was ready to leave it all behind, but I underestimated Tao's popularity. More people were coming in, slowing our getaway. A mob of people broke our joined hands, but I kept pushing forward.

"Rachel!"

I swung my head around, hoping to find Danny, but my eyes landed on someone else. For the first time since we broke up, I was face to face with Josh.

Chapter Seventeen

YOU KNOW YOU'RE REACHING MIDDLE AGE WHEN YOU CAN BREAK down your life into different eras. My early twenties were a blur between Berkeley and summer jobs to pay for school. As much as I thought I was exceptional at the time, it turned out that scholarship committees did not. Then I had the great luck of graduating during a recession.

Despite my super-practical business degree from a big-name school, there weren't any jobs. In a panic, I messaged almost everyone I knew, willing to take any job that would have me. It was Nat who helped me find my internship. It paid nothing, but it was my foot in the door in Hollywood, something I dreamed about. That dream kept me going through the years of instability and having no career ladder. I had to out-hustle everyone else and keep my foot in entertainment.

By the time I turned thirty, the questions about settling down and getting married became more frequent and serious. It was easy to brush off when none of my friends were married, but one by one, they were now finding someone to commit their lives to. I started to feel the pressure. By that point, it was hard to ignore that I'd had little success with dating. The occasional fling with an aspiring actor hoping to make it big never lasted more than a few dates. I was working at FreeStream by then. It was the beginning of my long-term relationship with my job, the only thing I was committed to taking all the way.

But then I ran into Josh in the most serendipitous way. I had been thinking about going back to school to get my MBA to get a leg up in my career. I was sitting at an information session when Josh took the seat next to mine. We were both career-minded and talked easily. There was also the fact that he still ran regularly and was built like a bodyguard. It was hard to find a reason why we shouldn't date and see where it went. We seemed to want the same things and were sufficiently attracted to each other. Thus began my Josh era, but it wasn't meant to be. Some things work in theory but not in real life.

"Rachel," Josh said, a little annoyed that he had to repeat himself. He had to give me a break. It wasn't every day that I ran into my ex-fiancé. He pulled me aside to a corner of the backyard, under a big orange tree, to get out of the way of pushy guests. "What are you doing here?"

"I was actually leaving," I said, standing on my tiptoes to look over his shoulder. I couldn't find Danny anywhere.

"How are you? I heard from my mom, who heard from your mom, that you were in town."

I'd have to remind my mom not to give Josh's mom so many updates.

"I didn't think I'd see you here, though," he added.

"Things are good," I said coolly. "I was laid off."

I spared him the rest of the details. He'd experienced his rounds of job insecurity, so I didn't think I needed to explain that part.

Josh gave me one of those friendly "cheer-up" pats on my arm. "You didn't tell your parents yet, huh?"

This was a rhetorical question. Josh knew that if my mom knew, that meant his mom would know, which meant that he would've known. We might not be together anymore, but we were still in each other's business, whether we wanted to be or not.

I shrugged. "I won't if I don't have to."

"I can ask around if anyone's hiring," he suggested. His way of being encouraging was offering solutions. He used to get upset whenever I rejected his ideas, telling me that actively working my way out of my predicaments was more productive than being sad. I was convinced that my feelings were a form of self-sabotage, but what if I considered the alternative? That instead of working against me, my emotions were telling me I wasn't ready to jump into next steps? It was perfectly fine to take a break.

"That's okay. I'll figure something out." I wasn't looking for more ways to stay entangled with Josh. When we broke up, we both agreed to part ways as amicably as possible. In many ways, our lives complemented each other's. We were both self-motivated and liked our own spaces. I thought it was great that Josh was understanding when I was busy during our MBA program or when I had to stay late for work. We were both doing it. But once we started talking about settling down, not as another milestone to reach but to build a life together, we quickly deduced that neither of us wanted to give up our ambitions. We started to fight about not spending enough time together. We weren't there for each other as much as we wanted to be, but neither of us wanted to make the sacrifice. We each thought our work was too important to give up. So, as much as I admired Josh for who he was, and even though I enjoyed his company, the writing was on the wall. It wasn't enough that we made good partners. There wasn't enough love to sustain what we wanted from each other.

Josh looked like there was more he wanted to tell me, but when he shifted his feet, an orange dropped from the tree and fell on his head. He ducked and rubbed his head as he bent down to pick up the offending fruit. "What the—"

I burst into laughter. The liquor had caught up with me and pretty soon I had a case of the giggles. Josh was so easily shaken up. He probably would've laughed too if I hadn't pointed at him, but he eventually cracked a smile.

"I could've been hurt," he insisted.

I removed a leaf out of his hair. "You're gonna live. I promise."

"Rachel."

Danny cleared his throat as his eyes darted quickly between Josh and me. "Hey, Josh, long time no see," he said with a friendly pat on the shoulder, even though they were merely acquaintances back in high school. "You okay there?"

I couldn't imagine what was going through Danny's head. His face was unreadable.

"Hey!" Josh said with a little too much enthusiasm. He wasn't subtle when he shot a questioning look my way. Josh was never good with names and faces. I mouthed Danny's name. "Danny!" he announced with a hint of uncertainty. "How are you, buddy? What are you up to these days?"

Buddy? I tried to keep my cool during this charade. They had nothing in common.

"Good." Danny stuffed his hands in his pockets, but his posture was stick straight. "Business is good. I run my own executive coaching business."

"Oh, do you specialize in anything?" Josh asked.

"No. I was doing a lot of team-building for a while, but I've recently limited my time to managers and executives who want individual coaching. They like to keep me on their schedules. I split my time a lot between here and the Bay Area. What about you?" Danny asked, prompting Josh to complain about tax season, which I remembered all too well. It was a perennial topic.

This was the most Danny had spoken about his job. Was he . . . bragging? The only time I'd ever heard Danny brag was when he landed a flip off a bench at Almansor Park. A visceral memory unlocked and suddenly I heard the scrape of his board in my ears. His hands catching me when I fell after my first skateboarding lesson. I hugged myself to help contain the overwhelming sensation.

"You okay there, Rach?" Danny's arm wrapped around my shoulders. "Are you cold?"

"I-I came straight from the office," Josh stammered at the same time.

"Ah, a late night for you," Danny commented before I could respond to his question, deftly returning to his conversation with Josh. I might as well have been invisible.

"Uh, yeah," Josh replied, then nodded. Danny nodded too. I was surrounded by bobbleheads.

"Um," Josh said eventually, ending this nod-fest, "there's actually something I've been meaning to tell you, Rach." Eyeing Danny, he added, "Privately."

"Yeah, okay." Danny let go of me, but snuck a glance, making sure I was going to be okay. I nodded, missing his warmth right away. "I'm going to see if Felix and Nelson are here."

"I'll be right there."

Danny replied with a half-hearted wave and dragged his feet as he left like he was on his way to get his wisdom teeth pulled.

"Is there something going on there?" Josh said, not taking his eyes off Danny as he walked away. Then, with a touch of amusement in his voice, "No way."

When we were still together, I once told Josh about my crush on Danny. I didn't think he'd remember it. "We're just catching up." Josh didn't believe me for one second, but he didn't need to know. I wasn't sure what was going on myself. "What did you need to tell me?"

Josh scratched behind his ear, which made me nervous because he only did that when he had bad news. "I thought I should be the one to tell you that I'm dating someone."

"Yes!" I clenched my fist. Now my parents could stop harassing me about us getting back together.

"What?"

"I mean, congrats!"

Wait a minute. If he was dating someone, how come my parents were still nagging me? "You haven't told your parents yet."

This was a recurring theme between us. We were children to our parents first, adults second.

"This is why I wanted to tell you. Our moms will take the news hard."

"They can still be friends," I said. "We'll sit them down and let them know that our breakup wasn't their fault." Josh and I had agreed that we were too alike to make it work long-term. We were too focused on ourselves to bring the best out in each other. "They'll get over it."

"I hope so." Josh gave me a single pat on my arm, the same kind he'd give one of his bros. "I'll see you around?"

"Sure," I said. I didn't plan to run into Josh again, but if this night had taught me anything, it was that anything was possible. I pushed my way back into the crowd. I said hi to a few people I recognized from Math Club. I caught a few stares from strangers who probably now recognized me as the person who gave the sad emo speech. I suppressed the urge to defend myself and save face. Viv somehow found me in the fray.

"I've been looking all over for you!" Viv unzipped a black pouch to display vials of a violent mix of fragrances. It had me seeing double faster than all the drinks combined.

"Not now, Viv." I had to get away from her before the smell poisoned me. "I'm trying to find Danny."

"Say less." Before I could stop her, Viv twisted my arm and dabbed a potent floral perfume on my wrist. "This is ylang-ylang, perfect for relieving blood pressure and a known aphrodisiac. Do you like it?"

I braved a whiff and I had to admit that it smelled nice when it wasn't right up against my nose. "Yeah." Surprisingly.

"Glad to be of service," Viv said, zipping her pouch of samples back up. "This is what I enjoy most—helping people in need."

I didn't give Viv enough credit. She had found her niche and she loved it. What more could you ask for? "Thanks, Viv."

"Anything for a friend." She handed me her business card. "Hit me up if you want to order a whole set. Use the code VIVSCENTS for an introductory ten percent off. And when you're free, I'd love to share how go-getters like yourself can take control of your own life with this opportunity of a lifetime."

I respected Viv's hustle. No one could deny her persistence. I flicked the card between my fingers. "I'll let you know."

I kindly removed myself from the conversation and power-walked away before Viv gave me a full sales pitch for a multilevel marketing scheme. I broke away from the crowd in case Danny was looking for me. There was no way we'd find each other within the mass of people. Danny must've been thinking the same thing because I spotted him alone in the far corner of the yard, leaning against the cinder-block fence, checking his phone. It wasn't like him to be a wallflower.

I sidled next to him. "Hey."

"Hey." He seemed happy, almost relieved, to see me, but he didn't budge from his spot. "You guys have a good talk?"

I shrugged. Running into Josh had dampened the mood. "Yeah."

Danny picked leaves off a nearby shrub. "I didn't know you guys were still friendly."

"We talk here and there, only because our parents still talk. I don't have any other reason to stay in touch with him besides that."

"I get it. You don't have to explain."

But I did. There wasn't anything to hide. It would do us more good to put it out in the open. "We weren't really a good match."

"You were engaged. That's pretty serious." Danny stood up, stuffing his hands in his pockets. "I saw the picture of you and Josh, showing off your engagement ring. You looked happy in it."

Danny saw the pictures? It felt like we were starting our conversation in the middle and I didn't know whether to go back to the beginning or forge on. The picture Danny was describing had been Josh's profile picture while we were engaged. Josh proposed to me on the beach, which had no special meaning to us other than it made for a nice photo. Everything was staged. We coordinated our outfits, and I had my hair done. We couldn't find parking because everyone went to the beach before sunset, so we had to rush through the proposal. It wasn't as romantic as the pictures led everyone to believe.

"Social media can be deceiving," I said. "That's what you do when you get engaged. You post a picture of the ring, let everyone congratulate you. But when you break up with your fiancé, you quietly disappear and hope no one notices." Danny must know this after getting a divorce. "But I wasn't happy."

"How come?"

"You know how I'm usually early?" Danny nodded. "Well, one time I was late." Danny didn't seem to catch on to what I was implying, so I continued. "I thought I was pregnant, and I took a test. I was relieved when it came out negative, which upset Josh. He thought, with our engagement, the next step was having children. That was when things fell apart. He had a whole vision that once I had kids I'd slow down from work to make more time to raise our family. He had all of these ideas without discussing them with me, and they didn't align with what I wanted."

I was raised with the Spice Girls shouting "Girl Power!" I couldn't give up my career so easily, and that expectation put a strain on our relationship.

"You don't want kids?" Danny asked carefully, like he wasn't sure if he was allowed to ask.

"I do, but not the 'picket fence, two-point-five kids' version Josh had in his head." I shrugged. "But I don't know. I'm almost forty." Having kids was still a possibility, but biology wasn't working in my favor. Once that window closed, that was it. There were no loopholes, and no amount of negotiating would keep that option open for me. "If I don't have kids, I'll be okay with being a cool aunt. What about you? Do you want kids? Do you *have* kids?"

Danny laughed, but his whole face turned a telltale shade of pink. "Not any that I know of." He rubbed the back of his neck. "I always thought I'd have kids, but my ex-wife didn't want any."

"Was that why you divorced?"

"Not specifically. We grew apart, and it made me realize that we were fundamentally different people."

I wanted to ask Danny a ton of questions, but I could tell I was the only one who wanted to dissect his divorce. Danny diverted his attention back to the party, with a faraway look in his eyes, tapping his fingers to the beat of the music on his thigh. It was like he was hiding in plain sight, appearing to be engaged while putting up his emotional wall. If we weren't standing inches apart, I might've missed it.

"This conversation got too deep, didn't it?"

Danny's mouth curved into a wistful smile. "Yeah. Just like old times."

April 2003

"You brought me here?"

Of all places, Danny brought me to Almansor Park, mere blocks away from Commonwealth.

"You told me I could decide," Danny pointed out.

Oh my god. I gave up perfect attendance for Almansor Park. I should be in Spanish class right now. "I thought you'd take me somewhere . . ." I stopped myself before I said "romantic," though it was on the tip of my tongue. ". . . I don't know. Fun?"

"It is." Danny grabbed his skateboard from the backseat. "You just don't know it yet."

I didn't become a truant to watch him skateboard across the big park where everyone in town exercised or got married.

"Do you come here a lot?" I asked. Danny swooped down the windy path like he had it memorized.

"It's a great place to skate. Do you want to try it?" He

steered away from the trail to the empty tennis courts. "How about here?"

"I don't know," I said, warily.

"Come on, Ms. Scholar-Athlete," he teased. "I saw those tennis letterman patches collecting dust on your desk. This should be easy."

My forehand skills weren't going to help me any, but I motioned at Danny to dismount his skateboard. I could never back down from a challenge. "What do I need to do?"

I placed my feet in the exact spots where Danny was pointing and immediately wobbled. I screeched and grabbed onto his shoulders for balance. "You didn't tell me that was going to happen!"

Danny laughed. "Try to even out your stance. Once you get your balance, try pushing with your right foot."

"How?!" That was physically impossible. I was going to fall flat on my face, which I wanted to keep intact. "I'm gonna get off—"

"No, wait—"

Danny's hand shot out to my waist, holding me in place. Then neither of us spoke for a long time. I may have forgotten how to breathe.

"It's okay," he said, looking up at me with shining brown eyes. "I got you." I hadn't noticed that he let me go, until he said, "See? You got it. Try putting your foot down."

I blamed my lack of sleep for not overriding my ingrained reflex to follow directions as I put my foot down and felt the momentum pushing me toward the net. As I glided slowly and shakily, a sense of awe and invincibility washed over me. "Hey. This is fun—"

I'd forgotten an important lesson from sports: always keep your eye on the ball. In celebrating my mild success, I didn't see the stray tennis ball on court. I tried to swerve and the skateboard flew out from underneath me. When my body hit the hard court, I never felt more like a bag of bones.

Danny rushed to my side, checking my head. "Are you okay?"

I hissed when I saw the gnarly scrape on my elbow. "I got ahead of myself."

"More like the skateboard got ahead of you," Danny said as he helped me up. He examined me from arm's distance, checking for any other sign of injury. His careful touch was more disorienting than the fall. "Come on. You should sit down."

We left the court and retreated to a shady spot on the grass not too far from the big gazebo. I winced as I sat down. My hip was banged up pretty bad. "How long did it take for you to skate better than that?"

"I don't know." He sat with his legs crossed, leaning back on his elbows as he watched the ducks swim across the pond. "A day or two?"

I picked a handful of grass and threw it in his direction. "Show-off."

He laughed. "Takes one to know one."

"Pfft, whatever." I carefully lay down. Good thing I'd retired from my tennis career. My coach would've chewed me out for getting injured over this. It was kind of strange to feel senti-mental about that now. I didn't even cry like my teammates did when the season ended in the fall. It didn't hit me that everything from now until graduation would be the lasts of my high school experience. I'd been so focused on hearing back from all the colleges I'd applied to that I hadn't thought much about it.

"Where did you apply to?" I asked Danny. I had never asked him about it before since he didn't seem so concerned about his grades.

Danny shrugged. "Nowhere. I forgot to apply."

My eyes widened. I couldn't even fathom what he said. It was all my classmates talked about during the fall. "What are you going to do?"

"Work for a while. Jimmy's been waiting for me to graduate so I can take more shifts at his booth."

"You sound really excited about it."

Danny side-eyed me for the sarcasm. "Not all of us want to go to Ivies. And what's wrong with working?" Danny replied defensively. "I don't know what I'd go to college for when I can make money now."

"I'm just saying . . . ," I said, backtracking. I actually didn't know what I was saying. I hadn't expected to touch a nerve, given how much Danny avoided talking about his brother. "I think you can do whatever you want to do. You're capable of doing more, if you wanted."

"Like what?" he asked, surprising me that he was entertaining this conversation.

"I don't know. Anything." I thought through my next response before I lost him. "You're good at listening," I offered, more earnestly. "You know how when you talk to some people you can tell they want you to hurry up? I never feel that way with you."

I might have embarrassed Danny. He looked away and silently picked at the grass.

"I thought about applying to community college," he said after a while. "I don't want to go far away in case Jimmy needs me. I don't want to leave him behind, not when he's finally staying out of trouble."

"But—" Danny watched me with heavy eyes, and I couldn't bring myself to finish my thought. He'd made up his mind. I didn't want to ruin things by arguing. "That sounds good too."

I wasn't going to fault him for wanting to help out his family. I understood the feeling. Coming from Cambodia, my mom and dad saw education as a luxury they wanted me to have, so I never took mine for granted. My mindset about it was, if I continued to be successful, then I could help my parents in turn and they wouldn't have to worry about my future. Everything should fall into place because I would make it so.

"That's it?" Danny asked. "I thought you'd put up more of a fight than that."

"It's your life. I don't think my opinion matters." I was so confused. I was trying to be supportive.

"You're wrong," he said. "It does."

That would've sounded nice if he wasn't defensive about it. "Well, that can't be true because I'm rarely wrong," I said to annoy him. "Do whatever makes you happy."

Silence fell between us and nothing seemed to move until a breeze swept through, rippling through the grass. I huffed, blowing out some steam, sending some tendrils away from my face while I stared at the sky through the tree branches. Then the quiet got to me and I couldn't stand it anymore. "What are you doing this summer?"

Danny didn't say anything. Instead, the tips of his fingers crawled over my hand and suddenly his face appeared in my view. I thought he might kiss me. Even though things between us had been strained, I would've let him. Kissing sounded like a good way to forget about this conversation. Talking about college reminded me how I wouldn't see Danny every day anymore.

I zoned in on his mouth like it was my next target, but as soon as I set my sights on it, he looked up and moved a foot away.

"Hey!" Someone was shouting from a distance.

I sat up and shook the grass from my hair. It was Felix, skateboarding down from the parking lot.

"Hey, what's up?" Danny was trying to play it cool, though he wasn't fooling anyone with his pink cheeks.

"Dude! I got into UC Santa Barbara!" Felix was so excited, he was out of breath.

I scrambled to my feet, ignoring the pain of my bruised body. "Admissions decisions came out already? Did it come in the mail?"

"Nah, it's all online. You have to log into your account."

"I have to go." I had to find the nearest computer. My future, everything I ever worked for, awaited. Fuck! What was my password? I was pretty sure I wrote it down in my planner. I took five steps before I remembered that Danny drove me here. I turned around to find him right behind me.

"What are you doing?" he said. "Let's go."

"What about—" I glanced at Felix, who seemed to think he was part of our conversation. He followed along with us, probably wanting to catch a ride too. "I can walk home."

"I'd feel better if I could take you home." Danny's skeptical eyes fell on my shaky hands. My nerves were getting to me. "Come on. You can tell me later."

Danny gave me a knowing look and he didn't need to say more. Later meant nine o'clock, on AIM. Our long-standing meeting spot.

After Danny dropped me off, I sprinted to my room. No one was home. My mom was at the salon, and my dad was showing a prospective buyer who was interested in the print shop. I wished Angela was there to calm me down as my shaky hands typed in the login information. Waiting for the portal to load felt like an eternity.

Dear Rachel,

Congratulations! I am delighted to welcome you to the University of California, Berkeley...

Tears spilled as I screamed. I did it. All the extra credit and extracurriculars I joined to curate the perfect application paid off. I clicked through the following screens to see my next steps. There were some forms to sign to accept my admission and fees to pay. That reminded me to check to see if I earned any scholarships. I searched for my financial aid package. I had some grants, but there was still an outstanding balance. There was information about loan options but nothing about scholarships. I kept clicking through, wondering if I'd missed it. Finally, I landed on the page that summarized my awards.

Scholarships: $0

I was confused. I was in the top 10 percent of my class, half of whom were valedictorians. My résumé spanned four pages of accolades and activities. Was it not enough? Or was *I* not enough?

Exhilaration was quickly replaced by worry. How was I going to pay for tuition? With Ba's print shop gone, there was no way my parents had enough money coming only from the salon to pay college tuition for Angela and me both.

I shut off my computer. I couldn't keep staring at the big zero any longer.

Chapter Eighteen

IT HAD BEEN A LONG TIME SINCE I'D STAYED UP THIS LATE AND IT didn't involve a movie premiere after-party or a *Gilmore Girls* marathon. I didn't make it a habit to have long conversations with anyone, not even Josh. Our conversations usually lasted over a meal before we went our separate ways to tackle our own to-do lists. Danny had always been the exception.

Danny and I stayed in our corner, watching Tao's party turn into something like a scene at an underground warehouse party. Strobe lights flashed across a mass of bodies moving in sync as they danced to "Sandstorm" by Darude.

"What do you think?" Danny asked. "Is this everything you thought Tao's party would be?"

"Is this it? Free beer and trance?" Danny wobbled his hand to say *more or less*. "I guess I'm not as scandalized by adults drinking responsibly while staying close to their partners," I said.

"Believe me. This was wild for us back in the day."

"I'm sure."

"It didn't meet the hype, huh?" Danny asked as I yawned.

"It's not that. You're going to think this is dumb, but after I was laid off, I thought I was entering my funemployment era. I envisioned that I'd be more spontaneous and do what I want."

"No offense, but you're not the spontaneous type." I glared at him, but there wasn't any heat behind it. It was true. "So, tell me. What have you done in your funemployment?"

"Spent a traumatic day at a spa," I griped, "and then I started working as Nat's assistant."

"Doesn't that mean you're technically not funemployed?"

"Yeah, I see where I went wrong with that."

It was hard for me to stay still. I had to keep busy or else I wasn't maximizing every minute of the day to meet my potential. Somewhere along the line, I started to believe that the inverse must be true—that taking time off meant I was wasting away. I didn't know how to relax. I'd been this way for so long, I wondered if I'd become a big knot tangled too tight to ever unravel.

The cinder-block wall was cold and hard against my back as I watched the party from a distance. "Do you ever feel like you're an observer looking in?"

"Like a stalker?" Danny was being a smart-ass.

"You know what I mean." I elbowed his arm. "You know why I never danced at a school dance?"

"Because you'd volunteer."

"I chose to volunteer so I wouldn't have to dance. I was afraid I was bad at it and I would look stupid. I talked myself out of trying things. No wonder I'm still trying to figure myself out."

"Are you trying to tell me you want to dance?" Danny started dancing in place, moving his arms in haphazard formations. "Pretend I have glowsticks."

"No. I'm saying what I want is that," I said, pointing at him. He was so unapologetically happy as he rolled his body around like those inflatable tube men advertising a fee oil change off the side of the road.

"Excuse me. I have a name," he said without missing a pulsating beat, sassy with his faux-offense.

"No." I tried to copy Danny, but my arms stayed closed to my wooden body.

Danny laughed as he assessed my moves. "Are you dancing or turning the steering wheel?"

I dropped my arms. "I wish I could be less self-conscious and take more risks, even if it meant being bad at it for a while."

"You're in a rebuilding year." Danny finally stopped dancing and hugged me from behind, resting his chin on my shoulder. "No one expects you to turn your life around overnight."

Danny didn't understand. When you consistently deliver excellence, people take it for granted. Anything less than stellar felt like I was letting people down. I wished it didn't take time for things to get better. I didn't feel like me without a sense of purpose when I woke up in the morning. I wanted to be that person again. I liked that person and I didn't know where she went. I needed a reset, a way to start over. I wanted to be a new and improved version of myself, one who wasn't afraid to be bold.

A group of dudes started howling, and I made the mistake of looking at them. After a few drinks and much cajoling, Winston had climbed the diving board and stripped down until he wore nothing but a pink sequined thong. Some things hadn't changed.

"Something tells me he planned this all along," Danny said. "So what do you think? Does it meet the hype now?"

I shushed Danny. I couldn't hear what Winston was saying until someone handed him a microphone.

"Winnie's back, bitches!" Winston backed his thing up, causing the crowd to go bananas over his pale ass. It was a full moon indeed. It wasn't pretty, but I admired the confidence.

Winston stopped at the edge of the diving board and teased everyone by dipping a toe in the water. "But I'm not going to do this alone. It ain't a pool party if it's only me in there. Which one of you bitches want to swim with me?"

The crowd murmured as some Daft Punk track started, building the anticipation. The night suddenly felt young again. Something came over me because I raised my hand. I could blame it on the liquor or the potent essential oil, but I was tired of feeling sad and this was my chance to do something a little reckless. I had nothing to lose.

"What are you doing?" Danny asked.

I dropped my purse on the ground and shuffled out of my jacket. Danny's eyes were glued to my exposed skin, making me feel invincible. "Watch these for me."

"Wait! Rachel!" he called out, but I didn't look back. All night, I had talked about wanting a fresh start. What better way to do that than with a splash?

I let the adrenaline take over as I weaved through the crowd, leaving surprised classmates in my wake. I didn't care if they thought I was crazy. My life was already out of control. I might as well let it take me for a ride.

I was a few feet from the clear blue pool when I leapt up and tucked in my knees. Shouts of awe and "What the fuck" soon garbled as cool water enveloped me, swallowing me whole. As my body sank, I temporarily left the noise from the party and my failures behind. I held my breath, letting myself feel weightless as I floated up from the deep end. It was quite peaceful.

My quiet solitude was interrupted by other people diving in. I spotted Winston right away with that scrap of shiny pink fabric covering him. But the rest of the bodies were swimming in my direction. It was like half of the water polo team and Nat, torpedo-ing toward me.

I kicked myself up, but Nat reached me first. She grabbed an arm to pull me up and then toward the shallow end. "Are you okay?" she said as she gulped for air. "Do you know how long you were under?"

"I'm sorry. I didn't mean to scare you," I said. I repeated this as the rest of my rescuers came out of the water. They waved me off and teased each other about their form. It was all fun and games to them. One of the guys gave me a high five.

"Dude, that was epic! You caught so much air!"

How about that? I'd never been called epic before.

Tao took over the DJ booth and shouted in the microphone: "Best reunion ever! Brought to you by the notorious T-A-O!" The crowd chanted his name like this was his altar. Except for Mari-ana. She threw back her drink and crushed her cup.

Nat wasn't too thrilled either, now that she knew I was fine.

"Rachel!" Nat slicked her wet hair back, smearing her blue makeup. "What the fuck are you doing?" she screeched.

"Felt like going for a swim," I said, earning a splash in the face.

"Not in my suit, you don't," Nat said. "You're going to get that dry-cleaned."

"Yes, boss," I muttered, annoyed that I'd created more work for myself.

Tao's aunts appeared and helpfully handed out towels as people got out of the pool. This must not have been their first rodeo. I waited in the shallow end for my turn.

Danny pushed his way to the edge of the pool, his eyes wide as saucers when he found me. "I can't believe you did that."

It was chilly now that I was out of the water. I slicked my hair back, squeezing as much water out of it as I could. "I felt like going for a dip."

"You felt like—" Danny clutched my jacket, shaking it in my direction. I'd never seen him this baffled. "I hope you got what you wanted out of that."

Other than the smell of chlorine, I felt refreshed and alert. Then again, that could be from the way Danny's eyes clung to my skin like my wet clothes did.

"Is this everything?" he asked, showing me the things I'd left with him. Danny tossed my jacket over his shoulder and hung my purse on his elbow. His eyes dropped to the water. "Where are your shoes?"

I looked down at my cold, bare feet. "At the bottom of the pool?" I guessed. I glanced back to the deep end, but Danny grabbed my arm.

"Don't even think about it," he said, more sternly than I'd ever seen before. Next thing I knew, I lost my sense of gravity. Danny had lifted me off my feet and was holding me like he caught a big fish. "Put your arms around me."

Danny was bossy. I liked it.

"I can walk," I insisted, though I did what I was told before I fell out of his arms and made a bigger scene. I never thought of myself as a damsel-in-distress type, but there was something to be said about being in the protective arms of a strong man.

The crowd parted for Danny, whispering among themselves as they watched me get carried out. Thank goodness I didn't have to see any of these people tomorrow in the school hallways as the center of gossip, although I supposed there was an upside. If the last memory people had of Danny and me was of us fighting on Awards Night, it could now be replaced with the image of Danny carrying me out of Tao's party. I considered that a win.

"Don't pay attention to them," Danny said. "Focus on me." That wasn't hard to do when his grip tightened, pressing me into his warm chest. His shirt was plastered to his skin, wet from holding me. His breath became more erratic the farther we walked. When I saw a bead of sweat trail down his straining face, I wondered if I was heavier than I thought.

After we made it out of Tao's and had crossed the street, Danny asked, "Can you explain to me what possessed you to jump into the pool?"

I shrugged. "Haven't you ever wanted to do something and not think about the consequences?"

"I think laws exist for a reason," he said.

"When at Tao's, right?" Danny shot me a look like it was the dumbest reason ever.

"If you wanted a shower, you could've done it at my place." This would've been a totally innocent and awfully nice gesture if Danny's ears hadn't turned pink, giving away the moment his mind went into the gutter. "I mean . . . you know what I mean."

I did, but I loved seeing him squirm. My fingers dug into the nape of his neck and played with the ends of his hair. "No. What do you mean exactly?"

Danny stole another glance at me, before responding with an annoyed, low grunt.

"I have to put you down to unlock the door," he said when we reached his house, though he didn't make any move to do so.

"Okay . . ." I wasn't sure what was holding him up. I didn't mind standing barefoot, or he could've put me down on one of the chairs on his porch.

"I can get you a towel and take you home," he suggested, "or you can stay."

"And do what?" I whispered conspiratorially into his ear, which was red-hot now. It was too easy to tease him.

His eyes lowered slightly, his voice soft and warm. "Anything you want."

The joke was on me because Danny slid me down against the length of his body, caging me while he unlocked the door. He took up so much space, somehow taller and broader than before as he closed in, his leg settling in between mine. His hands met at the small of my back, bringing me closer as he dropped a kiss on my shoulder.

"That seems to be your favorite spot."

"It is." He kissed it again, this time dragging his lips across my skin until he reached the sensitive spot behind my ear. "But I can find new ones."

My heart raced like the countdown on a stopwatch. There wasn't time to think. Only action. "Take me inside."

May 2003

AP exams were over and, effectively, so was high school. I still had to show up for attendance reasons, but the last few weeks were filled with senior activities to send us off in good spirits. The hallways buzzed with excitement for Grad Nite at Disneyland, and people were making plans for Senior Ditch Day. Nat invited me to go to Newport Beach with the Drama Club, but I declined. I couldn't tell her that I had to save money because my dad was having trouble selling his business. He was going to wait out his lease and close the print shop at a loss. I wasn't even going to prom, not that anyone asked.

Though we had moved past our last fight, things with Danny hadn't gotten back to normal. He came to tutoring for a while, but he had flaked this last week because of work. The topic of prom never came up, so I assumed he made other plans. Plans that didn't include me.

I curled into my computer chair late Saturday night, ignoring my homework. It was all busywork now that exams were behind us. My grades were so high that these assignments would have no significant impact whether I turned them in or not. I'd eventually do them, though, because it was strange not to.

I logged into AIM, but no one was on. Everyone was at prom. I stared at Danny's gray screen name. I wondered if he'd been online. Once I was done with studying for exams, I hadn't been online, trading my computer for sleep. I typed out a message, even though he wasn't going to see it until he logged on.

How've you been? I missed you.

I smashed the backspace button.

xxaznxbbxgrlxx: hope you're having fun at prom

I closed the chat window and got up to get a snack when a notification sent me rushing back to my computer.

SuperxSaiyan85: i'm at home. you too huh?

He didn't go? I heard all of his friends talk about getting a limo together. I assumed that included him too.

xxaznxbbxgrlxx: cost too much money

SuperxSaiyan85: same

SuperxSaiyan85: wanna meet up?

I was going to say yes anyway when he sent another message.

SuperxSaiyan85: movies?

My parents were already home, and they knew it was prom night, so I wouldn't be able to be out late without them questioning it.

xxaznxbbxgrlxx: I can't stay long

SuperxSaiyan85: how about my place? I have something for you.

Now he had me curious. He lived in an apartment complex near the school, but I'd never been there before.

xxaznxbbxgrlxx: send me directions

"Ignore the mess," Danny said when he opened the door. "It's all my brother's shit."

The apartment was small and spartan. It was impossible to disregard the piles of cardboard boxes lying around. It was quiet too, so quiet that I heard my socked feet shuffle on the carpet on the way to the couch. Danny sank into the seat next to me, inadvertently bringing me closer.

"Um, here." Danny reached into a paper bag, fumbling for my gift. I wasn't sure why. I could've opened my own present. That was usually how these things go. But then he produced a clear box. Inside, there were flowers resting on a bed of ribbon. "This is for you."

It was the prettiest corsage I'd ever seen, made up of bundles of creamy roses with pink along the edges, as if they'd been dipped in watercolor. When I didn't reach for it, Danny stammered, "D-do you want to put it on?"

I looked down at my outfit. I had come over in a T-shirt and cargo pants, thinking this was going to be a casual hangout. "I feel very underdressed."

"That's okay." He smiled as he opened the box. Long white ribbons unfurled as he lifted the corsage out of the box and slipped it onto my wrist. It took up most of my forearm. "The florist said this was a popular style."

"It's, uh, big," I said, unable to peel my eyes away from it. The ribbons flowed like streamers on a handlebar. "You didn't have to."

"You're welcome," he said, as if to correct me.

"Thank you," I amended.

"Sorry if it's a little bruised," he said, even though I couldn't tell. "I wanted to give it to you at school yesterday, but you left campus before I got to you."

"But why?" I'd hardly spoken to Danny outside of school in the last few weeks. I isolated myself when I went into study mode. After I heard that I wouldn't get any scholarships, studying was the only way I could be proactive. If I scored well, I could save some money by earning college credit.

"I heard you weren't going to prom," he explained with a sheepish shrug, though his answer left me more confused.

"No, I mean—why are you being nice to me?"

"Why wouldn't I be nice to you?"

I felt dumb for having to say it. "Because we had an argument. I didn't even say sorry."

"You don't have to. I could tell you were going through something. I figured you'd tell me about it eventually." Danny was being extremely generous. I might've told him everything back when our online chats were anonymous. It was harder to face Danny when he'd already seen the ugly sides of me.

"I am sorry."

Danny shot me a kind smile as he clasped his hands over his lap, so tight his knuckles were white. Words escaped me, so I gave him a friendly nudge with my arm. It was supposed to be platonic, but the heat of his skin lingered on mine like a small ember, catching the feelings I was trying to hide. It was painful to be this close to him, sharing the same air, for nothing to be happening.

On an impulse, I kissed Danny's cheek. "Thanks," I added later.

Saying that was an excuse, a safety net in case he wasn't interested. If he walked away from this like nothing happened, then I could live with having given him an innocent peck.

"What was that for?"

I hadn't counted on Danny asking me a question. "Um..." It was hard to think when Danny leaned in, like he had to do that to hear my answer. Lacking product for once, his hair fell to the side as he angled closer, stopping just shy of our lips touching. It left me nowhere else to look except his soft eyes, which implored me with something that felt a lot like hope.

"I just wanted to," I said, the words barely coming out of my mouth. It sounded lame and cowardly to my ears, but Danny must not have thought so. His gaze sharpened, like he'd found what he was looking for.

Danny dived in for a proper kiss that went deeper and deeper, like there was no beginning or end to it. We were free-falling. The kiss consumed me as the switch to my brain seemed to turn off and I let my body get lost in it. I kissed him back, trying to match his moves like a back-and-forth volley.

I needed him closer.

My back hit the sofa as I pulled Danny over me, letting my hands explore his chest and his shoulders. I wasn't sure if Danny was enjoying any of this until he let his body become flush with mine and he moaned in my mouth.

Things were going well until he squeezed my boob like a sponge he wanted to wring dry.

"Not so hard," I whispered.

"Sorry," he replied into my neck, tickling my skin. His ears were so red. All was forgiven when his hands slipped into my pants. Every inch of my body became ultra-sensitive to his touch, building momentum. But then his fingers began to move erratically, like he lost his place.

The break in momentum gave me a moment of clarity. "Um, are we . . . ? Do you, you know?" I cleared my throat. "Have protection?"

Danny looked like he was trying to solve a math problem in his head. "I don't."

My hands shot to his shoulders, putting some distance between us. In an instant, my brain flooded with every sex ed lecture showing images of squiggly sperm traveling to meet the egg. When *was* my last period? I was too young to be a mother!

"We should stop." I sat up and tried to smooth down my hair. Some petals fell on my lap. Our make-out session had done some damage to the flowers. A few roses flopped to the side. Danny's lips were swollen, and if I looked at them any longer, I'd do anything to kiss them again. "I'm gonna go."

"I can walk you out," he sputtered as I sprinted out the door.

I couldn't wait for him. I was a ball of nerves, mostly frustrated, unsatisfied ones. I didn't trust myself to make another smart decision. Being with Danny was thrilling and exciting and made me want to throw out every rule book. I couldn't be this reckless. Not now, not when I had so much ahead of me.

Chapter Nineteen

I LOVED HOW DANNY GENTLY PLACED MY BELONGINGS ON AN END table like they were something precious and then slowly emptied his own pockets, as if I wasn't creating a puddle in his living room.

"Turn off your phone," he commanded as he silenced his. "No more interruptions this time."

Oh. His voice was swift and decisive. He knew what he wanted. This wasn't the time for dillydallying. I had to keep up. My hands shook as I pressed the side button and then dropped my phone by the rest of my stuff so I could help Danny out of his shirt.

Danny clasped my hands over his chest. "You're cold."

"I bet you could warm me-e u-up." This would've sounded sexy if my teeth weren't chattering. I tried to convince him I was okay with a kiss, but he backed away.

"Hey," Danny kissed my cheek, taking away the sting. "You're freezing. Let me draw you a bath. There's no need to rush. Not like the first time."

I laughed, surprised that he brought it up. That had been so embarrassing. It shouldn't even count, since we didn't get very far. "You mean we're actually going to take our clothes off this time?"

"God, I hope so." Danny took my hand and led me down the hallway. "Come on."

Danny ran the water, checking the temperature as it filled the tub in the master bathroom. Waiting gave time for nerves to surface. It was one thing to get naked in the heat of the moment, but we were under bright, unflattering bathroom lights and the bathwater was clear as day.

I crossed my arms in front of my chest. The camisole was too small and too thin, now that I saw my reflection in the mirror. "Do you have a bath salts or something bubbly?"

Danny made a face like I was speaking a different language. It was pretty cute, though I had a feeling he'd protest the word, like he'd outgrown it. Maybe he could live with "adorable."

"I don't have anything unscented." Now I was the one making a dumb face. "You looked like you were about to pass out when we were at Noodle World. In the bathroom?"

Oh. He remembered that? That felt like a lifetime ago.

Danny rummaged through his vanity drawers. "Uh, I have three-for-one bodywash, or this pink-and-purple bath bomb that, uh"—he cleared his throat in a startlingly loud way—"came in some gift set, I think. I don't know how it got in there."

He didn't even need to take it out. I could smell it from where I was standing. It was like walking into a Bath and Body Works. I covered my nose with the back of my hand. "I'll use whatever soap you use."

Was that weird to say? Because we spent the next five long seconds staring at each other, while his ears stayed a persistent pink.

"Okay." Danny kissed my forehead and threw his thumb over his shoulder. "I'll give you some privacy." As he left, he adjusted the lights, so it wasn't so bright. "Don't go for any more swims. The tub isn't big enough for that."

"Ha-ha," I replied, but I was grateful. I undressed and lowered myself into the water. It was perfectly warm, just shy of hot. It took awhile to find a comfortable position and relax. I rarely took baths because showers were more efficient. I lathered soap in the water, recognizing the mild linen scent. I ran my hands along my arms and legs, each pass melting the stress of my day away. I realized I should listen to my body more. It was telling me to slow down.

I could hear Danny's feet padding around his bedroom and wondered what he was up to. If he wasn't busy, maybe he could help me release a different kind of tension. My own hands didn't feel quite enough anymore.

"Danny," I called out.

"You need something?" The door to the bathroom was behind me, so I couldn't see him, but he could see me.

"You were right."

"I'm sorry. Can you say that again? I don't think I caught that."

I rolled my eyes. "You were right."

"What's this in reference to?"

This guy was trying to milk "you were right" for all it was worth. "This bath is really nice, but"—I lifted my leg and arched my foot toward the faucet—"the water's gotten cold," I lied. "Think you can help me?"

"It hasn't been that long." The water sloshed when I dropped my leg back into the tub. Just when I thought Danny was hopeless, he announced, "Maybe I should come in and check."

I bit my lip to stop my smile. Danny could never make it as an actor.

He took two steps and stood still by the side of the tub, wearing the same damp clothes. His hands were squarely in his pants pockets as his eyes swept my body, which had more dimples and stretch marks these days. Not that Danny knew that. He didn't look like he cared.

Danny knelt beside me and rolled his sleeve to his elbow. His fingers swirled in the water above my belly button. "Seems warm to me."

"You should keep checking."

Danny squeezed my knee. "Nope. Warm here too."

"Danny," I warned. I didn't call him over to play games. "Are you done?"

"What are you talking about? I'm just getting started." His hand slid up my thigh, and I was groaning softly when he reached the center. I closed my legs to keep him there.

Danny smirked as his hand slipped away to rest palm flat on my belly. "You're so impatient."

"Oh really? Because I think you started something twenty years ago that you haven't finished." I, for one, would like to finish.

"We can't have that happen again, can we?" His hand wandered over my body, caressing the curves of my breast. "Tell me what you like."

Oh, so this was how he was going to play this.

"I need you lower."

I thought the message was clear until Danny asked, "And do what?"

"Do you want me to give you step-by-step instructions?"

"Well, you're the tutor." Danny massaged my inner thigh, frustrating me to no end. He was so close to where I needed him. "What do you want me to do next?"

"Touch me." I pushed his hand to the apex of my thighs. "Here."

Before I could say another word, a sigh escaped my lips. Danny ran his knuckle down the center, teasing me. He didn't even try to hide his satisfied smile. "Okay, what else?"

"More." My breath grew hot and heavy as Danny's steady

finger applied more pressure, changing the current in the water. "Harder." Apparently, I could only speak one word at a time.

Just when I thought this was all fun and games for him, Danny's breath grew ragged. "Like this?"

Danny kissed me, making me gasp in his mouth as he inserted a finger and then two. There wasn't anything for me to teach him when he was reading my face with heavy-lidded eyes, watching me fall apart. My thighs shook as pleasure climbed and climbed.

Danny groaned, hot and low in my ear. "Fuck."

It broke me. Every sound I made—every moan, every whimper—echoed throughout his bathroom.

Danny pressed his lips on my temple as I rode out the rest of my orgasm. "Enjoy the rest of your bath, okay? There's no rush."

He said that, but as he stood up to leave and I got a good view of the front of his pants, I saw that we had urgent business to take care of.

I dried my hair and wrapped a towel around me, then caught up to him in his bedroom. He was sitting at the edge of his bed, bent forward, his hands pressed on the back of his neck, staring at the floor.

I stood in front of him. "Are you okay?"

"I need a minute." His eyes dragged up my body as his head slowly turned up to mine. "Two minutes."

"Is there anything I could do?" I asked, taking a step closer.

"You've done enough." His hands flirted with the edge of my towel. "We don't have to jump right into bed. You need to give me a chance to make it last."

"What about you, though?" I palmed his hard length over his pants, earning myself a low moan from Danny.

"What about me?" His words came out strained as he continued to resist. "I'm fairly easy to please."

"Oh yeah?" I slowly unwrapped the towel and let it drop by my feet. Danny groaned like I was being unfair.

"You're killing me." His eyes grew hungry, taking advantage of the up-close view. He dropped his head, nipping the valley in between my breasts. "I want to live here."

His enthusiasm made me laugh until he gripped my thighs and lifted me onto the bed. There wasn't anything funny about the way he got rid of his clothes. His body was smooth and strong, a sculpture out of my own desires. Danny licked his lips as he crawled in between my legs.

"Danny. You already—"

He hushed me, spreading my legs wider with clear determination. "Just let me have a taste."

"A taste" was underselling it. Danny was savoring it with his languid tongue. I would've let him have at it and get seconds, but I was already wound up.

"Dan—" I swallowed my gasp. "Danny. I need you. Inside. Right now." This time he listened to directions. He sat up, wiping his mouth with the back of his hand.

"Are you sure?" The earnest way he said this reminded me of the boy I used to know, who always tried to make me laugh, the one who stole my heart without even trying.

"You like taking care of me." I saw it in the way he looked after me and put me first.

Danny reached for a condom from his bedside table. It was excruciating watching him roll it down slowly. "I want to make sure it feels good."

"Trust me," I said, pulling him over me. "It does."

He thrust slowly, letting me feel the entire delicious length of him. I loved how concentrated he was on me and having the weight of him on top of me. But as I ran my hands down his body, feeling the strain of his back and shoulders, I wondered how much he was holding back.

I dragged him down for a kiss. "I want to know what you like too," I said into his mouth. "Show me." There wasn't anything I wanted more than to see Danny lose himself to me.

"Yeah?" Danny kissed me, hesitating for a moment before he retreated. He sat up once more to reposition himself, gripping my hips as he slammed into me once, giving me a sample of what to expect. "Tell me if you want me to stop."

Not a chance. "Keep going."

As Danny picked up his rhythm, his sounds became raw and rough. I had to shelter my head from hitting his headboard, but it was a small price to pay when Danny felt this good. I rocked my hips, meeting him where he needed me until my mind went blank, free from past mistakes and failed attempts. Danny's hands followed the arch in my back, his mouth tracing the curve up my neck. I hung onto him as he buried himself into me, relentless until I surrendered my pleasure. My orgasm came hard and fast, more intense than the first time.

Danny kept going through my aftershocks until he found his own release.

"That was—" Danny blew out a deep breath without finishing his sentence, then collapsed beside me. I mumbled a sound of agreement. I wasn't exactly in a position to form insightful thoughts either. He rolled over and kissed my shoulder.

"Stop." I slapped him away. "I'm sticky."

"So am I," he said, bringing my attention to the sheen of sweat illuminating his flushed skin. "How about a shower?"

I laughed. I was still wet from my bath.

"Only a shower," I said, though I wasn't sure if I was trying to convince him or me.

I LEARNED SOMETHING new about Danny. He was remarkably energetic after sex. Yes, it was the most exciting shower I'd ever had, but it was past my bedtime. I could've easily nodded off in the soft T-shirt and sweatpants I borrowed from Danny. However, he knew my weakness: a late-night movie.

"We might as well watch something while your clothes dry," he reasoned as he picked up the remote.

I made myself comfortable on the sofa. Danny opened the search bar and entered his query one letter at a time. I was giddy as "Keanu" spelled out on the screen, until Danny selected a *John Wick* movie. "*Speed* was right there."

"My house, my pick." Danny slowly eased into the seat next to me.

"Is it your butt? Is it still sore?"

"For the last time, can you stop talking about my butt?"

"I could, *but* it's fun." I tugged his arm and patted my thigh. "Lie down so you're not putting any weight on it."

Danny hesitated, but he eventually gave in and rested his head on my lap. Instead of facing the screen, he looked up at me.

"You're not watching the movie," I said, playing with his luscious, luscious hair, still damp from the shower.

"I'd much rather look at you." From that angle? Did he like looking up my nose?

I rolled my eyes. "You think you're so smooth, huh?"

"No. Just trying to beat you at your own game."

"What are you talking about?"

"You're the one who always watches me to see how I react."

"Oh." I hadn't realized. "I didn't mean to be a creep."

Danny's body shook with laughter. "It's not creepy. I thought it was your way of including me, like you were letting me in on a secret." My breath hitched when he took my wrist and kissed my palm before pressing it on his cheek. "There's something I've been wondering, though."

I turned down the volume on the TV. "What is it?"

"Earlier you said you were sorry for breaking up our friendship, but I never thought it was broken."

What was he talking about? "On Awards Night, I told you that I never wanted to speak to you again and never returned your messages. I broke it."

"You didn't read any of the messages I left you," he said, like he was working that out as he was speaking.

He left me messages?

"I basically quit IM-ing people after," I explained, hating my dumb younger self. When I said I didn't want to talk to anyone again, my decision was final like a sale item on clearance. No returns. No exchanges. I was horribly stubborn that way. "Do you remember what any of them said?"

"Not really. I just wanted a chance to talk to you," he said. His sincerity broke my heart.

"How could you still want to be my friend after I got mad over your grades or how I basically avoided you after prom?"

"We'd been friends for so long. I wasn't going to give up on you so easy." Danny reached up and tucked my hair behind my ear.

"Still. I wasn't that nice to you."

"No, but it's like that one saying. Set something free and if it comes back, it's meant to be."

"So wise," I teased. I was pretty sure that wasn't how the saying went. "Is that why you give advice professionally?"

"Someone told me once that I was a good listener." He reached up and held my face. "It kind of stuck with me."

"It's true," I said. "I second whoever told you that."

Danny's hand went cold. "*You* told me that."

"I did?" I couldn't recall ever saying that to him. Was it over AIM?

"You don't remember?" Danny laughed, incredulous. "We were at the park. I got you to ditch school. You were lying on the grass, looking up at me like I'm doing right now." His voice grew more passionate as he tried to set the record straight. "We talked about going to college. You don't remember that?"

I squinted, like I was trying to squeeze out every ounce of memory, hoping something familiar emerged. "Uh, I remember wanting to kiss you."

"Oh my god, Rachel." Danny palmed his forehead, horrified. "That is one of my core memories."

"Same for me!" I insisted.

"Yes, but mine set the trajectory for my adult life. Yours was because you were horny for me. Actually, now that I think about it, I'm okay with it."

I smacked him with a decorative pillow. "You're an idiot."

Danny blocked my attacks as he sat up and tickled me in his defense until he had me underneath him once again. "Let the record show, Rachel Dang was horny for me!"

I laughed like I hadn't laughed in a long time. I laughed at the absurdity of this night, culminating in this moment, something I never thought I'd ever have again. It was more than I could ever have hoped for.

Chapter Twenty

FROM THE MOMENT I OPENED MY EYES IN THE MORNING, I KNEW two things. First, it was too early. Danny's living room was dark, but dawn was casting shadows, allowing me to make out the shapes and outlines of my surroundings. Two, my back wasn't going to forgive me for falling asleep on the couch.

I moved to get up when Danny's arms cinched around my waist.

"Go back to sleep," he grumbled, nuzzling his face into my neck, reminding me of the other sore places on my body.

I patted Danny's hands to let go. "I need to get up."

"Why?" Danny tightened his hold. "It's Sunday."

"I should go home," I said. My parents knew not to wait up for me anymore, but they were going to freak out if I wasn't there before they woke up. It didn't matter how old I was. If I was under their roof, I was always going to be their child first and foremost. That meant I still had to follow their rules. "What time is it?"

Danny lifted his wrist to my face so I could look at his watch. It was five thirty. I could spare a few minutes before I had to get up. My parents' house wasn't that far away.

"I had a great time last night, minus the cactus," he mumbled sleepily into my hair. "That scarred me for life."

"Send me your therapy bill." I laid my arms on top of Danny's. I couldn't stop touching him. "I had a good time too."

Danny and I were back on good terms, so in that way, I met my goal last night. Going to the reunion had brought not just a sense of closure to a period of my life but also the beginning of something new. Danny and Rachel 2.0.

But even with this shiny, brand-new optimism, there was a voice lurking in the back of my mind, telling me to be cautious. The new day brought me back to reality. It wasn't going to be as easy as seeing each other every day after school and holding hands in the hallway. We both had failed relationships and careers to consider. And the way my life had been going, I couldn't ignore this itchy feeling that I was going to say something stupid and ruin things again.

I slipped out of Danny's arms and searched for my phone to work off my nerves.

"It's on the kitchen counter," Danny said as if he read my mind. He yawned as he sat up. His hair looked like a ball of fire. "I charged it for you last night."

"Thanks." I couldn't even look at Danny when he was being so thoughtful and cute, whereas my mind was filling with doom and gloom.

I spotted my phone charging next to his on the counter, right where he said it'd be. Danny's kitchen was nice and cozy. I could tell he used it. His coffee machine had a timer set to brew at six thirty, and there was a small sauce splatter on the foil that lined his stovetop. It was very homey, not a place where Danny just slept and kept his belongings but where he was settled, where he'd made his life.

"Can we meet up after you get back from Austin?" Danny asked from the sofa.

He wants to see me again. More impressively, he remembered.

He remembered a lot of things. I didn't know why I was collecting these observations like I was storing them away for a long winter. I guess I needed some extra assurance to hold on to.

"Let me check my calendar," I said as my phone powered up. As soon as the home screen appeared, it was littered with notifications from last night.

> **unknown number:** it's Mariana. if you're still in town, you can drop off the award at CHS

I was close to replying with a middle finger emoji, but switched it to a thumbs-up. Mariana had no space in my life anymore, so I wasn't going to waste my energy on her. If she wanted the award back so badly, she could have it.

> **Nat:** Rach, there's a hot guy at Tao's. I need to know who he is.

Oh no. Not Bo!

> **Nat:** Don't wait up for me.

Noooo! I didn't warn Nat in time! I texted Nat to call me back. I swiped over to the next notification from my family group chat.

> **Mom:** Rachel

Since I didn't respond right away, my mom resorted to using my childish nickname.

Mom: 妹妹

Mom: 几点回来?

Angela: Mom. Leave Rachel alone

Angela: 她已经长大了. 不用提醒她

Dad: 大人还要提早回家

If they wanted me home early, they should've given me a curfew. *Nagging is their love language*, I reminded myself, repeating it in my head as I looked at my next notification. It was from *TMZ*, which I normally would've ignored, except Nat's name was in the headline.

NATALIE HUANG LEAVES BTD SET
AMID CANCELLATION RUMORS

Shit. Even if it was reported as a rumor on *TMZ*, readers were going to take it to be as good as true. I quickly googled Nat's name. *Deadline* reported the official cancellation news thirteen minutes ago. Nat's agent and publicist were probably calling her right now.

Danny tapped my shoulder, startling me. "Rachel?" I put my phone face down on the counter or else I would have kept looking at it. His face softened as he smoothed my hair. "I can take a rain check if you're busy."

"I'm sorry," I said, dragging a hand down my face. "Something came up. I need to find Nat." I had to find her and get back to our apartment so we could square out all her talking points. It was going to be tough on her to promote her movie when journalists were most likely going to bring up the cancellation. I left for the bathroom, where my clothes were hanging to dry. The cream suit was still damp in some spots, but it would have to do.

My phone rang as I changed into my clothes. It was Nat.

"Rach." Nat had left her carefree attitude at Tao's too. She sounded tired. "Where are you?"

"I'm at Danny's." My eyes snagged on my reflection in the mirror as I zipped my pants. There was a nice glow to my skin, offset by the dark circles under my eyes. I was low on sleep but high on anxiety. "The perfect combination," said no one ever.

"You need to come home. I have too many people in my ear right now, and I'm too hungover to deal with this." Nat groaned. "What were in those damn drinks?"

"I'll be there as soon as I can." Maybe my mom would let me borrow her car, if I could get my ass back home before she woke up. I spread a line of toothpaste on my finger and did my best to brush my teeth. It was a desperate reach at my normal routine to try to calm my nerves. There was so much to do. When I opened the door to leave, I came face to face with Danny.

"I can give you a ride," he said. He had changed his outfit. Now sporting a dark gray cardigan over his white T-shirt, he'd traded his pajama pants for jeans. He looked nice and fresh while I looked like I washed ashore.

"Okay. Thanks." I wasn't in a position to refuse. I had no other mode of transportation available. I stopped at the front door to double-check that I had all of my things while silently dancing around the fact that I hadn't answered Danny's original question. Last night was a nice break from my real life, but I couldn't ignore it any longer.

"Here." Danny placed a pair of flip-flops by my feet. "You're going to need these."

Oh right. My shoes were at the bottom of Tao's pool. "Thanks," I said as I slid my feet in. The sandals were too big, but I wasn't going to complain. Beggars couldn't be choosers. "I'll get them back to you."

"Okay. Bring them the next time we see each other," he said as we walked to the car.

"Are you sure?" I wasn't sure when we could meet again. I wasn't planning on being Nat's personal assistant forever, but I couldn't quit now that the *Beyond the Dark* cancellation was blowing up.

"I have other sandals," he replied breezily, misinterpreting my worry. He'd been so kind to me throughout last night's unpredictable events. With Nat's schedule and my unforeseeable future, it didn't seem fair to Danny to start something I couldn't give 100 percent to.

While Danny drove me to my parents' house, I rehearsed all the things I wanted to say in my head. I didn't have grand expectations for a sweeping romance. Danny had said himself that there wasn't any rush and we could take our time. That sounded perfect while I worked on getting my life in order. I wanted to be in a better place so that I could be the best partner I could be. Once Danny parked the car in my parents' driveway, I recited my speech, word for word.

"I had a great time last night," I reiterated. "I'd love to see you again, but I don't know when this shit with Nat is going to settle down. I don't know what's going to happen in the next week or month or year. Everything in my life is in the air, and no matter how hard I try to grab something, it slips through my fingers. I think I need some time to get my life back on track before jumping into this . . ."

Relationship? Courtship? Some other word that ends with -ship? Damn it. I need some coffee.

"... this thing with you. Is that okay?"

Danny nodded as he took in everything I was saying. As I braced myself for a yes or no answer, he posed a question instead. "There's something I've been meaning to talk to you about. Do you remember Awards Night?"

I thought we were going to have a conversation about the future, but we were still rehashing the past. "What does that have to do with this?"

"I think we both have different memories about what went down."

I wasn't sure what he was getting at. I remembered it very clearly. After our failed hookup, I couldn't look him in the eye without blushing really hard. It was like my body was announcing to the whole world that I almost had sex with him. It was unbearable.

Awards Night had happened a few days after. I didn't remind my parents to go because Awards Night was a bragging competition for top students to tout their scholarships and other high honors. I wasn't going to make them sit through a long ceremony where I wouldn't even walk onstage. The only reason I went was to see if I won Student of the Year.

When our principal invited Mariana to come up to the stage to accept her award and share a few remarks, she had walked up confidently, without any hint of surprise. Her speech was delivered perfectly because she had time to prepare and rehearse for it. I held out hope for nothing.

By the time I saw Danny afterward in the hallway outside of the auditorium, I was a dangerous mix of feelings, ready to explode.

"I was crushed, and I took it out on you. I said some things I didn't mean, like that I never wanted to see you again," I replied with my summary of events.

"That's not all you said." I closed my eyes. I'd said a lot of things in a fit of rage, and it couldn't have been pretty. "I apologized for being late," Danny continued, "and then you said something I never forgot. You said, 'Danny. You always have excuses, and I never said anything because I thought we were friends. But I don't know what's going on with you anymore. I thought I was the smart one in this relationship, but I'm the dumb one waiting for you to try harder."

I didn't remember things quite as clearly, but that sounded about right.

"Do you know why I was late?" he asked. I shook my head. I never gave him a chance to explain. "After school, I went to work at my brother's stall, like usual. I was going to ask if I could leave early. Except, it wasn't there anymore. It was gone. I looked everywhere for Jimmy. I went back home, and none of his stuff was there. He left without telling anyone."

"I didn't know that." If I had, I wouldn't have been so harsh. Or maybe I would've. I wasn't great at containing my emotions like Danny was.

"I didn't say all of that to make you feel bad," he added.

Too late.

"Don't get me wrong, I *was* hurt. But over time, I understood where you were coming from. I wasn't a good friend to you. I wasn't doing well in school. I wasn't putting my energy in the right places. I didn't handle things well, and I paid for it."

I was stunned into silence. We'd been apart for twenty years, and not once had I ever expected to hear Danny say all of that.

"What I'm trying to say is that I want to do this 'thing' with you. I'm walking into this with eyes open, Rach. I want a chance to do things right. You might be worried, but I'm not. I know you. You've always had high expectations for yourself. You don't just reach your goals. You want to smash them. When you have your sights on something, I think the best thing I can do is step aside and get out of your way. So if you need to get your life in order first, I can wait. But I want to be there for you too, if you'll let me. Don't push me away."

I'd been doing that, hadn't I? How many times had I tried to run away when things didn't work out the way I wanted? I'd search everywhere for answers. Everywhere and anywhere, except within myself. "So what do we do now?"

"How about we start with exchanging numbers?" Danny held out his phone, urging me to take it. "I don't want you sending me a message on Facebook. I only used it to invite people to the reunion." Danny watched me as I typed my information. "Fill in all the boxes while you're at it," he added.

In that case, I entered my apartment address, my parents' address, and my birthday too before I returned his phone. I was nothing but thorough. "And now what?"

"What do you mean, 'now what'? Do you want a detailed plan for dating?"

That didn't sound half bad, even though he was joking.

Danny saved my information and sent me a text, so that I had his number. "There's this thing called texting? You may have heard of it. And then . . ."

"And then what?" I egged him.

Danny smiled with a little twinkle of mischief in his eye. "And then let's see if you can stop yourself from falling in love with me."

"Ha!" I laughed facetiously, though I couldn't help the bubbly feeling in my stomach. As if I'd accept a challenge like that. I wasn't trying to set myself up to fail.

Chapter Twenty-One

BA WAS SITTING IN HIS FAVORITE CHAIR, READING THE SUNDAY edition of the *World Journal* on his tablet, when I came home. He nearly spit out his tea when he saw me walk into the house at six a.m., wearing wrinkled clothes. "You're just getting home?"

"You didn't know I've been gone?" That earned me a light smack on the arm.

He grunted as he went back to reading the news. "Go change before your mom sees you like that." I ducked into my room as my dad continued to mumble in Mandarin loud enough for me to hear. *"What good is flaunting around designer clothes if you look like a crumpled piece of paper?"*

I chuckled because I was used to it, but I never understood my parents' logic. They griped about how it was time for me to grow up, but they still insisted on treating me like a kid. I changed my clothes and packed the rest of my things. If I'd brought my laptop, I would've been able to get some work done from here. There was only so much I could do on my phone. My clunky old desktop would probably crash from software updates alone.

I opened the door to the hallway at the same time Ma walked out of her room, stretching her arms. "You're going back already? Bù xiān chī zǎocān ma?"

I wasn't planning to eat, not when Danny was waiting for me, but this was a test. The wrong answer would earn me a guilt trip that would last much longer than the time it'd take to sit and have breakfast. I nodded. "Okay."

While Ma milled around the kitchen, I managed the influx of emails in Nat's inbox, deleting any that requested a comment.

"Put that away." Ma set a plate of steamed scallion buns in front of me. "Eat first."

My mom always had these buns on hand for a quick grab-and-go breakfast, so she must've picked up that I couldn't stay long. Her mother's intuition was strong.

I peeled a piece off my bun, eating it layer by layer like string cheese. "I have to go soon. I have a lot of work to do."

This, she didn't hassle me about. We were a family that valued work. She knew as well as I did how much time she used to spend at the salon. "But when you have some free time, you should come over more."

It wasn't like Ma to make such a request. Did she find out I was laid off? Now that I thought about it, Ma was watching me eat every morsel of this bun. Had she even blinked since I sat down? "Okay," I said, treading carefully. "I'm going out of town for the next week, but I should be free after."

"Good. It's important to spend more time together, you know? As a family," she added.

This was really strange. Was she trying to break some bad news? "Ma. Is everything okay?"

"Your mom misses you," my dad chimed in from the living room. Ma shushed Ba, like she was embarrassed at the sentimentality. God forbid she missed me!

"Ta," she warned. My mom called my dad a grandpa in Khmer only when she was annoyed. "What's wrong with spending time with family? That's how we know what's going on with each other."

Something was up. This wasn't the usual reminder to call more.

"Are you sick?" I swallowed my bun so fast that I got the hiccups. I pounded my chest, which didn't help at all. "Is Ba sick?"

"Nobody's sick!" Ma wagged an accusing finger at me. "Don't you have something to tell me?"

Oh, she must know about my job. I should come clean. It was time. They had always trusted me when it came to managing school and work. They should trust me now when I was figuring things out. "Ma, I'm sorry I didn't tell you—"

"I knew it! You were hiding something from me. Okay. Tell me." She sat up straight with both arms flat on the dining table. I steadied myself with a deep breath and opened my mouth to speak, but unable to hold it in any longer, she broke in. "Are you dating someone?"

Wait, what?

"Where did that come from?" I asked.

She pointed out the window. Danny was walking around the driveway like he needed to stretch his legs. Why didn't he wait in the car? My mom gasped when I sent Danny a text, like it was all the confirmation she needed.

> **Rachel:** Hey. If you need something to do, can you help me with my bags?

From the window, I could see Danny search his surroundings until he finally turned to the house, looking slightly alarmed that he'd been caught. Did he think no one would see him?

"So?" My mom patted my arm to get my attention. "Are you dating?"

"Yeah," I said. There wasn't any point in lying when Danny was right there. Besides, this just might be the thing to get my parents off my back about Josh. "Do you want to meet him?"

The shock on my mom's face was priceless. I wished I could've taken a picture of it.

"Why would I want to meet him? Is it that serious already?" Ma was fishing for information under the guise of old-school dating formalities. She needed to chill out.

I went to open the door. "Can't you just say hi?"

Danny had said he wanted to walk into this with eyes open. Well, he was in for a rude awakening.

"He . . . ey." Danny's smile tightened when he saw my mom loitering behind me at the doorway. "Everyone's up early." He offered my mom a small wave. "Chào cô. I'm Danny."

"Why is he dressed like a professor?" my mom asked in Khmer. It was an observation in the form of a question.

"You're still in your pajamas, Ma," I pointed out. Ma crossed her arms, affronted as she tried to hide her clothes. I picked up my overnight bag. "He's dropping me off at the apartment."

"He knows where you live? How long have you been dating?" Ma sputtered as more questions came out of her mouth. "W-wait, what happened to your car?"

My dad stood up, shaking his tablet in the air. "Hey, mèimei! What's this about your company laying people off?" He must've reached the entertainment section of the newspaper. "Do you still have a job?"

That was my cue to leave. I handed Danny my bag and shooed him until he turned around and started walking back to his car.

My parents were so shocked that they didn't register that I was hugging them. "Don't worry. Everything's okay."

My dad didn't fall for the bullshit. "Mèimei. Bùyào kāiwánxiào."

"I'm not," I insisted as I walked toward the driveway. It wasn't a joking matter to me either. I was going to give them all the answers they wanted. But first, I had to get to a safe distance. "My car got totaled and I don't have a job right now, but I'm handling it."

"What?!" Ma and Ba shouted at the same time.

I have everything under control, I thought as I jumped in the car and told Danny to step on it. It wasn't the most mature way to go about it, but so what? Maturity was overrated. I'd told my parents the truth and that was the most important thing.

"So that went well," Danny commented as he drove off. "You couldn't have, I don't know, sent a text that I'd be meeting *your parents?*"

I waved my hand dismissively. "It was like two seconds."

"Two awkward seconds. They're probably comparing me to Josh as we speak." Knowing my parents, the chances of that were good.

"You were the one who said I shouldn't care what people think."

"I meant society at large. People who don't matter." Danny rolled his hands as he tried to come up with another explanation. "Not your parents!" He shook his head, scolding me. "I think you drank too much pool water last night. It made you unhinged."

"But you like it, don't you? Because you *liiiike* me."

"Yeah, I do," he said without skipping a beat. I was teasing him, but his direct response made something inside me flutter, like my heart was warming up to take flight. "Try not to forget it while you're gone."

"I won't." It was all I was going to think about while I was away.

Getting Danny back was the only thing in my life that was on the upswing, but I had to press pause. Even though a week wasn't a long time, after twenty years apart, the idea of waiting any longer felt like a punishment.

A lull fell between us when we arrived at my apartment. There was no white noise from the car as we drove and no music from the radio to break the silence. I had to keep this short and simple. This wasn't a goodbye. It was a see-you-later.

"Thanks for the ride." I got out of the car and threw my bag over my shoulder before Danny could get to it. I didn't want to prolong this. Everything that needed to be said had been said. Or so I thought.

Danny didn't let me leave without one last kiss. It was a steady press on my lips, like he wanted to sear it into my memory, adding to the list of things not to forget. When we broke apart, Danny stayed close, so all I could see were his brown eyes, searching mine through a dreamy haze. It made it all the harder to walk away. "Text me later."

Chapter Twenty-Two

GETTING TO LAX WAS A BEHEMOTH TASK. NAT WAS FRAZZLED from the constant notifications she was receiving from her own team. Her publicist kept texting a variety of talking points to control the narrative because news outlets had moved on to theorizing about the demise of *Beyond the Dark*. In addition to FreeStream getting folded into ABN, there were baseless rumors that Nat was a diva on set. According to some "sources," Nat fought with directors and rewrote her own lines. The rumors spun out of control from there.

A group of fans created an online campaign for another streamer to pick up the show, which Nat found endearing but which also brought a whole new level of attention that would have to be addressed. Nat was going to be asked about it, and she wouldn't have any answers. Entertainment didn't move that quickly, even for shows with a devoted fan base. When it came down to it, if it didn't bring in a profit, *Beyond the Dark* was unlikely to find a new home.

I had to help Nat pack her clothes and make a last-minute call to her stylist to confirm that I had the right shoes and accessories. I wrote down all the designers' names so that Nat could credit them properly when she inevitably got hard-hitting questions about her outfit on the red carpet. This left me with no time to curate my own suitcase, so I threw whatever I could into it. Nat and I thought we'd be safe once we got to the airport, but as soon as she stepped out of our Uber, paparazzi swarmed around her.

"Natalie!" Cameras flashed from every direction. "Look here!"

"Natalie!" some pushy man shouted from behind a camera. "Sorry that your show was canceled. How are you feeling?"

"Sad, of course," Nat said, pushing up her sunglasses. "There were more adventures left for our space crew, but hopefully we can find a new home." She smiled politely and waved off any questions as she walked in.

I extended my arm and acted as a human buffer, clearing the way for Nat. Luckily, the assholes didn't follow us inside. They were probably staking out, hoping to catch someone more famous going to South by Southwest.

Once we were a safe distance away, Nat dropped the facade. "Damn. That's never happened before. Are you okay?" I nodded, though if I never experienced that again, I'd be happy.

I directed Nat to the PreCheck line. "Does this mean you've made it? Have you graduated to the B list?"

"Does it?" Nat's eyebrows lifted. I couldn't tell by her expression if she was excited or scared. "If this is a preview, I better be on top of my game for the red carpet."

We made it to our flight. Nat took the window seat and inserted her earplugs. "I need to center myself. Flying makes me nervous." She closed her eyes, but left one last instruction. "Let me know when they come by with drinks."

Wow. I made the choice to come on as her personal assistant out of friendship, but somehow I didn't think I'd actually feel like her assistant. It wasn't as nice as accompanying her as a plus-one.

"Nat." Only her left eye opened. "I was thinking about flying home after South by Southwest."

I had Nat's full attention now. "So you can get back to Danny?"

"That's not why," I said as I put my phone on airplane mode. A text from Danny came through right before I disconnected from the Wi-Fi.

Danny: Text me when you get there ♥

Nat hovered over the armrest. "Is that a *heart* I see?"

"That's not the whole reason." I flipped my phone around before I stared at the text any longer. "I need some time to focus on myself for a while."

"Isn't that what you've been doing?"

"No, not really." I had thought that going to the reunion would open up some clues to regaining my confidence. What it really showed me was that I'd been too afraid for too long to make the changes I needed to in life. There was no joy in dedicating my energy to meaningless awards or places that didn't value me. Why was I spending so much time feeling like I'd failed for not advancing my career in a company that cared more about the bottom line than it did about me? I had to redefine what would make me happy. The only person who could answer that was me.

"You're free to join me in meditation," Nat offered, shutting her eyes once more.

"Not to sound ungrateful for the invitation, but listening to my own breathing isn't my thing."

"So what's your plan? Are you going to find a younger man and get your groove back? Or will you be eating, praying, and loving through your self-discovery?"

Nat knew I never needed an excuse to stuff my face with pasta. "Are you done?"

"Aw, come on," she said in between breaths. "Let me have a little fun."

"What about the fun you had with Bo?"

Nat had dodged every question about Bo since the reunion. That could only mean one thing. It was either really good or really bad.

Nat shushed me as she ducked in her seat. "Don't say that so loud. I don't want to see that in *TMZ* tomorrow. That was strictly a onetime thing."

Nat was a good actress. To an onlooker, she was the picture of serenity. Her face was content and her breath even, but I heard that dreamy sigh. She couldn't fool me. "It was good, wasn't it?"

"Oh my god." Nat hid behind her hands. "Part of me is so grossed out that I—you know—with *Bo*." Her body clenched like she might dry-heave. "But why is he so hot now?"

It was one of life's wonders.

"There, there," I said, pretending to comfort her. "There are worse things than having a night of passion with a hot man."

"You cannot tell a soul!" Nat groaned, but soon her body shook with laughter. "Why do we do this to ourselves?"

I put my headphones on and selected my in-flight movie. "I guess we're never too old to be young and dumb again."

ONCE WE GOT into the hotel room, I started unpacking. Nat sat at the end of the bed and immediately popped back up after checking her phone. "The cast is getting together for dinner. Do you want to come?"

The Illustrious Five, the movie that Nat was promoting, had been filmed over a year ago. From the stories Nat told me, it seemed that their fictional heist crew had become a tight group.

I didn't want to impose. I'd be the lone assistant/friend sixth-wheeling their reunion.

I hung one of Nat's shirts. "I'll grab something later. I'm drained from the flight."

"Let me know if you change your mind. When you have a sec, can you check where we can get a green juice around here and a good breakfast sandwich? Gluten-free, of course." Nat made her way toward the door, but came to a halt behind me. "Ooh, can you iron that for me?"

I signed up for this. I signed up for this. "Yes. No problem."

My time as an assistant was going to be over soon, so I wasn't going to stress over the niggling annoyance of dealing with Nat's laundry. After she left, I finally had a chance to text Danny.

> **Rachel:** Hi. I made it to the hotel.

> **Danny:** Good. How is it so far?

> **Rachel:** Good

Minutes passed. It felt like a black hole had opened and my message fell into the void. What happened? We used to be good at this.

> **Danny:** Sorry. I'm not as fast at texting

I smiled, imagining Danny fumbling on his phone. I couldn't compare it to our AIM days. We weren't sitting around typing on our keyboards anymore.

Danny: Will you get to watch any films while you're there?

Rachel: Doubt it

Unfortunately, Nat's days were filled with press and events. If I hadn't been obligated to keep her on schedule, I would've tried to attend a screening. I'd only been to South by Southwest once before, when a producer friend of mine offered me a pass to the film and TV festival. I finally used some PTO to attend and spent the whole time watching movies. Those were the days.

Danny: You can't sneak out?

Rachel: You're a bad influence

Danny: Says the person who ran from the principal

Danny: and jumped in a pool

Rachel: don't you like it when I'm wet

Danny: dang Rachel Dang

Rachel: have I tainted your virgin eyes?

Danny: where else would you like to taint me?

My thumbs paused. What had gotten into him? I checked the time. Wasn't he at work?

I wasn't used to seeing this side of Danny, but I liked it. I started typing all the things that made Danny sexy. The confidence he had in his own skin. It showed in the way he moved easily wherever he was. How his mouth always landed somewhere that'd make me pause to savor it a little longer. How his arms were my favorite place to be. How being with him made me excited about what was next.

I stopped myself. I'd written a thesis by texting standards. Seeing the words on my phone screen gave me secondhand embarrassment. What started as a playful attempt at sexting had turned into something that made me feel even more naked. There was a level of commitment involved when putting feelings into written words, and I wasn't sure if I could do that just yet. I backspaced as fast as I could.

My phone rang. It was Angela. I'd been anticipating her call. My parents had been eerily silent since I left their house a week ago. That could only mean one thing. They were complaining about me to Angela.

"Rach. Mom and Dad keep calling me, and it's getting annoying," she said, jumping right into it. "What do you want me to do?"

"Ignore them," I said. I didn't need her to be my PR person. "I'll handle it."

"That's easy for you to say. You're not the one they've been calling." Angela paused as some fumbling and tapping sounds came through. "See? They're calling me right now." She sighed. "Rach, they just want to know if you'll be okay. If not, they're going to tell you to move back home to save money."

It was a generous offer, but I wasn't jumping at the chance to be treated like a kid 24/7. It was enough to know that I had somewhere to go if it came down to it. "No, I'll find something soon."

"I'll keep my eye out for any jobs," she offered. "If you need to, you can crash at my place."

"No, that's okay," I replied. The truth was, even though the entertainment industry had chewed me up and spat me out, I couldn't imagine doing anything else. I'd put too much into it to let it go so easily. But I still had to figure out how to make work a part of my life instead of my entire life.

"You know that's not even half of it. Who's the guy who showed up at the house that Ma keeps going on and on about?" Angela gave herself away with that sly tone. She was asking for herself as much as she was asking on my parents' behalf.

"Danny."

"Am I supposed to know who Danny is?"

"He's a friend from high school."

"A friend from high school who drove you home early in the morning after you stayed out last night? Who, according to Dad, waited for you like a puppy in the driveway?"

There was no use denying it, so I gave Angela a truncated version of our relationship timeline. "It's still very new."

"Uh, I don't know how new it can be if you've known him since you were fourteen and you slept over at his place. I'm assuming you showed him your flower."

"Oh god," I muttered while Angela cackled like an evil witch. "You're the worst."

"I can tell you like him," Angela mused once she settled down. "You never talked about Josh like that before."

I wasn't sure if I should be worried that Angela picked up on that so quickly. Danny was different, though. He occupied his own section of my heart. But since she seemed to know me so well, maybe she could help me figure my life out. I could use a blueprint. "Can I ask you something?"

"What?"

"How do you do it all? You're married. You're a parent. You have a whole career." I only knew how to do one of those things. "How do you juggle all of that?"

"Uh . . ." Angela laughed. "I don't do it all well, and I don't do it all at the same time. There aren't enough hours in the day. You know that. You've seen my messy house. Why are you asking me all of a sudden?"

"I want to have it all too," I admitted. "I don't know how, though. Nothing seems to stick these days."

"I don't know what to tell you, Rach. There are no right or wrong answers with this stuff. You can only plan for so much. My only advice is, once you find a good one, whether it's a job or a person, you hold on to them tight for as long as you can. After that, it's kinda like anything else you've ever done. You have to keep working at it, and ideally, you get better at it. That's all we can ever do."

"I guess," I replied. None of that helped me feel better, but Angela was right. She couldn't give me a clear answer because it wasn't hers to give. I had to come up with it myself. Texts started coming through, so I ended my call with Angela. "I have to go. Don't pick up any more of Ma's phone calls."

Angela scoffed. "Like that would solve anything. Call me if you need anything."

"Will do." I hung up and swiped my screen.

Danny: that bad huh? it sounded better in my head.

Was it bad that I laughed?

Rachel: sorry. my sister called

Danny: I was starting to think you forgot about me

Rachel: never

But given Nat's hectic schedule in the coming days, I had to set Danny's expectations straight.

Rachel: I won't be able to check my phone as much once Nat starts her appearances

Rachel: but don't let that stop you, if you want to send me a reminder every now and then

Danny: is that your way of requesting nudes?

Rachel: I was thinking more of a hello, how's your day kind of update but by all means.

Danny: your virgin eyes are about to get tainted

Rachel: can't wait

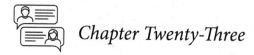

Chapter Twenty-Three

March 10
7:28 a.m.

Danny: good morning. I'm having avocado toast for breakfast

Rachel: so millennial of you

Danny: this the kind of riveting update you asked for

Rachel: keep them coming

Danny: a good motto to live by

11 a.m.

Rachel: omg I just figured out what you meant

Danny: you're still slow

Rachel: what do you mean, still?

Danny: do you remember the first day we met?

1:29 p.m.

Rachel: in the AOL chatroom, SuperxSaiyan85?

Rachel: or at the internet café?

Danny: no. at school, before the internet café.

Danny: it was my first day. we got paired up for tutoring

Danny: you don't remember, do you?

Rachel: i do! you were the new kid.

Rachel: mrs chang reminded you not to skateboard at school

Danny: your eyebrow arched like, "this fool?"

Rachel: and I was right

Danny: I was afraid of you

Rachel: that's because I made you do your homework

Danny: I thought you were pretty

Rachel: this is some revisionist history

Rachel: I had thick glasses and
I didn't wear makeup

Danny: you had me with your natural beauty

Rachel: I don't think so

Rachel: fine. thank you

Rachel: omg omg OMG

Rachel: Keanu Reeves is on the red carpet

Danny: remember. he's a
person like you and me

Rachel: that's a lie and you know it

Danny: what's he promoting? Do you
know what he's gonna be in?

Danny: rach?

Rachel: trying real hard not to
make a joke right now

Rachel: brb he's walking closer!!!

1:50 p.m.

Danny: Rach?

Danny: you there?

3:19 p.m.

Rachel: we made eye contact and
I couldn't even say hello

Rachel: I forgot my own name

Rachel: my life will never be the same

Danny: Dang, calm down

Rachel: if you don't hear from me,
it's because Keanu and I ran away
together to start a new life

Danny: let me know where you'll be registered

DANNY ATTACHED A PICTURE. IT WAS A NOTEPAD, SITTING ON top of the desk in his home office. I'd passed by it a few times during my short stay at his house. On the top page, Danny had drawn a heart with the words "Keanu + Rachel" inside, something my younger self had doodled before. Now a new picture had appeared. He'd modified the drawing, crossing out Keanu's name and replacing it with his own. This innocent scribble of our names together had me cheesing so hard. What was going on? This felt so easy. Too easy.

"Rachel!"

I stowed my phone away in my purse. Nat was coming off the stage from a panel with the rest of the cast. "Did I sound okay? Some journalist asked me about some alleged on-set drama with *Beyond the Dark*. I tried to redirect the questions back to the movie we're actually promoting. I didn't come off like a bitch, did I? Or am I going to see headlines tomorrow that I 'snapped back' at someone?"

"I don't think so," I replied, though I had no idea what she was talking about. I was engrossed with texting Danny and must've missed that part of her interview. Nat's interviews had always gone fine, so I had a hunch this one went well too. I unscrewed the cap of a water bottle for her. "It's fine. If the journalist was an asshole, then they probably deserved it."

"'Probably?'" she repeated after a loud chug. "Were you even listening?"

I put my hand on her shoulder, guiding her out of the auditorium. We had to get back to the hotel for hair and makeup. *The Illustrious Five* screening was in a few hours. "That's not the point," I said, trying to cover my own ass. "We've gone over this. Follow the script your publicist sent you. The rumors are fake news. You're sad about the cancellation, but holding out hope that another network will pick it up. Pretty standard stuff, Nat."

Nat said her goodbyes to her castmates and waited until they dispersed before confiding, "The cancellation is hitting me hard, Rach. Being a series regular made me soft. It was supposed to be my big break."

"Uh, Nat. Your movie is about to premiere at South by Southwest. I think you've broken." We stepped out of the side of the building and waited for our ride.

"You know nothing's a guarantee in this business. What if this is it?"

Here was Nat, asking the same question I'd struggled to answer for myself. Danny was onto something. It *was* easier to look at someone else's problems than my own. My response to Nat was immediate. "You have a pile of scripts waiting for you at home. People want you in their films. In lead parts," I added. "The show might've put you on the map, but this film is going to make you a bona-fide movie star. Trust me."

Nat shrugged this off. "I still have to audition. What if people forget about me?"

"Impossible. There's so much buzz around *The Illustrious Five*." Whenever Nat walked through a crowd, I heard more people talk about the movie than *Beyond the Dark*. If she couldn't feel the hype, then I had to really gas her up. "No one's going to forget you, Nat. Not when they see your ass in that dress."

Nat filled her chest with a deep, meditating breath. "Yes. More of that."

"You want me to keep telling you you're hot?" Nat nodded. I could do that. It wasn't that hard. "You're going to walk out there tonight and make people fall on their knees. You will make someone question their sexuality tonight."

That was enough to revitalize Nat. She squeezed my hand hard.

"Thanks, Rach. I needed that. If I say something stupid on the red carpet, come save me, okay?"

"I will. I'll pretend like I'm your handler and drag you away. I'll wear all black and put on my sunglasses, like I'm your bodyguard." I posed like I was The Rock. "No one will wanna mess with this." It was great to hear Nat's laugh, but was it *that* funny? "You don't think I can be your bodyguard?"

Nat easily pushed me aside when our car pulled up to the curb. "Don't quit your day job."

Point taken.

Nat's spirits stayed up, amplified by her sleek hair and makeup as she changed into her evening look. Her sexy red mini dress was dotted with jewels that sparkled under the camera flashes. The outfit's best accessory was her patent leather boots, which told everyone that she didn't come tonight to play. Nat was a standout against the yellow step and repeat.

I held on to Nat's purse and stood off to the side, outside of the camera's frame, while Nat was interviewed by various news outlets. She was such a pro, delivering fresh answers to the same questions over and over again. If this movie didn't win her more fans, then these interviews should.

"Excuse me, but I think you're in the wrong place."

Gloria Miller's chain-smoking asphalt voice caught me before I felt her hand on my arm.

"Gloria! Hello!" I didn't dare try to hug her. She wasn't the touchy-feely type, and I never knew if she was trying the latest diet fad, which usually left her cranky. "It's me, Rachel Dang."

"I know who you are, Rachel. I may be an old broad, but I never forget a face."

I thought that only applied to Gloria's deep Rolodex, not former interns. She could pluck out a weathered card and remember every detail of the person—how they met, who they were related to, and most importantly, if they had money. I wouldn't be surprised if she still used her Rolodex. Gloria was a visionary as a producer, but the lady wasn't tech-savvy. Last I heard, she still faxed contracts. Regardless, I was honored that she remembered me.

"I also saw your picture in *TMZ*," Gloria added.

Ah. That was it. I knew it was too good to be true.

"I almost didn't believe my eyes," she said, following me out the side as I shadowed Nat. "What are you doing, pushing paps away? You trying to get in front of the camera now?"

"No," I said. "I'm not hot enough to make up for my poor acting skills."

Gloria's laugh sounded like an engine turning over. "It's funny because it's true. Listen," she said, speaking louder. She was competing with the shouting photographers. "I always thought you were better behind the scenes. You had great instincts when we went over scripts, and you know your way around the biz now. Have you ever thought about doing something more creative?"

I hadn't. As much as I loved being on a set, I was never inclined to pick up a camera or write a script. Creating something out of thin air was a foreign concept to me, and getting it made was a different beast. The very nature of fighting for every project, not knowing what was next, had scared me when I was just starting out. But what did I know? The younger version of me had no idea how to take a chance.

I wasn't that person anymore, was I? Getting laid off was like waking up from a disorienting dream and not being sure yet what was real or not. It made me wonder if my life had flown by or if I wasn't paying attention to it as I was living it. This whole time since being laid off I'd thought I had to start my next chapter from scratch, but it wasn't possible. No matter what I did, even if I wanted to leave my career behind and do something completely out of left field, nothing could take away everything that had led me here. I'd been looking at my work in the industry as a burden, a waste of time, when I should've been looking at it as an asset. I had options. If there was ever a time to pivot into a new role, this was it.

"I'm considering it," I replied. Gloria was a busy woman, but if she was willing to impart some words of wisdom, I'd take them. "If you have time, I'd love to meet up for coffee when we're back in LA."

"Set it up with my assistant. And then you can tell me how I can get your friend Natalie Huang attached to one of my films. Her agent is a pain in the ass."

I kept my mouth shut, but I didn't disagree. From the few brief interactions I'd had with Nat's agent, Joel, I'd found him to be a smooth talker. A little too smooth, if you asked me. But now that her career was on the rise, Joel approached new projects more strategically with Nat. From what I had gathered in their recent email correspondence, a significant number of scripts coming her way were similar to her character on *Beyond the Dark*, and neither of them wanted Nat to be typecast.

"Not sure how I can help," I said. "I'm just her friend."

"A friend who could tell her to read the script I sent."

Oh. I'd never considered myself someone with any leverage, especially with someone like Gloria Miller. She must really want Nat if she was going to try to go through me.

"I'll see what I can do." I wasn't going to make any promises. Gloria was a little old-school and rough around the edges, but she knew where to find the money for her projects. Meaning, her projects had a stronger likelihood of getting made. That was a plus in my book.

Nat finally got to the end of the red carpet and waved as she stepped out of the spotlight. "That was intense," she said as her smile dropped. "If I have to answer one more question about trading my skintight catsuit for the disguises in this movie, I'll lose it. Do you have something to drink? I'm parched."

"Nat!" I said quickly, before she let her guard too far down. I hoped the extra cheer in my voice was enough of a warning. I stepped back so she could see we had company as we inched closer to the theater. "Have you ever met Gloria Miller? I used to be her intern, way back in the day."

"Oh my—" Nat's hand shot out to shake Gloria's. "You're an icon!"

"Tell that to your agent," Gloria shot back, meaning every word. The woman didn't kid around. She threw me a wink, the signal that she was going to take over the conversation from here on out. I walked ahead of them, creating a path in the slow-moving crowd to let them talk. I couldn't hear everything since the theater was full of chatty patrons waiting for the film to start, but from the snippets I did hear, it sounded like Gloria was pitching a fun action-adventure about a modern-day battle for some fabled hidden treasure.

By the time we arrived at the row reserved for the cast, Nat and Gloria were exchanging their "have your people call my people" pleasantries. Over Nat's shoulder, Gloria gave me one more wink, which I took as a good sign.

"Next time, can you give me a warning before you introduce

me to Gloria freaking Miller?" Nat whispered as we climbed over a few people to get to our seats. "The rumors are true. She's a tough lady."

"I didn't have time! She ambushed me." An announcement came over the speakers for everyone to get to their seats. The screening was starting soon. I dug into my tote bag filled with all the things to keep Nat happy and gave her a pack of gummy bears. "But was it good? It sounded like it went well."

Nat's eyes lit up like sparklers on the Fourth of July. "Rach. I can't believe Gloria even thought of me for this part. She says she sees me playing the desperate broke sister who tries to secretly swipe the treasure before the rest of the family finds out."

"You'd be playing the villain?"

"It's more complex than that, but it's different than anything I've done before. I can't wait to read the script." Nat couldn't contain her excitement. "It'd be nice to dive into a character that didn't require so much makeup and costumes."

I nudged her with my elbow. "See? What cancellation?"

Nat elbowed me back. This time she didn't wrinkle her nose at me for saying the c-word. Maybe her superstitious tendencies kept her from broaching the topic, but Nat's smile remained bright when the lights faded on the audience as the movie began.

I could only imagine how surreal it must be to watch yourself on-screen, but Nat was beaming. The audience, a mix of critics and festivalgoers, loved *The Illustrious Five*. People cheered and laughed at the right moments. After the credits rolled, the applause lasted a full minute. If I were to guess, I'd bet the reviews would call the movie "whip-smart" or "the slickest heist movie since *Ocean's 8*." It was that good.

Nat had to believe the hype now. People were surrounding her at the after-party to snag a selfie. I let the clout-chasers have at her and snuck off to the bar to check my phone.

10:33 p.m.

Danny: how's the movie?

He'd sent it an hour ago. Was it too late to text back?

11:45 p.m.

Rachel: so fun!

I regretted the exclamation point. It was loud at the party, and it translated somehow into shouting in my text. My insecurity washed away as soon as Danny replied.

Danny: what are you doing now?

Rachel: drinking a Break-In Bellini

Danny: what does that taste like

I took a sip. Break-ins tasted like peach, apparently.

Rachel: better than a Pilfer Pilsner

Gotta hand it to the publicity team. They were really sticking to the theme.

Rachel: how are you up right
now? Isn't it a school night

Danny: i was dreaming about you
and then you texted me

I refused to dignify that corny line and ignored it. Good thing
he couldn't see the stupid smile on my face.

Rachel: go to sleep. i'll talk to you tomorrow

Danny: can't wait to see you again

There was that flutter in my chest again.

Rachel: it hasn't been that long

Danny: still

Rachel: wish you were here

"Can I have my purse?" Nat was pulling at the top of her dress so
she didn't land in the tabloids with an "oops" censoring her chest.

"You escaped your adoring fans?"

"Oh please," she said, taking her stuff from my hands. "Are you
texting Danny?"

"How do you know?"

"Let me see," she said, tapping her lip. "You're at a party and
instead of scoping out all the hot people, your eyes are glued to
your phone with a big smile on your face."

"Stop it."

"I bet if Keanu Reeves walked in right now, you wouldn't have known because you're texting your lover."

"Shut up." God, why was I blushing over this stupid teasing? "It's not that bad."

"Sure." She swatted me with her purse. "Get out of here. Go home."

"Like, to the hotel?" I checked the time. "The party just started."

"Go home," Nat repeated. "I'm not going to stand in the way of love by making you stay. Go, before I have to fire you."

"I already quit," I reminded her.

"Then get out of here, quitter," she said, stealing my drink. "Go back to your love-ah."

"I need you to stop calling him my lover."

"Isn't that what he is?" When I didn't answer right away, Nat added, "Don't you want him to be?"

"Yes, but when I left, I told him I needed time to think, and he said okay. That's it." Our relationship status was yet to be determined.

"What?" Nat replied in mock horror. "You have a man who listens to you? How dare he?"

"I'm not complaining about it." It was one of the things I loved most about Danny. "I don't know. Isn't going back to see him the opposite of taking things slow? I'm supposed to be using this time to reflect and grow. I don't want to send mixed signals. And it's not like he's going out of his way for me. We're just texting."

"Rachel." Nat placed both hands on my shoulders. "You were the one who ended things last time. Shouldn't you say something that would give him more confidence than a 'let's wait and see'? If you want to be with him, then tell him, dummy."

"It isn't that easy," I shouted. Did the music have to be so loud?

"Isn't it? If he liked you after the reunion, then I don't think he's looking for perfection."

Danny had seen me at my worst, hadn't he? What was I doing, standing around at this party where no one knew I existed? When there was one man—one good man—waiting for me to get my head out of my ass?

"I have to go," I said. Nat shooed me out, but I couldn't leave without giving her a tight hug. "Thank you."

"Break a leg!" she shouted, but I was halfway gone. I beelined out of the party and ran out to the curb. Tasks piled into my brain. There was so much to do. Call a ride. Pack my things. Book a flight. I had a man to catch.

Chapter Twenty-Four

IF MOVIES HAD TAUGHT ME ANYTHING, IT WAS THAT GRAND GES-
tures usually involve a lot of running. I tried to circumvent that by
calling for a ride, but it seemed like everyone at South by Southwest
was trying to get home. I jogged back to my hotel in heels, which had
given me blisters by the time I made it to my room. If running was
supposedly good for me, why did I feel like a chewed-up paper straw?

I searched for flights out of Austin, but nothing was available
until the next morning. Which meant I ran all that fucking way
for nothing. I tried to sleep, but I couldn't without having some
sort of game plan. So I stayed up rehearsing what I would say
when I saw Danny. It was hard to condense years of feelings into a
meaningful summary. I wrote messy notes into my planner to try
to form something cohesive, then edited it down to a nice para-
graph that told a story about how I felt about him.

There was one problem with cramming the night before an
early flight: it was completely erased from my memory once my
alarm went off for the third time.

"Fucking shit!" I scolded myself, stuffing my clothes into my
luggage. Nat was out cold since she'd returned to the hotel room
only a few hours ago. So, being a considerate roommate, I kept my
swearing to a low volume as I scrambled to pack my things.

I made it to the airport and by some miracle got on the next
flight to LAX. Finally, something worked out for once. But as the

plane took off, my body felt heavy. All that running that was sup-posedly good for my health, combined with the late nights I'd been pulling, had me falling asleep before snacks came around.

When my eyes opened, I was back in California, walking through LAX like a zombie. I was wearing an old pair of leggings and an oversized sweatshirt that I wore only to sleep. My hair was half curly from the night before and half flat where I'd slept on it. It was useless to fix it, so I left it alone. I spent the long Uber ride to Al-hambra reviewing what I wrote in my planner. I couldn't decipher my own writing. Words trailed all over the page, crossing over lines like they were a mere suggestion. A sentence starting with "I loved you before I knew who you were" was immediately followed by an unfinished "your fine ass is . . ." These notes read like the unfinished thoughts of a stalker-y teenage girl writing in a fever dream.

I crossed everything out. No one could ever see this.

I arrived at my parents' house and dropped off my luggage in my room. "Ba, can I borrow your car?" I ran my fingers through my raggedy hair, trying to get it to behave. I gave up when my fin-gers got stuck in a web of knots. "Can I borrow the shower too?"

Both of my parents stood at my doorway, arms crossed like a human barricade.

"Don't you think you have something to say to us first?" Ma asked. She might have been small, but she was scrappy. She un-apologetically threw those sharp elbows of hers at restaurants whenever we fought over the bill.

"I'm sorry for dropping big news on you and then skipping town." I tried to go in for a hug, but my parents didn't budge.

"No, that wasn't good"—Ma's face crumbled with disappointment—"but I mean about Josh. You knew about his girlfriend?"

Ah. She finally found out.

"I did kind of tell you," I said, though I was making it up at the time. "It's been three years, Ma. It's time to move on."

She tsked. "It's not that. I lent Josh's mom my big pot. How am I going to get it back?"

"You two can still be friends," I assured her. "Josh and I don't care."

Ma considered this for a while, but then shook her head. "No. Her new daughter-in-law probably won't like that."

I wanted to tell Ma it was too early to refer to Josh's new girl-friend as a daughter-in-law, but she was distracted. Using the fingers on her hand, she mumbled to herself as she took inventory of the things Josh's mom had borrowed over the years.

Ba kept up his tough exterior. "Where are you going, looking like that?"

I gathered a clean pair of jeans and a nice top. "I'm going to see Danny."

"Is that the boy who picked you up last week?"

"Yes."

"Does he have a job?"

"Yes."

"Is he nice?"

"Yes."

"Is he nice to you?"

"*Yes.*" I didn't have time for this, and I was too tired to go through more rounds of rapid-fire questions.

Ba tossed his car keys to me. "Don't get in an accident."

That's it? That was easier than I thought. "That's all you want to know about Danny?"

"Dāngránle." He shrugged in a "What are you gonna do about it?" kind of way. "If you like him, then okay."

"Really?" This was unlike him, so I had a right to be suspicious.

"You don't listen to me anyway. If I said no, it makes no difference." So Ba was surrendering to my stubbornness. I'd finally worn him down. "Next time, introduce him properly. Your mom was upset for days that he saw her in her pajamas."

That I could do. "Thanks, Ba."

"Not a scratch on the car," he reminded me.

That was the least of my worries.

I STOOD IN front of Danny's house with nothing but thoughts and prayers. I should've texted first, but of all things, I'd forgotten my phone charger in Austin. I worked up the nerve to press the Ring doorbell when it spoke to me.

"No solicitors," Danny called out.

"It's me." I knelt down until I was eye level with the camera. I thought I heard a snicker, but I could have been wrong. All that traveling and lack of sleep had me feeling delirious.

"You could've called."

I held up my phone. "It's out of battery."

"How convenient." The door opened. Danny leaned in the doorway, arms crossed. The top half of his body read C-suite executive, with his crisp, white dress shirt and gray tie, while his bottom half had gone on vacation in pink board shorts decorated with hibiscus flowers.

"Were you working?" I asked. He wasn't looking too pleased. "Did I interrupt something?"

"I wrapped up early," he said. That must be nice. It wasn't even noon. "What are you doing here? Why aren't you in Austin?"

He sounded more curious than mad, so I kept rolling with my plan, even though I wished he was a little happier to see me. Then again, I did drop by unannounced. "Can I come in?"

Danny made space for me to pass through, so I hurried in before I made a declaration on the lawn. I wasn't trying to be Lloyd Dobler. I didn't have a stereo or a trench coat. I didn't try to sit down and risk tarnishing the nice memories we had on his couch, but paced around his living room instead.

"I have something to tell you, and I had to tell you in person." I swallowed and fished out my planner from my purse and shoved it in Danny's face, flipping the ink-stained pages so he could see. "I wrote everything down, but it's such a mess, like me."

Danny pressed a finger in my planner and smoothed down the page. His eyebrows shot straight up his forehead. "You put me on your to-do list?"

"That's irrelevant!" I shut my planner. "That's not why I showed you. You know I don't handle change well. I plan things out. I like to be in control, and when I'm not, I can't function. But you were there for me when I was clueless and I had no idea where to turn. I'll always be grateful that you messaged me online, even if it was out of boredom." I gulped for air. I was talking too fast. "But when things changed between us, I didn't know what to do, so I ran away. But I'm here now because I don't want to run away anymore. I don't know what's ahead of me, but I do know one thing and that's you. I want you with me."

Danny's eyes widened ever so slightly, whether from shock or fear I couldn't tell. Trepidation flooded my veins, and the desire to run out of the door was at an all-time high. But I dug in my heels and let the words tumble out of my mouth before I lost the courage.

"At fourteen, you were the one I wanted to talk to about my day. The small everyday things that I found exciting. At eighteen, you knocked me off my feet, literally. You helped me look up from my books once in a while, showed me what I was missing out on. I wished it didn't take me so long to tell you how amazing you are. And I'm not saying that because you have a career and a house and that damn good head of hair. I mean"—indulging myself, I gently brushed his hair back—"it's pretty great, but that's not why. I love the way you remember random things and call me out on my shit, but in a caring way. I want you so much, but I'm so afraid that I'll fuck things up again."

"You will," Danny said matter-of-factly. "You have."

"I have?" He nodded, smiling slyly as he wrapped his fingers around the handle of a carry-on that seemingly appeared out of nowhere. I pointed at it. "What's that?"

"This?" Danny glanced down as he gave his suitcase a twirl. "I was going to go see you in Austin."

"Shut up." I couldn't help it. First I was seeing things. Now my heart was going haywire. "Why?"

"You said you wished I was there, so"—he shrugged—"I bought a ticket."

"You were going to see me?"

"Yeah, but you ruined my plans. I have things to say to you too." Danny folded me into his arms and dropped two light kisses on my forehead. It was like he was tapping on the window to my brain, telling my thoughts to calm down in there. "Ever since I drove you home last week, I've been kicking myself for letting you go like that. I wish I'd said more."

"What are you talking about? It was perfect."

"Maybe," he said, brushing my hair behind my ear. "But I wasn't completely honest. If I had been, I would've asked you to stay." He held my face, sure and steady. "Rachel. You and I have both had long-term relationships. We know there's always going to be ups and downs. There's no rule that says we have to be in a good place in our lives to be together. Things will get messy. We will make mistakes. It's inevitable, but making it work is not impossible."

"That sounds great, but actually, I'm glad I went."

Danny's face fell. "Oh?"

I nodded as I hugged him tighter. "Because I got myself a meeting with a big producer and I quit being Nat's assistant."

Danny's face lit up with a contagious excitement. "Rachel." He kissed me, leaving me a little breathless. "That's great. Does that mean—"

"Yup. I'm staying and my schedule's completely open."

"Well, what do you know?" Danny's hands gripped my hips and turned me around for a back hug. "So is mine. I cleared the rest of the week to go to Austin."

"What shall we do?" I asked innocently, though Danny was already walking us toward his bedroom.

Danny kissed my neck, sending a shiver down my spine. "Oh, I have a few ideas."

"I bet you do." I let him help me out of my shirt. His joined mine on the floor soon after.

"There's one other thing I've been meaning to run by you." Danny's arms tightened around my waist. "Rachel Dang. Will you go out with me?"

"Like on a date?" I turned around to see if he was serious. We were literally half-naked. "I think we're past that."

"So we're doing things out of order. Who cares? I don't want to miss out on anything. So what do you say? Dinner and a movie?"

With Danny? That sounded perfect. "Okay, but my pick."

 *Epilogue*

A Year Later

THESE DAYS, TIME WAS MY CURRENCY OF CHOICE. TOO BAD I WAS always running out of it. I knocked on Nat's trailer door.

"Come on, Nat. We need you on set." I stepped back, narrowly missing it swinging out at my face. With Nat's shabby costume and graphic eyeliner, she carried a threatening aura born out of her character's desperation. I would've been shaking in my boots if I didn't recognize Nat's grumpy face. I must've woken her up from a nap.

"I liked you better when you were my assistant," she grumbled.

"Those days are long gone, my friend."

After I quit, I gave myself permission to do whatever I wanted. I slept in until ten and watched movies all day. That lasted a good three days before I was bored. I gave resting a good college try, but I wasn't built to stay still and that was okay. I didn't have to fight it, but I couldn't go back to a life that prioritized work. Not when I had someone to spend my time with.

I scheduled that meeting with Gloria while the offer was still fresh. She brought me on to help her read scripts, and it was a dream job. Gloria let me shadow her and showed me how she shepherded projects to fruition. It was a great education, but staying in the office all day wore me down. When there was a call for help on set for the movie Gloria convinced Nat to star in, a quirky murder mystery à la *Knives Out*, I jumped at the chance. A week later, I was on a plane to Vancouver to handle the day-to-day logistics. It was an added bonus to see Nat tackle a new role.

Gloria warned me it was going to be tough. The director was running behind and costs had ballooned, so it was up to me to overhaul the schedule to make it as efficient as possible. It was a headache, but it was thrilling once things were back on track. The shoot was almost over. We'd flown back in LA the night before to get some exterior shots. Now if only the talent would cooperate.

Nat huffed as she came down the stairs. "If you want to fight, I'll have you warned that I have a green belt in tae kwon do."

"Geez, did you miss your meditation session this morning? I'm just doing my job."

"Oh," Nat said, trading in her tough attitude for something sweeter. "Rach. I was practicing my line."

She got me there. That was good. "Save it for the set," I said, fighting through a yawn.

We were pushing through a late-night shoot on location in Chinatown, a cliché choice for a film with a predominantly Asian cast, in my opinion. According to Mike, the director, this was his way of paying homage to one of his favorite films, *Rush Hour*. Though if that were the case, I wondered why he insisted on using the same building used in *Freaky Friday* instead of Foo Chow Restaurant. It didn't add up, but I wasn't hired to question artistic decisions. I was hired to make things happen. It took some creative budgeting solutions and the right permits to get us here. The caveat was that we had to get the shots tonight. There was no time or money to do this again.

Nat replied with her own yawn. "Stop doing that. You know I yawn if you yawn. You can't hang like you used to."

"Nope." This project had to wrap tonight. I couldn't handle any more late nights.

"So is that a no for drinks after?" she called out as she walked backward to her mark.

"Rain check," I said, taking my seat in the back of video village. I was going to leave as soon as the director called cut. I couldn't wait to get back home and crawl into bed with Danny. I'd been in Vancouver for a month, and I'd hardly seen him since I came back. I had so much to tell him.

Lanterns and neon signs appeared on the monitors set up in the front. I rubbed my watery eyes, creating trails of electric red and teal in my vision as I fought another yawn. Mike glared at me over his shoulder.

"Sorry," I mouthed before he turned back around to call action. Maybe if he wasn't so particular about his takes, we wouldn't be up this late. I kept that thought to myself.

I sat up when I felt my phone vibrating in my pocket, thankfully not loud enough for anyone to notice. I quickly pressed the side buttons to silence the phone before checking my messages.

Danny: babe when are you coming home?

Danny: it's getting late

Danny: are you going to be okay driving home?

He must've forgotten that Nat and I commuted to set together.

I'd crashed at her place after our flight from Vancouver to stay closer to downtown.

Rachel: don't worry about it

Danny: I'll pick you up

Danny: don't argue with me

Rachel: you're so bossy

Danny: you like it that way

Rachel: only sometimes

Danny: then stay put

Danny: can't wait to see your face

And I couldn't wait to see his.

On-screen, Nat stormed out of a red building, ruthlessly pushing people out of her way as she chased her costar through historic Central Plaza. I'd read the script multiple times with Nat, but it was one thing to read the words. To see actors breathe life into their characters was nothing short of magic. Nat finally apprehended her costar, and after an exchange of threats, the plot twist was revealed. The shot closed in on Nat's face as her eyes grew frightened, understanding that she'd gotten the whole thing wrong—that the person believed to be dead might actually be alive. After one last, shuddery breath, the director called cut.

"That's a wrap!" he shouted into the bullhorn.

Cheers erupted across the set.

"Shhh. We have to keep it down or residents will complain," I reminded them, but no one listened. I couldn't really blame the cast and crew. It'd been a journey to get here, so I gave in to the festivities. It was going to be my problem anyway, not theirs.

After a rousing farewell speech from our director and a few pictures with the cast and crew, I walked down the block to make sure all the equipment was getting loaded. We had to get out of there before the city shut us down.

Danny appeared like something out of a dream. He was leaning against his car with his hands in his pockets, so he was a little slow to catch me when I ran to him.

"What are you doing here?" I said, clutching him tight. "Aren't you cold?"

"Oof," he said when his back hit the passenger door. "Take it easy. I thought you'd be happy to see me."

"I am!" I said, peppering his face with kisses. "I hope you weren't waiting too long."

"Nah. I just came from your parents' house."

My parents' house? "What were you doing there?"

"Helping them clean out their junk."

"Why? You still think my parents don't like you?" Danny thought I'd put him at a disadvantage when I sprang him on my parents, but that was hardly the case. My parents liked him. They told me so every time I called.

"I gotta give Lucas a run for his money on this favorite son-in-law business."

"We're not married yet." We weren't even engaged. "I'll remind my parents not to call you that."

"Don't," Danny said. "It's only been a few months since your dad stopped calling me 'Rachel's boy.'" I laughed, though Danny wasn't as amused by my dad's hazing. "You know, I turned on your old computer before I took it to recycling. Guess what I found?"

Danny unfolded a piece of paper covered with lines and lines of code. It was hard to make out anything until Danny turned on the flashlight on his phone. To my horror, it was a copy of our old AIM chats.

"Nooooo." It was pure teenage cringe from 1999. "How did you get this?"

"There was an archived log of our messages."

I took the paper and read it, holding it close to my chest. If there was anything embarrassing, I could easily destroy the evidence.

> **xxaznxbbxgrlxx:** who really thinks that they'll get money from sending an email to 10 friends?

> **SuperxSaiyan85:** don't click the link. it's a virus

> **xxaznxbbxgrlxx:** have you heard that Got Rice song

> **SuperxSaiyan85:** they better take that shit down before tupac sues them

> **xxaznxbbxgrlxx:** do you think he's still alive?

> **SuperxSaiyan85:** I don't think. I believe.

"Oh my god." Did we really have nothing better to do? "Why did you print this?"

"It's the start of our fated relationship. I thought it'd be nice to have." Danny's shy smile had me backpedaling, but then he added, "There's plenty more where this came from. I backed up the files before I dumped the computer."

"Oh no," I protested. "No one can ever know about this."

"Okay. It'll be our little secret, then." Danny folded the paper and stuffed it back in his pocket. "You ready to go home?"

We'd only been living together for two months before I left for Vancouver. It still gave me a thrill to hear him call it our home. "Wait. I have something to tell you. It's kind of important."

"Let's get in the car." Danny moved to open the passenger door, but I stopped him.

"No, I have to tell you now. It's probably best before you get behind the wheel."

"Uh, okay." Danny eyed me warily. "What is it?"

I'd thought about waiting for a special time to share my news, but seeing his face after this long night, bright with love and affection, I couldn't hold it in any longer. "I'm late."

"To what?" Danny looked over my shoulder, where the crew was still packing up. "Is there a wrap party or something?"

Danny wasn't catching my drift. It was probably hard for him to understand, since it was coming from someone who was prompt to a fault.

I palmed his cheek. "Remember when I told you that I wanted to produce this movie? And that I'd be gone for a whole month?"

"Uh-huh . . ."

"And then we . . . *you know* . . ."

"*Oh*." Danny pressed his hips into mine. "I remember," he

purred as he kissed me. I had to stop him before we got sidetracked.

"Well, I'm *late*."

It took a few seconds for the words to sink in, but when Danny got it, unadulterated joy washed over his face.

"Are you sure?" Before I could answer, he lifted me off the ground. It was hard not to beam right back at him. He spun me around but quickly came to a halt. Happiness was replaced by worry. "Should I have not done that?"

"It's fine—"

He knelt down and pressed his face on my stomach. "Is this for real?"

I ran my fingers through his hair. "According to three tests, yes. What do you think?"

This past year with Danny had been one of the best of my life. We were still getting to know each other, but we knew enough to discuss a future together. We'd talked seriously about having kids since we weren't getting any younger. While we weren't actively trying, we weren't preventing it either.

"What do I think?" Danny asked my stomach. "I think I'm already in love with this baby. What about you, though?" He stood up. "You had goals for this year."

I tried to hold back my tears before he got the wrong idea. They weren't tears of sadness or regret. This was my goal too. To find joy and love. This was more than I could hope for. "Yeah, I'm good. I'm right where I'm supposed to be."

Acknowledgments

I came of age in an era when Asian Americans were finding each other online. In the late 1990s and early 2000s, the internet was the place I could discover artists, musicians, and bloggers who were creating media that was distinctly Asian American. I wrote this book in part to celebrate that period of time and the Asian Americans who were (and still are) contributing to our culture through art.

A manuscript doesn't turn into a book overnight. An incredible team worked behind the scenes to make this book what it is today. To my incomparable editor, May Chen, for seeing the vision for this story when it began as a short pitch. Thank you for your confidence in me. It's such a blessing to work with you. To Allie Roche for answering my questions and keeping me on task. To Cynthia Buck for copyediting my manuscript and fixing my many errors. Thank you to Jess Cozzi and DJ DeSmyter for shining a light on my books. Thank you to everyone at Avon, from marketing, sales, design, publicity, and production, who worked on this book that I haven't had the pleasure of meeting yet. I appreciate you!

Thank you to my agent, Laura Bradford, for championing my books and taking them farther than I could have ever imagined.

Joyce and Laura, thank you for holding my hand through my first draft until I was ready to finish it on my own.

To my author friends who heard me whine the most: Suzanne

Park, Carolyn Huynh, Michelle Quach, and Alicia Thompson. Thank you for keeping me grounded.

Special thanks to Munika Lay and Shay Fan for letting me interview you about your entertainment experience. Thanks to Jes Vũ, for inviting me, an introverted author, out to CAPE events. It's such a privilege to meet other creatives and hear their passion for storytelling.

Cheers to my local boba shop for serendipitously playing a 2000s emo playlist instead of the usual K-pop rotation the day I was brainstorming this book.

Big thanks to the librarians, booksellers, bloggers, Bookstagrammers, and readers for supporting my books. Your passion for books makes me excited to read and write. Shout-out to Amanda at Bookish Brews (@amandasbrews), Viviann (@vietgirlreads), and Sarah (@sarahs.thoughts.on.books) for highlighting diverse book recommendations. My TBR is never-ending because of you.

Last but not least, to my family. Ba, the idiom was for you. Ma, sorry for all the times I ran up the phone bill because I stayed up late to chat with my friends on AIM. To my sisters, Phuong and Sue, for giving me a blueprint when I needed one (and letting me borrow clothes, even when I ruined them).

To David, for loving me even when my deadlines turn me into a gremlin. Alice and Sophie, thanks for not touching Mommy's computer. I wish nothing but for you girls to be the most likely to achieve your own dreams in your own time. I love you with my whole heart.

About the Author

JULIE TIEU is a Chinese Cambodian American writer, born and raised in Southern California. When she is not writing or working as a college counselor, she is reading, on the hunt for delicious eats, or dreaming about her next travel adventure. She lives in the Los Angeles area with her high-school-crush husband and two energetic daughters.

READ MORE BY
JULIE TIEU

"Tieu's tumultuous but believable plot combines heat and heart, bolstered by a diverse cast readers will want to spend more time with. The close friendship between Elise and Rebecca is an especially nice touch. Tieu should win some new fans with this one."

—*Publishers Weekly*

Opposites attract when an always-the-bridesmaid florist and a grumpy caterer mix business with pleasure in this swoony romantic comedy in the vein of *27 Dresses*, from Julie Tieu.

"Endearing, unabashedly tropey. . . . Cadence and Matt's very different, but equally loving, family backgrounds only enhance their romance. This breezy outing is sure to please."

—*Publishers Weekly*

Julie Tieu, an exciting new voice in contemporary romance, returns with a hilarious and sexy new novel about colleagues who decide to take their relationship outside the office.

"Donut miss this tasty treat! Julie Tieu is going on my auto-buy list. Her writing is as fresh and warm as a newly baked glazed. You need this book now."

—Meg Cabot, author of the Little Bridge Island and *Princess Diaries* series

Julie Tieu sparkles in this debut romantic comedy, which is charmingly reminiscent of the TV show *Kim's Convenience* and *Frankly in Love* by David Yoon, about a young woman who feels caught in the life her parents have made for her until she falls in love and finds a way out of the donut trap.